The Madame, Contessa and the Dollhouse

Written by Jonathan White

Jonathan White

Published by Tavares Entertainment, LLC.
(www.tavaresentertainment.com)
Printed in the USA by Kindle Direct Publishing
Cover by Germancreative-Lesia T.
ISBN 979-8-218-31863-5

CHAPTER ONE
Sweet Sixteen

There was a knock at Contessa's door. "Come in," Contessa said. Standing in the doorway was a tall woman with skin the color of ebony, hair tight in a bun, and two sapphire dragonfly clips in her hair. "Yes," Contessa said. "You have everything ready for tonight? Your dad said the party is at midnight, and he will be up at nine to get you." said her mother. "Yes, mama," said Contessa. As her mother walked out of the room, she looked at her daughter on her 16th birthday and thought to herself, I made that beautiful baby girl. But, of course, Contessa looked nothing like her mother, with her beautiful milky skin and deep emerald eyes, which have golden iris freckles almost artistically placed.

The thing that made Contessa stand out from everyone else, though, which her mother disliked the most about her, was the voluptuous curves that hit her in all the perfect places. She is gorgeous inside and out, but she always felt that her parents overshadowed her. Her father was a tall man with ivory skin, brown hair, and emerald-green eyes. The Coven and her mother supplied potions to all the local do-good housewives. She thought that nobody truly saw the real her until that was. Of course, tonight is the Winter Solstice, but that is not the only unique thing happening tonight. Tonight is Contessa's 16th Birthday, and not only that, but it is also her initiation ceremony into the Coven, something she has waited forever for. "Grace," came a voice from downstairs. Contessa's mom shut the door to her daughter's bedroom on the second floor.

She quickly walked over to the banister, where she saw her husband, Frank, the head of the Dragonfly Coven, standing in the foyer. Frank was tall, with ivory skin, brown hair, and emerald-green eyes. At this time, it was extremely rare for a person of color to own a home, let alone one of the most gorgeous homes in Black-wood, Mississippi. One of the things that made Ms. Grace's home so beautiful was the foyer. Unlike most of your southern planta-tions, Dragonfly plantation had something special. The foyer. Walking into this fantastic home was like walking down a catwalk with all the past owners looking down at you from the cherry wood frames they sat upon. Then it opens up suddenly with a big glass-domed ceiling above you where the heavens just stare down at you in all their glorious beauty. At the back of the foyer was a beautiful spiral staircase that led up to the second floor.

Then, leading off to the left was the library, which is basi-cally Frank's office because that's where Frank conducted all his business anyway. To the right was the parlor where Mrs. Grace took care of all those Bible-thumping Christians who were too tired of waiting on God to answer their prayers. Because of these Chris-tians, the Montgomerys could even own their 8-bedroom, 2-story house on 3 acres of land. You see, back then, the only time you saw colored folk on a plantation or in the main house was when they were working on it. The Montgomerys were given a free pass be-cause of what Mrs. Grace did for all the town's ladies, in secret, with her spells and potions. No one wanted their dirty laundry aired, so they let the Montgomerys be and looked the other way at their skin color and their other worldly practices.

Mrs. Grace would do anything and everything to keep their home. She did because she loved doing her incantations and making potions in the privacy of her own home. Of course, without the prying eyes of all the self-righteous gossipy hens of the town. Even though they were the first to come and knock on her door when God stopped answering. Like when the preacher of Blackwood's wife, Hannah, showed up late one Saturday evening because God wasn't giving her a child, so she figured Mrs. Grace could. When that knock came, Grace did as she always did. She answered the door, stifled a laugh, took the lady's money, and handed over the potion. And just like that, nine months later, out came a beautiful, healthy baby boy named Jeremiah.

Hannah became somewhat of a regular client after that, at least when she wanted another baby, which is how Isaac, Sam, Matthew, James, and Isaac were all conceived. So, no one, and I mean no one, wanted to upset the Montgomerys because who knew whose secrets could be spilled? "Are you even listening to me?" said Frank. "I'm right here, Frank; what do you want?" said Grace. "Good God, seriously, woman? Tonight is the most important night in Contessa's life. Not only is my baby turning 16, but she is also being inducted into the Coven. So, everything, and I mean everything, needs to be extra special and perfect for my sweets." said Frank. "Well, I called the caterers, and they said they would arrive around 5:30-6:00. I also called the Coven. Molly Remise told me that the ceremonial mask had just arrived and that she would bring it with her when she came around 5:00 to help me set up for tonight.

"Contessa's upstairs. She should be starting to get ready at any moment and be ready for you by 7:00. Then the moon will peak around 9:00; everything is getting on just fine. On another note, I need to take care of something in town before Molly arrives, so I best be heading out." Frank turned around, staring daggers into Grace, and said, "Where in the hell are you going?" "As I said, Frank, I'm going into town. Lenny will be driving me. If you must know, I am taking Jessica Branston her cream and a candle for good luck for her cousin, which seems like she will need." At this comment, Grace didn't even try to stifle the laugh that came bursting out of her. "Fine, but please, God, do not be late. I am counting on you to ensure that this night goes perfectly for our baby girl."

Back upstairs in Contessa's room, she is getting all her clothes set up for her party. She grabbed her black dress from the closet, placed it on the back of her vanity chair, and then set her ballet slippers down on the floor. Looking back at her vanity, she saw a silver box with a black silky ribbon tied around it with a note attached. She picked up the note and read it: Something special for a special someone on their day. Happy Birthday, Sweets! She wondered why she hadn't seen the present before but didn't pay much mind to it. She pulled the ribbon, letting it fall onto her vanity, and opened the box. What Contessa saw inside brought tears to her eyes. It was a silver dragonfly charm with blue sapphires inlaid on the wings and rubies for the eyes. As she picked it up from the box, she saw the gorgeous pearl necklace it was hanging from. She quickly removed her dainty gold chain and placed her new necklace around her neck. It fit her beautifully, lying just low enough that it sat perfectly between her breasts.

It wasn't so much the beauty of the necklace that had brought tears to her eyes but what the actual dragonfly charm meant. It symbolized her officially being a part of the Coven. Not just any coven, but the one her family had run and helped make into one of the strongest covens of the south. As Contessa took one last look in the mirror, she decided to grab the black ribbon and tie it to her hair. As she walked toward her bedroom door, she turned around to make sure she had everything laid out that she would need for her special night. Once she was convinced that her outfit was all laid out and ready for her, she opened her door and quietly closed it behind to make sure no one heard her leaving. She took a left and started to head towards the back stairway that led down into the kitchen and out the back door.

She grabbed hold of the railing and began to descend, and when she was just about to enter the kitchen, a voice came out of nowhere saying, "Where do you think you are going, little miss?" With that, Contessa scanned the kitchen, looking for the voice's owner, and froze. "Who is it?" "Santa Claus," said the voice, "I'm kidding. It's me, Celeste, the woman who changed your diapers and wiped the snot from your face." Celeste was, for all intents and purposes, Contessa's mom, not by blood, but because she was the one who was always there for her and raised her. Celeste was also everything from the head cook to the maid, to the therapist for Contessa's parents, and the nanny/ second mom to Contessa. It wasn't that Contessa's mother was a lousy mom. It's just that she couldn't be bothered with childish things.

She was the first lady to one of the strongest covens in the South. She ran several socialite committees and her own business. Contessa would sit in the kitchen playing with the rag doll Celeste had sewn for her, watching Celeste go about her daily duties, which included loving Contessa. "Now I asked you a question: where are you going?" Celeste said. "Out!" Contessa said with a firm but respectful voice. "Now you know tonight is extremely important for you and your parents. You have three hours to get washed, dressed, and ready for tonight," responded Celeste. "You are going to meet up with that boy, aren't you? He will break your heart, but hopefully not before your daddy breaks his legs. Honey, you know the rules, no dating humans, especially the preacher's son. Isn't he supposed to be with that other girl Tilly? Yeah, he really loves you, baby girl." "But he really does, Celeste, he told me last night. So, I will meet him behind the Cantina Bar in town tonight so that he can give me my birthday present". "Fine, sugar. Still, please be back in time, or both of our hides will get a tan for you not being ready." "Don't worry, Celeste, I already have everything all laid out and ready upstairs. I promise I will be ready when my dad comes up to get me."

CHAPTER TWO
Forbidden Love

Contessa made it out the backdoor and across the yard to the barn without anyone else seeing her. As she quietly opened the barn door and went inside, she immediately stopped and was taken back with memories from over the years. One of her favorite things about the barn was the smell. Most people do not understand how someone could enjoy the smell of a barn, but those people were probably never around horses. A mix of hay, leather, and horse dander makes up the aroma. She stood there taking in the smell and sights for a few seconds longer and quickly made her way through the barn and to her horse's stall. Snow was a giant Friesian who was as white as freshly fallen snow, hence the name. She picked his reins up from the rack outside his stall and hastily opened the stall door.

As she stepped inside, she said, "Hey, Snow, we are in a bit of a rush, so we need to hurry." She had already put Snow's saddle on him earlier that day to save time, so all she had to do was get his reins on, and they could be on their way. It is a fifteen-minute ride by horse from the Dragonfly plantation to the actual town of Blackwood. Blackwood was where the crème del a crème lived, where everybody knew everybody, and where dirty little secrets came in spades. The roads were paved, which was a good thing because there were more cars than horses in Blackwood these days.

I mean, not even the town over Lansbury had paved roads, let alone a streetlamp, which made sense because most of the population was made up of colored field workers and maids. In contrast, Blackwood was made up of white doctors and lawyers. As Contessa rode through the middle of town, no one looked her way. That was because of who her parents were and because of the side business her mother ran. No one dared to let anyone know that they had been to see Mrs. Grace. She made a left onto Eagle Lane and headed straight towards the Cantina diner. When she got there, she stopped right out front by the tie-off posts. She dismounted Snow, wrapped his reins around one of the posts, and walked around the diner's side and down the back alley.

As she walked past the trash cans, a hand suddenly covered her mouth; the other pulled her close, and this mysterious person whispered, "Hey there, beautiful." At that, Contessa remembered what her father had taught her. She quickly jabbed her captor in the ribs with her elbow. He immediately released her, and she spun around to see who it was. "You didn't have to elbow me so hard. Damn, that will probably leave a bruise." "Well, that's what you get for grabbing me like that. You better start acting like you have the sense your mama gave you, or your ribs will not be the only thing that is hurting and bruised," Contessa said as she stared into the eyes of the man she loved. James, the preacher's son, stood at about 6'1. He was thin but had an excellent muscular definition. He had impeccable cheekbones, beautiful wavy brown hair, silver eyes like the moon, and slightly bruised ribs.

"I had to grab you; someone might have seen you," said James. "Well, if you had actually broken it off with Tilly and told your mother about me, we wouldn't have to be sneaking around like this," Contessa responded. "I don't see you being as forthcoming with your parents about me. Or have you just not told me yet that you told your folks you were in love with a human? Also, ever since my mom became the head of the Thousand Stars committee, I barely see her, so I haven't had the chance to say something yet." James said as he grabbed her again. She slapped, grabbed, and pulled him in for a kiss. "Happy birthday, Contessa," he said as he reached into his pocket and pulled his hand back out in a fist. When he opened his hand, there laid a beautiful crystal, "I know you collect them, and so I thought this would be perfect for adding to your collection." "Yes, I do. It's gorgeous, thank you!

He gently caressed her cheek, stopping at her chin, and leaned in for another kiss. It started off slow and intimate, then grew more passionate, like a shooting star building momentum as it fell from its place in the heavens. It felt as though lightning was passing through them. James pushed his body up against Contessa so that she could feel him getting hard against her, which caused them to back into the door of an empty store. With his lips still locked with Contessa's, James reached around her and felt for the doorknob. He opened the store door because nobody locked their doors in a small town where everybody knew everybody. As soon as the door opened, Tessa fell backward, causing James to fall forward, and they both tumbled to the floor, like falling through a rabbit hole. "Ouch," Contessa said, laughing in between their kisses.

Both of their feet dangling from outside the doorway. The rest of them lay inside, and at that moment, James grabbed Contessa's hands and pinned them above her head. They both lay there for a moment, staring at each other, their passion hot enough to melt snow. Finally, James took his free hand, reached between their trembling bodies, and unzipped his pants. He loosened his grip on Tessa's wrists so that she could free a hand and remove James' shirt for him. At that moment, Contessa knew that this was right. The energy between them was electric, and it seemed they were both magnets being drawn to each other, locking together, never to break apart. What they were feeling was undeniable, so she would say fuck the rules and would keep him safe and throw caution to the wind. He was hers, and she was his.

Jessica Douglas lived in a beautiful Victorian-style home smack dab in the middle of town. It had a wrap-around porch with an old wooden swing in the front right corner. The house was sur-rounded by a white wooden fence lined with the remnants of Jessi-ca's rose garden, which had won her several awards from the town fair. As Grace approached the home, she thought these women did-n't have to work for a damn thing, that everything they had was just handed to them, unlike herself, who had to work for everything she had. "Stop the car. We're here," Grace told Lenny, "Yes, mama." Lenny had worked for Mrs. Grace for years because of his affilia-tion with Frank. He was a slender old man who was completely bald, and his skin was so dark that it looked like he had just walked out of the coal mines. Lenny stopped the car right in front of Ms. Douglas's fence gate and got out to open the door for Grace, stick-ing out his right hand to help her out of the car.

A delicate hand shot out of the car, slapping Lenny's hand away, "I might be aging, Lenny, but I am not decrepit. I can get out of the car by myself, thank you. Now get my bag out of the trunk." As Lenny hurried to the back of the car, Grace yelled, "Hurry up, Lenny," as she walked towards the front door. "I am already late because you drove like there was a pack of children playing in the streets, in no hurry at all, not caring if I am late or not for my appointment." Lenny grabbed the bag from the trunk and ran ahead of Grace to open the gate for her. They walked up between the bougainvillea and ivy wrapped around the columns that framed the stairs leading up to the front porch.

Lenny stepped ahead to ring the doorbell. Moments later, a short, stout, Negro man in a black suit opened the door and stepped aside to let them in. Grace stepped inside, took off her coat and gloves, and handed them to the butler. "I am here to see Jessica and her cousin Tilly," Grace said demandingly. "They are in the parlor having tea and sandwiches," he responded. With that, Grace turned to Lenny and said, "Give me my bag and go and wait in the car till I am done. It shouldn't be long, so just keep the car running. Do you hear me?" Yes, mama, I hear you," Lenny responded as he handed her bag and then turned and quickly headed back towards the front door. With that, the butler shut the front door and led Grace into the parlor. As she walked in, she saw Jessica and Tilly sitting on the couch. Both girls were petite and white, dressed in their Sunday best. They looked like they were trying to be grown-ups, but all Grace could see were two spoiled rich girls who would do or pay anything to get what they wanted with Daddy's money.

Grace despised people like this, who didn't lift a finger a day in their life to earn a single penny but took from everybody because they felt entitled to everything. Jessica was just plain ugly. No ifs, and, or buts about it. She had caramel brown hair and dull brown eyes. She was a big girl, but in all the wrong places, so she just looked frumpy. On the other hand, Tilly was an attractive girl in her own right, with her dirty blonde hair and brilliant blue eyes. "Grace, please sit down. Would you like some tea or maybe a sandwich?" Jessica offered. "Sorry, Jessica, but I am in a hurry to get back to the house because I still need to finish setting up for Tessa's birthday celebration." Grace politely responded.

Even though this was true, Grace wouldn't have wanted to stay anyway. Even if she had nothing else to do, she would rather have her eyes pecked out by ravens than be bored to death by these pretentious bitches she thought to herself. Grace walked into the room and over to the couch directly across from the two girls. She sat down and placed the bag beside her. "Not to be rude, but let's get down to business since there is no time to be wasted here," Grace said as she reached for the gold clasps on her bag. She popped open both clasps and reached into the bag, feeling around for the special items she had brought for these nitwits. The first item she pulled out was a jar, which she gently placed on the glass table between the couches. She reached back into the bag and, this time, pulled out a smaller jar, placing it right next to the other one on the table. "That will be $70 for you, Jessica, and $110 for you, Tilly." At that, Jessica leaned over, grabbed a silver bell off the table, and rang it.

Only 3 seconds had passed when the butler came into the parlor, "Go and get mine and Miss Tilly's purses from the hall closet and bring them to me now," she demanded. He left the room, returned with both of the girl's purses and handed them to the girls. They both snatched their purses and began to rummage through them to find their wallets. One at a time, they pulled out their money, counted it, and then handed it over to Grace. "Pleasure doing business with you young ladies," Grace said with a slight tone of annoyance. "Same time next week, Grace," Tilly said. "No, I will give it to you on Saturday at the Thousand Star Ball committee meeting," Grace retorted. "Very well, have fun tonight at your daughter's little party," Tilly said sarcastically. Eyeing Tilly like she wanted to put a hex on her, Grace said, in the most pleasant tone she could conjure, "Now I must be off ladies, no time for small chit chat." Both girls said their goodbyes as Grace stood up, but neither bothered to get up and walk their guests out. They both just sat there looking like the stuck-up princesses they were raised to be.

CHAPTER THREE
Witches trial

As Grace walked away, she opened her bag and put their money into her wallet, thinking to herself how her Contessa would never turn out like these two disgusting girls she had just finished doing business with. Grace entered the foyer where the butler was standing and waiting with her gloves and coat in hand. He handed them to her and opened the front door. She thanked him genuinely and walked out of the house and down the porch steps towards the little walkway leading to the fence. She walked down the path, and when she got to the fence, she opened the gate, walked through, and let it shut behind her. She walked to the car and got in, "drive, Lenny, we haven't a minute to waste," she said as she slammed the car door shut.

As they drove back towards the plantation, she wondered what she would do if Tessa ever befriended any of these hypocritical Christians. However, she didn't think about it too much because she knew her daughter would never be caught dead with any human, let alone one from this town. "Well, I should go. I am supposed to meet James at the diner for burgers and shakes," Tilly said. She took one last sip of her tea and yelled out for the butler to grab her things and meet her by the door. She stood up from the couch, leaned over to give Jessica a kiss on the cheek, and glided towards the front door. The butler stood by the door begrudgingly with her coat, gloves, and purse. She snatched them from him without even a glance in his direction or a thank you.

She walked out the door and started down the porch steps. As she walked down the path towards the gate, she thought living in the middle of town was very convenient. It made her walk to the diner much easier. Had she been coming from her house, she would have made sure that she had her driver take her because a girl of her status does not walk. Walking was for poor people and the help. While walking down the block, several women from her mom's circle of friends tried to stop and say hi to her, but all she did was say hi back and kept going. She was not going to deal with the annoyance of having to play politely with the bitter old women her mom surrounded herself with.

As she passed Colonial Drive, she could see the side of the cantina diner, and as she got closer, she heard noises coming from the alleyway behind it. She stopped for a second, assuming that it was most likely the miller's son taking part in yet another sinful activity. She was going to investigate when she remembered that she was meeting her James and started walking again. She only got a few steps away when something made her stop. She didn't know what it was, but something told her she should turn around. She knew that James was most likely waiting for her. However, something in her gut told her she needed to see what was happening in that alleyway. As she turned around and started walking down the alley, she wondered what she would stumble upon. The miller's boy was known for getting into trouble, not that an upstanding lady like herself would know about these sinful activities firsthand, but she had heard the stories.

And if it was him and, say, a lady, if you could call any woman doing sinful things in an alley a lady, she wouldn't look, but then she would at least know the cause for the noises she was hearing. It wasn't bad noises like someone screaming in pain, but the complete opposite. It sounded like someone enjoying something greatly. She didn't know exactly what would cause someone to make noises like that, but she at least knew that nobody was in trouble. If anything, she knew that whatever she came upon would make for great gossip at the Thousand Stars Committee meeting on Saturday. As she tip-toed down the alley, like a cat preying on a rat, she passed several rows of trash cans. They had stunk so bad she wanted to turn around; the noises suddenly came to a crescendo and stopped.

Not hearing anything other than what sounded maybe like heavy breathing, Tilly decided to turn around. Still, she saw it. Two sets of feet dangling outside a closed shop's doorway. The excitement started to build up in her chest. She knew she was about to catch somebody doing something that they should definitely not be doing and that she would never do. She crouched down behind one of the trash cans so that she wouldn't be seen by whoever was in the shop and slowly stuck her head around the edge of it so that she could get a better look. She was so anxious to see who it was that she felt like a detective about to crack a case wide open. Suddenly, she heard a girl's voice giggling and then said, "Stop it, you are going to make me late for my party." The mystery man responded, "You are just so beautiful. I can't keep my hands off of you. You want to go for round 2?"

Suddenly, everything started spinning because the voice of the man she had just heard sounded eerily familiar, as if it was someone she knew intimately. "James, please, my mom will kill me if I am even one minute late. Let me up so I can get myself together." James? No, it can't be my James, she thought to herself, but honestly, how many James did she know?

At that, she started looking over the top of the trash cans when her world came crashing down around her. The man not 10 feet in front of her wasn't the miller's son but her love, James. She dropped back down to the ground, dizzy and nauseous from the sight she had just witnessed. As her heart was breaking and the anger was growing, she wondered who the hell the slut who was trying to steal her James. She sat there going over the girls' names that it could be when she heard whoever the whore was started to giggle again, followed by what she assumed were kissing noises. "James, stop; you have to go meet Tilly, remember?" The mystery girl said. "Ugh, fine, but I would rather stay here with you than have to spend time with her, my beautiful Contessa." Contessa? That witch that lives outside of town. She thought to herself.

Tilly had never felt so many emotions at one time. Part of her felt like she was breaking from the betrayal and injustice she had just suffered, but another part was so angry she felt like she could just kill somebody. She peeked back over the trash and saw James and Contessa getting to their feet, buttoning their clothes and fixing their hair. As Contessa went to walk away, James grabbed her by the hand, pulled her close, and gave her a long, deep, passionate kiss.

He has never kissed me like that, Tilly thought to herself as she sat there staring at them, mouth agape. Suddenly, James looked in her direction, and she dropped back down, praying he did not see her. She sat there waiting to see if he had noticed her, and when she didn't hear anything to make her think he had, she peered back at them. They hugged and said their goodbyes, and then they both turned and walked away in different directions so that no one would see them together. That's when Tilly realized that James was walking right towards where she was hiding.

She started to scoot as close to where the trash can meets the stone wall, trying to become one with the wall, and closed her eyes real tight, praying to God once again that he wouldn't see her. As she sat there frozen with fear, she tried to get her heartbeat to slow down because it was practically beating out of her chest. She worried that he might hear it, and she would certainly be found. She heard his footsteps getting closer, and then he was right there, so close she could smell him and the scent that that whore had left on him.

Finally, she heard his footsteps going further away, so she opened her eyes a little bit and saw James turn the corner and leave the alleyway. Once she saw this, she stood up, which she had to do slowly because her legs were still shaky from what she had just discovered, wiping the dirt from her dress and trying to compose herself. She walked to the alley entrance just in time to see James enter the diner. She took a minute to get her bearings and breathe when the prickle of hot tears started to sting her eyes. She wiped them away with the back of her hand and turned in the opposite direction of the diner towards James' house, the preacher's house.

So, with vengeance in her eyes and hatred in her heart, she started walking. First at a lady-like pace, then in a full-out run, not caring who saw her at this point. When she arrived at the preacher's house, she ran up the front steps and banged on the door like a madwoman. She heard the scraping of chairs on the other side of the door and a voice calling out to someone. After what seemed like a lifetime, the door finally opened, and standing in front of her was the preacher. He was an average man all around; his height, his looks, his personality, everything. He had a heart for God and never got his hands dirty or went against God. That he left up to his wife. "I'm sorry to intrude, but there is no time for formalities. I need to speak to your wife about James now!" Tilly said as she pushed past him and towards the sunroom. "Tilly, what is going on? Aren't you supposed to be with James? Is something wrong? Is he okay?" the preacher said as he followed behind Tilly.

Ignoring the preacher, Tilly walked into the sunroom yelling, "Mrs. Hanna, Mrs. Hanna." "What in God's name do you want child? Do you not see that I am busy? Better yet, do you not see the time?" Hanna replied. Standing in front of Tilly were two older women. The preacher's wife, Hannah, was the heavier of the two and had long red hair that flowed past her shoulders. The other woman was much shorter, barely pushing 5'3", and weighed 90 pounds, soaked and wet. She had dirty blonde hair, just like her daughter, Tilly. On seeing her mother, Tilly stopped and was taken back for a second. "Mom, what are you doing here?" Tilly asked. "I'm here to discuss committee matters, not that it concerns you, young lady."

This made sense because the two women had been best friends since grade school, and her mother was Hannah's right-hand woman. "Now, what is the matter? You said something about James. Is he okay?" her mother inquired. "Everything, mama, that devil, that witch Contessa Montgomery put a spell on James." "Now, Tilly, that is not very lady-like language, and you can't go around making such accusations." Tilly's mother said. "I'm not making things up, mama. I saw James and her behind the Cantina diner; he was on top of her. They were both nearly naked and committing sins against God," Tilly said without even taking a breath.

"No!" Hannah and Tilly's mother said in unison. "Yes! I was at Jessica's house and had left to meet James at the diner to discuss marriage. I was almost there when I heard noises from the alleyway next to the diner. I didn't think much of it, but something told me to go investigate. At first, I thought maybe someone was in trouble, but then I realized that the noises I heard were not that of despair but pleasure. Sinful pleasure. I was walking down the alleyway when I saw them together on the ground in the doorway of one of the shops. That witch is trying to steal MY JAMES!" Tilly screamed.

Boiling over with anger, her cheeks turned crimson, and tears filled her eyes. Hannah grabbed Tilly and pulled her tightly against her chest, "There, there, child, everything will be alright. I will fix everything. Thomas, will you come here, please." Hannah said. "What is it, dear?" Responded the preacher. "I need you to call the flock and tell them to meet at the church. We have a snake in our midst." "Yes, dear." The preacher turned and went to the kitchen, grabbed the phone, and started dialing.

While still holding Tilly, Hannah began to instruct her best friend." Go and grab your things. Take your daughter home, and I will see both of you at the church in one hour. The Lord will make things right. Tilly, do not worry. Tomorrow, you and my son will be right back on track. Talking about marriage and having children. So do not fret." At that, Tilly shifted away from Hannah and to her mother so that she could help to support her. The maid entered the sunroom and handed Tilly and her mother their things, leaving without saying another word.

Back home, safe in the barn, Contessa took the saddle off of Snow and walked him back to his stall. "You barely made it," said a voice from behind her. Tessa turned around, coming face to face with Lenny. "Ms. Celeste sent me to find you before your mama does," Lenny said. She started to hand Lenny the reins when she said, "Well, here I am like I promised I would be." "I see. Now take your butt upstairs and get ready before Celeste gets on the both of us." She leaned over, kissed Lenny on the cheek, and ran out of the barn. "Use the back stairwell," Lenny yelled after her.

Tessa ran across the yard and up the back steps, avoiding eye contact with Celeste even though she heard her mumble something under her breath. She got to the second floor and headed straight for her room's third door on the right. She opened the door quietly and then shut it just as quietly so as not to draw attention to herself. She turned around to face her room when she noticed it was much cleaner than she had left it. Her bed was made, and her clothes on top of the bed were folded. Her closet door was shut, and her vanity was organized.

"Thank God for Celeste," Contessa thought to herself. She threw off her shoes and unbuttoned her pants, letting them fall down to her knees, using her feet to get them off the rest of the way. This instantly brought back the recent memory of James taking off her clothes and touching her in her most private places. Shaking away the thought, she continued to undress, standing in the middle of her room. She walked over to her vanity and picked up the short black dress she had laid out for herself. She slipped into it and grabbed her hair, starting to brush her hair. Finishing, she set the brush down and then sat at her vanity.

Almost done getting ready, she started to apply her makeup. She got up from the chair and went to the antique mirror when she was done. It had once been her grandmother's and was given to her after she passed away. She approved, giving herself the once over, her black dress clinging to her curves in the best way, with her hair brushed with the black silk ribbon still in it. As she was about to turn around, the new present that her dad gave her caught her eye. Looking at the dragonfly that now hung around her neck, she thought about its significance and how important it was. It was the symbol of the Coven, which made her love it even more. A knock at her door brought Tessa back to reality, "Who is it?" "It's your father. May I come in?" "Yes." At that, Tessa went back to her vanity, bent down, picked up her pink ballet slippers, and went and sat on the bed to put the first one on. She laced it all the way up her calf. As her father entered the bedroom, he asked if she was ready. "Almost," she replied, starting to put the last slipper on. "Here, let me."

Her father bent down in front of her and gestured for the slipper. She handed it down to him with a smile. He slipped it on her foot and laced it up her leg. He tied the ribbon and then leaned in and kissed her knee. Getting to his feet, he let her know she was all set. Contessa stared into her father's honeysuckle-brown eyes. She thought about how lucky she was to have a father who was always around whenever she needed him. Unlike her mother, who was only there in passing. She knows that her mother loves her, but she is just too busy to be there for her. I mean, you would think that she ran the damn Coven with how busy she is. "Meet you at the front stairs in ten minutes, sweets." Her father said. He got up, headed towards the door, turned around, and told her he loved her. "I love you too," she replied.

Alone again, Tessa got off the bed. She walked over to the door next to her vanity, opened it, and walked out onto the balcony. She headed over to the railing and stared out into the backyard. She watched the caterers and event staff getting ready for her party. To the left was a large white tent with dozens of tables under it and more than three chandeliers hanging from the big top. Twenty or so men in white suits set a long table with food. Then, to the right, she saw twelve chairs with men and women sitting there, setting up their instruments. Next to them in the center was a stage and a dance floor with a long wooden table on the edge of it only illuminated by torch light. In the corner between the stage and the tent was a bonfire. A man was standing next to it, roasting what looked like a pig.

Before going back inside, she looked up at the night sky, staring at the moon and the abundant number of stars. She smiled, thinking about how this would be the perfect night. She turned on her heel and headed back into her bedroom, shutting the door behind her. She headed out of her room and down the stairs, heading towards the foyer.

Standing at the top of the stairs, she looked down the foyer and saw her father smiling at her. She started to descend the grand staircase, her father holding out his hand for his daughter to take hold of when she got there. Grabbing Tessa's hand, he leaned in and kissed her on the cheek, "You look lovely, sweets." Contessa and her father walked around the staircase into the kitchen and headed out the back door. The villagers in the center of Blackwood sat on an old white church that had been there longer than most of the current population.

It had been built by the past generations of families in Blackwood since it was first established. It had black shutters and elaborate stained glass windows. A white fence wrapped around the church and the cemetery at the back of the building. It is a sacred place where people usually come to worship their God, but tonight was not your normal church gathering. Inside were the restless town folks outraged by what they were hearing. "There are more people here tonight than any given Sunday," Tilly whispered to her mother as they sat in the front row, listening to Hannah speak. "Unbelievable," came a voice on Tilly's left, which made her turn her head away from her mother and towards her cousin Jessica, who sat down next to her.

"Did you hear what happened?" Tilly asked. "Yes," Jessica responded. "Mrs. Crow filled me in about James when I saw people headed this way and stopped her to ask what was happening. Once she told me, I stopped everything I was doing and followed her straight here. I am so sorry about James, Tilly." Jessica said sympathetically. "Don't be. It's that witch's fault. She put a spell on him, and that's why he was with her. We are all here doing our Christian-like duty to try and save him from that whore's clutches." Jessica and Tilly turned their attention back to Hannah and continued to listen to her speak.

As they both sat listening, Jessica turned to look at all the town folk behind her. She thought how ironic it was that almost everyone in the church had received help from Contessa's mother at one point or another, including her own mother. The latter was sitting next to Tilly's mom in the front row. At this moment, everyone was trying to discuss a plan to storm the plantation with guns and other weapons, demanding that the witches hand over one of their own. Not only one of their own but their leader's child; this would not end well. "Everyone sits down, and we can calmly talk about this like civilized people," Hanna said. "Hun, this is our son. What do we do?" Hannah asked her husband. "Darling, this was a long time coming. This has gone too far. Knowing what those people have been doing on the outskirts of OUR town. Grace and her kind have gone too far this time. We have turned a blind eye to their blasphemous actions for too long. I think they forget that we let them stay there, and at any moment, we can take whatever we want from that witch and her devil-worshipping husband.

We have let the devil in, and now we must get him out. Any suggestions?" inquired the preacher. "Well, the party they are throwing tonight will be at its highest point around midnight," came a random voice from the crowd. At this, the preacher's wife spoke in her most commanding voice, "Tonight is the night. Ladies, take your kids home and lock your doors. Men, get your horses and a weapon to protect yourself with. We will ride out tonight asking them to hand over Contessa and demand she releases my son from her tangled web. Everything will be okay if they give her to us quietly and without hesitation. If not, then we will be sending more than just one witch to hell tonight." Hannah instructed with such passion that it made everyone feel as if it was their son who had the spell on him. "YES!" screamed the crowd.

Suddenly, the church door flew open and made a loud banging noise as it hit the wall with some force. The crowd all turned to find a young man making his way down the aisle, and as he passed by the congregation, several of its members whispered the Lord's Prayer to him. James found Tilly in the crowd and walked straight towards her, stopping at the edge of the pew. Tilly slowly looked up and locked eyes with James, the love of her life. Several seconds passed as they both stared at each other until finally, James spoke, "Why did you not meet me at the diner, and what in the hell is going on here?" At that, he motioned for Jessica to move over. She released her cousin's hand, got up, and moved over next to her mother.

"I saw you with that witch!!! Behind the Cantina diner, but don't worry, I am not mad at you because I know that you are not yourself, that that witch put a spell on you. We will save you, though. Your mother has a plan to free you from her clutches." Tilly said. James turned to look at his mother, fear building in his gut, "Mom?" "Child, you are not yourself, but don't worry, I will save you from that she-devil." Looking around for someone to help him, to make these people see that this was crazy, he saw his dad. "Dad, please, you have to stop this before someone gets hurt." Standing there, face white as a ghost, beads of sweat dripping down his forehead despite the draft in the church.

As his heart raced faster and faster, he looked around again, trying to figure out a way to explain to these people that they were wrong. After seeing that no one was using the sense that God gave them, he realized that he was the only person who would be able to save Tessa and her family. Looking back at his father, he gave him a pleading look to please help him. "James, were you or were you not behind the Cantina diner on top of that witch, undressed for everyone and God to see?" His father asked in a stern voice. "Yes," said James, dropping his gaze to the floor, panic building in his chest. Tilly grabbed James' hand but pushed it away with an intense force, with no love anywhere in the movement. "But you don't understand!!!" Now, he is shouting at his parents, the congregation, and Tilly.

"No buts, son, is any of what Tilly saying not true?" James's mother asked. "Yes, what happened behind the diner is true," James said, but his mother intervened before he could finish talking. "Then you leave us no choice, young man. We love you, and if we don't save you, no one will." "ENOUGH! I will not let any child of mine be taken away by some demon into the depths of hell." His father said sternly. "We raised you to be pure and to follow the word of God, and we will not let this heathen rob you of everlasting life. You are meant to be with Tilly. To start a family of your own, and one day, when you do, you will realize that we are doing the right thing by doing this tonight." His mother said in a loud, snapping tone. She passed in front of the stage with her hands outstretched towards the heavens.

James could not believe the insanity he was witnessing, not that it should have surprised him with how religious his family was. He turned away from the stage facing the door and went to take a step towards it. His father put a hand on his shoulder and began to speak again. "Now, we can't have you going and warning Contessa and her family about our plan." As his father said this, his grasp tightened on his shoulder. So, what do we do? James thought to himself as he quickly ran through his list of options. Scratching his head, he looked back at the cross on the wall. He thought about how many were killed in the name of the Lord, innocent people. "Here is what is going to happen," his father said as he looked out to the crowd to find his three other sons.

He gestured for them to join him up by the stage and instructed, "Take your brother home and lock him in the closet. Do not let him out, no matter what he says, until we get home. I am counting on you three, and so is your brother's soul. Even if he doesn't know it, he will thank you all one day for saving his soul." "DAD, you can't do this!!" James yelled as his brothers made their way to the front of the church to detain him. "I am sorry, my son, my mind is made up."

With that, James looked away from his father. He started to head over to the ends of the pews by the church wall. He climbed up on top of one. With his brothers slowly surrounding him, like a pride of lions surrounding a zebra, he quickly jumped from one pew to the next, trying to make his way to the door. "Spread out," his oldest brother yelled, "grab him," he shouted at the flock. People were screaming, trying to escape James as he jumped over their heads as if he were contagious and would spread this awful spell.

This made it harder for his brothers to get to him, so they started pushing people out of their way, forcibly trying to corral him as a dog would to sheep. His one brother Jeremiah was getting closer to him and tried to grab out for him, clasping onto his shirt with his fist. James pushed him off when his other brother, Matthew, appeared on his left side, blocking his way out. At that moment, James knew it was over. There was no escape. He tried to fight, but it was no use. Matthew had come up and hit him over the head with such force that he collapsed over the pew, landing upside down. "Stay down, brother," Matthew said as his two other brothers came up and high-fived him.

Isaac, the oldest, grabbed James's limp body, threw it over his shoulder, and started walking towards the church door with his other brothers in tow. "You know your orders," their father shouted after them. As they exited the church, the preacher looked over his flock and said, "Go with God. We will meet all of you tonight at the edge of town and ride out to the plantation." Then, like a herd of cattle, the people stomped out of the church, and you could hear car doors slamming and engines revving as people drove away and then silence. The only people still in the church were the preacher and his wife. He looked at Hannah, staring at her with worry in his eyes, only to see the same look on her face. "All will be fine, my dear. I will save this town, and I WILL save our son." The preacher said with conviction. Hannah stared at the cross and then back at her husband, saying, "No, we will save him together."

CHAPTER FOUR
The Solstice

As Contessa and her father walked out onto the back porch, they saw Celeste crying on Lenny's shoulder, and her mother was walking toward them. Grace reached out for Tessa's hand, and with both her parents on either side of her, they walked down the porch steps and towards the massive white tent. As they walked, Tessa looked up at the stars, thinking that she should have worn a sweater, and was brought back to reality as she heard the band start to play classical music per her mother's request. They reached the tent and made their way to the center of it. She saw the other coven members dressed in their ceremonial robes as they did.

They were laughing, drinking, and watching the leaders of their Coven lead their daughter into the middle of the celebration. Looking over the crowd, she spotted her best friend, Lexi. A petite white girl, two years older than Tessa, with long black hair and eyes the color of the forest. When they reached the tent's center, the coven members started cheering, some yelling Happy Birthday Contessa while others whistled. Her father lifted his free hand in the air, silencing the crowd. He then raised his hand that was holding Contessa's above her head, spinning her in a circle so the members could see how beautiful his daughter looked. As her father did this, her mother let go of her other hand and started to spin in her circle with a big smile.

Grace hated not being the center of attention and couldn't bear that Tessa was getting all of it, which pissed Tessa off that her mom could not give her one night in the spotlight. Usually, she hated having all eyes on her because it made her feel like a prize-winning pig at a state fair. Still, tonight was different, and it hurt her that her mom could not go without all the attention for just a few hours. The only person that didn't make her feel this way was James. When he looked at her, it made her feel strong and beautiful, which is one of the reasons she loved him so much. This made her blush because the memories from earlier that night came rushing back. She knew she could never tell anyone about them, including her best friend Lexi, because of the Coven's law about human interactions.

Once she stopped spinning, a waiter walked up to her and her parents, handing the three of them glasses of champagne. Her father cleared his throat and began speaking. "My friends, family, and fellow coven members, tonight is a memorable night for all of us, especially for my wife and me. Tonight is not only our daughter's 16th birthday but also the night that she joins the Coven. We are all here to celebrate this monumental occasion with her. We could not be prouder and more excited for the smart and beautiful woman she has become. I love you, my sweets." He said this as he lifted his glass in the air and added, "So after dinner, when the moon is at its highest, we will start the ceremony." "Stop fidgeting," Tessa's mother whispered to her. "Now eat, drink, and enjoy this gorgeous night."

With that, her father drank from his glass, grabbed Contessa's hand, and led her to the head table, her mother following closely behind them. Her father pulled out Tessa's chair for her, and once she sat down, he pushed it in and then walked over and repeated this respectful gesture for his wife before taking his seat. As soon as they were seated, a waiter came rushing over. He filled her glass with water and then her parents. While doing this, he asked, "Would you like the roast pig with mashed potatoes and collard greens or the blood orange duck with roasted red potatoes and green beans?" Contessa thought to herself for a moment and responded, "I will have the duck, but no green beans, please."

She knew this would piss off her mother because she was always on her about losing weight, but she didn't care because this was her night, and she would have whatever she wanted tonight. The waiter nodded and then added, "Would you like the dragonfly? It's the specialty cocktail this evening." Tessa leaned over to her mother and asked, "What is that?" "It is pink liquor with a little something special added to it from my potions cabinet to help people relax and lower their inhibitions so they can have fun." "Okay, I will have a glass of the dragonfly, please," Tessa added. The waiter nodded and then walked away. Dinner was amazing. The duck fell off the bone like butter, and the blood orange sauce complimented it very well, but she didn't like the potatoes, so she took two bites and then pushed them aside. For dessert, they had cloud cakes, which were Contessa's favorite. They were a warm puff pastry with powdered sugar and vanilla sauce drizzled on top.

It was literally like eating a cloud. She enjoyed them so much that she had two, making her mother give her a disapproving look and feel like a stuffed pig. As she finished the last cake, Lexi came over, said hi to her parents, and then grabbed her by the arm, pulling her up and out of her seat. They headed through the crowd, some patting her on the shoulder. They then made their way out of the tent. Once out under the night sky, they heard Tessa's father announce to everyone to make their way to the dance floor. "Come on, Contessa," Lexi said. "I'm coming. Hold on," Tessa responded. As the rest of the Coven filled the dance floor, Tessa headed to the long wooden table in front of it. Her parents waited until everyone had filled the floor and walked through the crowd and into the center. "Let the ceremony begin!" Her father said in a booming voice.

Her mother walked onto the stage, towards the microphone, and began singing. With that, the flutists began to play, followed by the clarinets and the rest of the orchestra. The sound was magical, like the wind blowing through the trees and the water rushing over the rocks. Her father raised his hands towards the sky, and out of his palms came a spark of something blue followed by a flame, which he threw out towards the crowd. The flame morphed into the shape of a dragonfly that flew around the members of the Coven. It was almost like it had a mind of its own, flying up towards the sky. BOOM, POW! In the sky, the dragonfly exploded into an array of beautiful colors. First, electric blue, ruby red, and finally, a beautiful grape juice purple. Contessa stared up at the sky in utter amazement. Then, the other men from the Coven joined her father, repeating his actions, ending in the same explosion of color.

Once the men had finished, the women joined in, releasing their own flames from their hands. The fire was the yen to the men's yang, and you could not tell where the flames ended and the exploding dragonflies began. Contessa felt a tug at her hand and looked over to find Lexi pulling her toward the center of the dance floor. The two of them moved around the other members of the Coven and their flames, making sure never to collide with their beautiful magic. Reaching the center of the floor, they ended up right next to her father, and when he saw her, he handed her a chalice, which she took. She looked into the cup and saw the pink liquid she had ordered earlier but never drank; without hesitation, she pressed it to her looks and drank it.

The liquid had an acidy taste, but she finished her sip, handed the cup to Lexi, and began to dance. She started to spin and was moving around between Lexi and the flames. As she did this, she realized that this must be what the sun and moon felt like. She spun until she lost her balance, and her father caught her. While she lay in her father's arms, she asked if she could go lay down. Her father raised his hand and gestured for the men to start moving the crowd to the ceremonial table. He carried Tessa over to an old wooden table and laid her down. Then, as she lay there, the men encircled her, and the women walked off the dance floor, leaving behind wisps of color and flame, and stood behind the circle of men. The men started chanting and placed their masks on one by one, a man handing her father the largest of the masks. And with that, Tessa closed her eyes.

CHAPTER FIVE
The last stand

The community met up on the edge of town to ride out to the Montgomery plantation. Once the preacher and his wife arrived, he honked his horn and stuck his hand out the window, gesturing for the others to follow him. They all drove in a row down the countryside towards the plantation. When they got to the edge of the property, the preacher turned off the car, got out of it, and walked over to the other side to help his wife get out. The other vehicles killed their lights and joined the preacher, forming a half circle around him and Hannah. Then the preacher spoke, "Tonight, we rid ourselves of this evil! We will free my son, save our town, and, more importantly, our souls. I have been told that they will be setting off fireworks around midnight, and when they do, that will be our sign to attack. So, get ready because it is almost time for our plan to be set in action."

As they stood there, all you could hear were guns clicking as people loaded their weapons. For what felt like hours, the congregation sat in their cars, anxiously waiting for the fireworks to light up the night sky. Finally, a BOOM went off as they saw a giant dragonfly explode in the sky. The preacher grabbed his wife by the hand and kissed it as he honked his horn, started his car, and drove towards the Montgomery plantation. Lenny was sitting on the front porch, listening to music and watching the magic above him, when he heard the first gunshot.

He looked up and saw the mob that was now heading toward him. At that moment, Lenny leaped up and ran inside the house, running towards the kitchen, hitting his hip on the table on his way. Now half running and half limping, he started screaming for Celeste at the top of his lungs. "Ms. Celeste, Ms. Celeste, the end is near, the end is near!" Entering the kitchen, Lenny kept repeating, the end is near, over and over. "Hush up, you old goat. Take a breath, sit down, and explain yourself." "What I am trying to say is go pack your shit. We need to get out of here. The villagers are coming, and I don't think they are coming for a piece of cake and to say happy birthday." Lenny said as he gulped air down. "Now move! Woman, MOVE!"

A look of sheer panic overcame Celeste's face, turning white as paper. She looked around. "What are you looking for?" Lenny asked. "A weapon. We may have to fight our way out of here. Now go upstairs and grab some of Frank's and Grace's things, and I will grab whatever I can from Grace's cabinet and some of Contessa's things. Lenny, hurry, we have to save baby girl." She said firmly. "Lenny, GO! We haven't a moment to spare." Lenny turned and ran up the back stairs. Celeste looked around again, grabbed up the first knife she saw, stuffed it into her apron, and ran after Lenny. As Celeste reached the top of the staircase, she saw Lenny's foot disappear into the master bedroom. She made a left and headed straight for Tessa's room. Shutting the door behind her, she grabbed the brown leather bag off of the floor and started stuffing whatever she saw into the bag.

Then, as she opened the door to leave the room, she saw Lenny running back down the hallway. "Wait, Lenny," said Celeste. "What?" "Go back down the stairs, go to the barn, and pack the horses. We don't have much time." Celeste instructed. He nodded and continued down the hall towards the stairs. Once Lenny was out of sight, Celeste entered the master bedroom and headed straight toward the armoire. She dropped to her knees and opened the small cabinet on the bottom right-hand side, where Grace kept all her liquids, herbs, and other things she needed to make her potions. She stuffed whatever she could get her hands on into the bag and got to her feet when she heard a commotion from downstairs. She slowly headed towards the door when she heard footsteps coming up the stairs and a voice saying, "We need to find the girl." "Not, baby girl," Celeste said to herself.

As she opened the door, she met the town baker, a tall, slender man with a double chin and a balding head. "I don't want any trouble, you hear me!" Celeste warned him. "Listen to me; you have two options here. You could go quietly and surrender Contessa over to us and let her be tried for witchcraft. Or you could not and burn with her. It's your choice." On hearing this, Celeste's face went from being as white as a ghost to as red as a lobster. She said, "Now you listen to me, you no good motherfucker; I will give you two options." The baker moved closer. "One, you could go home and stop blindly following these Bible thumpers, or two, I can slaughter you like a piece of meat, your choice." "SHUT UP!" he yelled back at her. "No, you shut up! I am not backing down!

Why are you here? The only reason your bakery didn't close down was because of Mrs. Grace. She used her special spices and herbs to save your bakery and kept food in your baby's tummy." Celeste said with an overwhelming rage. "So, what is it going to be?" The baker asked with a sinister smile on his face. "I will take my chances; I will never hand over baby girl." "Well, then, it was nice knowing you, Celeste." Celeste nodded in agreement and, in a flash, was standing in a defensive stance, ready for a fight. The baker lunged forward at Celeste, who moved quickly like a cobra to the left, causing him to fall flat on his face. She dropped the bag and reached into her apron, wrapping her fingers around the knife. She turned on her heel while the baker tried to get back up, plunged the knife deep into the top of his spine, and then pulled it down to his butt, filling his back.

The baker let out a horrific scream as she did this. Celeste pulled the knife out, flipped him over, and said, "No one will ever hurt my baby girl, NO ONE!" And as she said this, she plunged the knife into his gut repeatedly, blood splattering all over her face, body, and the walls, turning everything a dark crimson red. Realizing he had gone limp, Celeste stood up, grabbed the end of her apron, and wiped the knife clean as best she could. Picking up Tessa's bag, she turned and ran down the hall towards the back staircase. She was running down the stairs when she stopped abruptly at the bottom. Standing in front of her was the judge with a revolver pointed at Lenny. Fear growing inside of her, she remembered the potions she had packed.

Opening the clasps on Contessa's bag, she reached her hand inside and started rummaging through until she felt the small vial she had been looking for. She then removed the vial, and in one swift motion, she threw it at the feet of the judge. The bottle shattered into pieces, and green smoke began to rise. BOOM! The revolver went off in Lenny's direction, hitting him in the shoulder, which made Lenny spin around and fall back onto the kitchen floor, blood seeping out of the wound. Lenny, now heavily breathing, tried to get to his feet but could not. He ended up leaning against one of the lower kitchen cabinets. "Have you lost your mind?!" the judge yelled at Celeste. "No, but you're about to," she responded with an evil smile. She walked down the last of the stairs. She then headed over to where the judge was standing, with the revolver shaking in his hand. "You stay where you are." The judge said.

The green smoke was now reaching his nose, and as it did, he breathed it in. Slowly, it began to change him. The judge's brown eyes began to glaze over, and he seemed to relax and become immobile, like a toy soldier waiting for someone to move him. With the gun still pointing at Celeste, the Kitchen door swung open. A man came through and went straight over to the judge, grabbing his arm and saying, "Come on, sir, the fun has begun, and we are in charge of taking Contessa." This was all Celeste needed to hear, "KILL HIM!" She screamed with anger steaming off of her and a piercing look in her eyes. The man looked from the judge to Celeste with a puzzled look and then again turned back to the judge. "Come on, judge, she is joking, right? You wouldn't shoot me. Now shoot her, and let's go." "You threatened my baby girl. Believe me, this is no joke. Now, I order you to kill him!"

Venom spewing from her mouth. The judge turned the gun on the man who was once his ally and raised it to the man's head. BOOM, the gun went off, and the bullet found its destination right between the man's eyes. Blood came gushing out of the wound, covering his face in a thick red liquid, and then he fell back onto the kitchen floor. Now, with the immediate danger behind her, lying on the floor dead, she turned, grabbed a rag, and ran to Lenny's side. Lenny pushed the rag against the wound, "Stop, Celeste, you have to go and save baby girl. Keep her safe." "Right now, all I have to do is to stop the bleeding, you old goat."

Tears began to fill Celeste's eyes as she turned to ask the judge for help. He walked over and bent down. She took his hand and placed it on the rag. "Now you listen to me, take Lenny to the barn, load up the horses, and get him ready for travel, you hear me?" Celeste ordered him. "Okay, now that he is helping me, you need to go, NOW!" Lenny shouted. The judge got Lenny to his feet, and Celeste leaned over and kissed Lenny on the cheek, leaving a wet spot where her lips had been.

She then brushed herself off and took a deep breath. As the two men reached the door, Celeste told the judge one last thing. "Judge, you shoot anyone threatening you and Lenny, do you understand?" The judge nodded, and then he stepped through the doorway with Lenny, out into the chaos erupted. "Think, girl, think," Celeste said aloud. She looked around the kitchen and saw the cooking oil, an idea creeping into her mind. She walked over to the oven, turned it on, opened the oven door, and then reached over for the jug of oil.

Lifting the jug, she opened it and poured it onto the counter and then the stovetop. Using her other hand, she wrapped it around the bloody dish rag and threw it into the oven. She took one last look around the kitchen and thought, "damn, I'm really going to miss this kitchen." she threw the open jug of oil into the oven. As she turned and ran out the door, the kitchen exploded into a blazing inferno.

Race against time

The world was spinning, and all James could smell was the musky smell of his brother's cologne. Then, there was a slight pain in his chest and rock-like pressure in his stomach from being carried by his older brother. The cold breeze made his face sting, where his brother struck him. He listens to his siblings talking about the plan for the community to meet at the edge of town, where they will attack. Getting that witch and burning her and the plantation down when the fireworks light up the sky. James stood very still, thinking of a way to slip out of his brother's tight grip. "Man, I need a break. You take him," Matthew said. So, his brother Sam said he would take over. Mathew laid his brother down, stood straight up, yawned, and stretched when Sam bent down to pick up James. James moved quickly, head-butting his brother. This made him stumble back. James rolled back to his feet. Matthew and Jeremiah lunged forward but could not grab him. They collided, giving James a split second to find his escape. He went down an alley, running past a few trash cans. He bumped into a man in a white apron, stumbling but not losing his balance.

The Madame, Contessa and the Dollhouse

The shouting of his brothers rang in his ears, and the crunching of broken glass beneath his feet. Running as fast as he could. Reaching the other end of the alley. Scanning the nearly dead street for his next move. He spotted a man stumbling around his truck across the way. The man told his friend that he was headed out of town to take care of some business, so he had to close up early. So, noticing the man from the church as the backer, he moved quickly, running across the street. Watching the two men exchange friendly banter.

James reached the man's truck, hopping into the bed and scrunching himself into a ball. Praying that he would not see them. He waited a moment and then heard the door slamming, then the engine started up, and the car started moving. Jeremiah, Sam, and Matthew reached the entrance of the alleyway. Dad is going to be so mad, said Sam. Dad is who you're worried about. Really, he is a sheep compared to Mom. "We have to find him," said Jeremiah, and we will know where he is headed, so let's go to the witch's house and intercept him there.

CHAPTER SIX
Reinforcements

The air was colder at this speed, stinging James' face. He gripped the side of the truck every time the backer made a turn and bounced every time he hit a rock or pothole. James looked over the side of the truck, knowing they had to be close since all he saw was the fields and the moon in the clear sky. James laid back down and did not peer his head up until the revving of other engines and the truck came to a complete stop. All next to them, he could see a blue truck. Dropping his head down, he heard men and women shouting and talking about what would happen.

Then the crowd settled, and his father was the only voice he heard. "Tonight, we rid ourselves of the evil. We will free my son. When the fireworks light up the sky, we move in." Hearing the last words touch his ear, James was frozen, analyzing things in his mind on how to save his beloved. So, he waited, lying still against the cold steel of the truck. Listening to the murmurs of the villagers taking bets on who would take the last breath of Contessa, James clenched his fist at this. He waited to see what was supposed to be a majestic sight of colors light up the night sky. Then, the still night was interrupted by the sudden boom of the fireworks, and electric blue spilled over the night sky. He heard the slamming of doors and engines starting all around him.

The car started to move, and he could watch the night sky be painted with the most beautiful colors James had ever seen. Then he heard his mother speak. Backer, Mr. Mayor, you two go through the house, and the rest of us will head around back. James waited and counted to thirty, lifting his head up and peering over the edge of the truck's bed. When he saw the coast was clear, he hopped out of the truck and crept across the driveway. Tiptoeing up the steps, moving ever so slowly, just in case he saw one of the men that entered the house. As he got up the stairs, he saw the front door cracked open. Walking towards it, he peered inside and saw the backer and the mayor parting ways at the staircase. The backer headed upstairs, and the mayor went into the study. James was ready to pounce, standing in the doorway on the balls of his feet.

Watching the foyer becoming empty again, James moved to his left first over the threshold. Bam and James were no longer looking at the foyer but his brothers' faces. "Miss us, little brother?" Jeremiah said. "Nope, can't say I have," said James. Then Sam dragged James to his feet, the three boys leaning back down the stairs. Sam reached for the door of their parent's truck. Matthew grabbed the keys from the ignition and moved out of the way so they could shove James into the passenger seat. "What do we do now?" "We wait until they have his little girlfriend, and when they string her up, we will bring him out so he can watch. Then, by night's end, he will be our brother once more." As they stood outside guarding the truck, there was silence for about ten minutes until they heard a series of gunshots coming from the house.

"They may need our help," Jeremiah said. "You two stay here and watch James while I check it out." James could not see anything through the open front door when he reached the house. So, he walked closer, and out of nowhere, a boom and a blast of heated light rushed towards him, throwing him into the air, landing just feet in front of his brothers. Sam and Mathew raced towards their brother's side. James, without even thinking, slid over to the driver's side door. He opened it and ran out, racing past them. With the house burning before him, he raced to the side, moving at a running pace. He dodged debris, reaching the back of the house where he saw the Montgomerys dressed in their masks and party attire. While standing across from them are his parents and members of the church. Two men held him down while another threw a rope over a branch.

The man on Lenny's left grabbed the rope with his free hand and put it around his neck. Then he and his comrade joined the man who threw the rope over the tree and helped him heave up Lenny. At this horror, James moved towards the crowd until there was a thud. He landed on the cold ground, rolling over to his side. He stared back at a familiar face. It was the face of the mayor lying there, lifeless and cold. He retreated back, turning back over onto his knees. He then stared at black dress shoes. "Don't you dare move, you asshole!" The voice was familiar but distorted, though. He, despite the warning, lifted his head and spoke. "I have to stop them. I love her. I have to save her," said James. "Haven't you done enough? They're stringing up Lenny as we speak. And now I have to think how to save baby girl," said Celeste.

"Let me help you. I love her; I swear this was not me. This was Tilly. She saw us in town today and got our parents involved; now, it is all my fault." Celeste pondered for a moment. Holding the knife firmly in her hand, she said, "Fine. Get up, and let's get down there and do something. Come on. With my magic, I can get us close enough, so maybe you can talk to your parents and get them to end this crusade," said Celeste. "Let's go," said James. As they moved closer, they saw the lifeless body of Lennie up in the tree. Contessa slapped a stunned Hannah, and the preacher picked up the gun. He then pointed it at Frank's chest at the site of Contessa and Grace running into the woods.

Frank, standing between them, stopped abruptly, James slamming into her. "Damn child, wait a second!" she said in what was almost a whisper to not draw attention to herself. She raised her hands, purple and pink sparks spreading across her fingertips, strangulating. The sparks raced from her fingers and across the yard, reaching the preacher as the gun went off. "Dad!" yelled James. "Don't get soft on me now, kid. You need to choose a side. Now, we need to save my family, and if you truly love baby girl, you have to sacrifice for her." "Also, could you imagine if she ever found out that you could have saved her father and did nothing to do so," said Celeste. Despite all that has happened, that is still my family, but I'm with you. They lost their way and have to face the consequences. The sight was of the two men lying on the ground. One lifeless and the other clenching his shoulder.

The Coven was able to raise their hands, ready to battle, firing at the crowd as they retreated towards the woods. "Come on, boy, we have to get to Mr. Frank," said Celeste. They both started to run, sparks firing from her fingers. Racing in front of them and freezing the people to the ground. The villagers were now statues. Finally, the two of them reached Frank and dropped to their knees. "Mr. Frank!" Celeste cried out. "I'm okay. We must get the Coven to safety and find my wife and daughter," said Frank. "Mr. Montgomery, I'm sorry for the trouble I caused, but I truly love your daughter. It wasn't a spell that she put me under. I swear it." said James. "Hush, child, I know it is not your fault. You can't help who you love. This is the fault of a jealous little girl who could not get her way. But none of that matters now. My family is the top priority," said Frank. "Let me help you up, Mr. Frank," said Celeste.

She then asked, "What about them?" "I will spare them; unlike them, I believe in God's word about forgiveness, so I think I will make them forget us, and you and all of us will move somewhere else. James, let me lean on you and Celeste. You heal the coven members and get them together. We move out before sunrise," said frank. Celeste moved over a few feet, helping a woman who was shot in the leg. "Have you seen Lexi? Celeste, where is Lexi?" Asked the woman. "I don't see her. She must be in the woods." Hold still, the closest rubbed her hands together, letting the magic sweep over the wound. Moments later, a silver ball emerged from the wound, and the ball hovered over the wound while the skin started to sew together. "Come on, let's go find the others."

Helping her to her feet, they watched Frank and James move slowly toward James' mother. Frank put his hands on her face. The words left his lips then a cloud of smoke covered her face. She stood like a statue, and Frank spoke. "We are now a figment of your imagination. You will go home forgetting everything and only believing you have three sons instead of four." Frank turned towards James, saying, "Let's get to the barn and get Snowy and the other horses. They will be much easier in the woods." Frank picked up the gun and handed it to James as he spoke. "I hope you're ready. The night is not over." The men went into the woods with some dogs. "We have to hurry; they're gaining on my family." "I am with you, Mr. Montgomery. I'm with you."

CHAPTER SEVEN
Separated

With her eyes tightly shut, Contessa could hear the screeching of tires as the angry mob surrounded the house and party. The coven members were becoming restless, buzzing around like a swarm of bees in their hive. Tessa, with eyes still closed, had no idea what was going on, but she realized that everything that had been going on around her had stopped. Her mother wasn't singing, the orchestra had stopped playing, and the men had stopped chanting. Suddenly, someone was shaking her like a rag doll. "Come on, sweets, open your eyes." The person shaking her said.

Still feeling the effects of the drink, she let her eyes slowly creep open and saw her father standing before her. Looking at him, she saw the look of horror on his face; she had never seen him look like that before. "What is it, dad?" Contessa asked. "I don't know." Using her elbows to sit up, Contessa lifted herself up and turned her body so that her legs were dangling off the table's edge. She saw her mother walking over to them as she took in her surroundings. A hand touched Tessa from behind, sending a chill up her spine, making her turn around to see who it was. She quickly realized it was Lexi, who looked equally scared. She stared at her best friend and then looked back to face her father. As the drink continued to wear off, she realized they were being illuminated by something blinding them. From the sound she was hearing, she assumed it was a car. Her father stepped in front of her as they sat there waiting.

Still Not knowing what was going on or happening. Somewhere in the distance came a voice saying, "Where is she?" At that, Tessa tried to look from behind her father. "Is that you, Hannah?" Tessa's father inquired. "Yes, Frank. I'm sorry to intrude like this. My quarrel is not with you. I am here for your daughter. She put a spell on my son, trying to seduce him. She needs to pay for her crimes." At this point, the other members started to get out of their cars, joining Hannah. Realizing what was happening, Tessa jumped down from the table. She clawed at her dad to get in front of him. He held up his hands to keep her from going anywhere.

Tessa looked over at Lexi in a panic, and in a low whisper, Lexi said, "James? The preacher's son? Oh, girl, you are in so much trouble. You know the rules. Don't you think I know who Hannah is? Did you put a spell on him?" "NO! We love each other! Also, we didn't finish the ceremony, so I haven't even come into my full power. You know I can barely do the simplest of spells, let alone one as complex as a seduction hex." "She poisoned my son and tried to taint his spirit," said Hannah. "You got some balls. Your daddy will kill you if she doesn't do it first," said Lexi. "What are you talking about?" said Tessa's father, looking bewildered at Hannah. "We all know what you people are and what evil you are capable of. I thought you could control your kind, especially your daughter, but I can see now that you can't, so I am here to take matters into my own hands... into God's hands." The mob of villagers stood behind Hannah, screaming and shouting at the Coven in front of them.

"You dare come on my land and threaten my daughter, my people! Leave now, and I promise to take care of my daughter properly. As you keep saying, my kind has our own laws and punishments for breaking said laws. so, if what you say is true, then she will be tried for breaking our laws," her father said. "DAD, I love James. I have never used magic on him. He loves me with a free heart. What is going to happen to him?" She said with fear creeping out of her words.

"ENOUGH!" her father said to her in a voice she had never heard him use with her, making her shrink back in fear. Hannah stood there chewing her lip, considering what Frank said when she added, "Also, you must leave. All of you." In the same voice, but with more intense anger, he said, "NO FUCKING WAY! We will not leave, and I WILL not hand over my daughter to you. If she says she didn't put a spell on him, then she didn't." "Then you leave me no choice. You have condemned you and yours to hell," Hannah said. Then she turned around and yelled, "George!"

Tessa stood there wondering what would happen when she saw a man come from the back of the crowd, pulling a man behind him with a bag over his head and in his other hand, he had a rope. Tessa thought that even though she couldn't see the man's face, something about him seemed oddly familiar. "You people have brought the devil to Blackwood, and I intend on saving this town from you demons. George, bring him to me." Tessa looked at her father, panic thumping in her throat. "I didn't want to have to do this, but seeing as you will not cooperate with our demands, you have forced my hand," Hannah said as she reached over and pulled the bag off the mystery man's head.

Tessa heard her father gasp as she, too, realized who was standing in front of her, Lenny. "We found this one hiding in the barn, and it seems that Celeste put a spell on one of my people to protect this man, so sadly, we had to kill the judge. George the rope, please." George walked over to the massive elm tree that Tessa grew up playing in and threw the rope over one of the branches, and at that, she saw what was at the rope's end. Tessa could taste the acid in the back of her throat that was trying to make its way up from her stomach to her mouth. She knew what was about to happen, and it seemed that everyone else did, too. George walked back over to Lenny and grabbed him by the arm. Lenny winced in pain because that was the arm where he had been shot.

Tessa tried to run over to him, but her father grabbed her and wrapped his arms around her. She wanted to kick him to get away, but no matter what she did, her father's grasp only got tighter. "Hannah, do not do this. You are a God-fearing woman; your God would not condone you killing an innocent man!" Tessa's father pleaded. Hannah threw her head back and laughed, "God will not punish me for this. On the contrary, we will all be rewarded for ridding our home of you devils. George, will you please." George took the noose and put it over Lenny's head, tightening it around his neck. Two more men came over from the crowd, grabbed the other end of the rope, and started pulling. Tessa let out a sob and started screaming. She looked around, trying to find anyone who would do something, but everyone looked just as scared and fearful as she felt. She saw Lexi crying, standing next to her mother, with complete shock on their faces.

Tessa looked back at her father, pleading when she saw the blue sparks twirling around his fingers. He moved his hand in Lenny's direction when she heard a loud pop. Tessa looked up and saw Hannah standing there with a gun in her hand. "Don't even think about it! You're in love with the devil. Try using your magic, and I will shoot your daughter and wife right in front of your eyes." Tessa looked back at her father and said, "Daddy, please do not let them do this. Give me to them so that Lenny does not die for me." Her father looked at her and said, "Sweets, I will not hand you over to them. They came here looking for blood, and whether we give you to them or not, they will not stop killing. They want us gone and will do whatever it takes to make that happen."

Tessa stood there in horror, unable to do anything but watch. The two men kept pulling the rope, and as Lenny's feet left the ground, his body started contorting in pain as he tried to take a breath. All around her, Tessa could hear the screams and cries from the other coven members as they all watched in horror as Lenny was slowly dying. As Lenny hung from the tree branch, fighting to breathe, he started trying to say something. "K-k-keep ba-a-a-aby g-g-gir-r-rl s-s-saf-f-e." His body went limp with that. As Lenny's limp body hung there, all you could hear was silence, and then shrill screams erupted from the coven members from the horror they had just witnessed. Tessa and her father stood there. They listened to the mix of emotions the members were dealing with, and there came laughter from the mob. At first, a small snicker, and then they all broke out in an uproar of laughter.

It was horrendous; Tessa could not fathom how they thought this was funny. At hearing this, Tessa completely lost it. She started screaming and cursing at the church congregation. "You all are fucking monsters!!!!! You come here out for blood, thinking I have hexed someone from your group of people when we are in love. You say you are here to save the souls of your people when you have just condemned them all to hell with this atrocious act of violence. Lenny did nothing to you people!!! Even though I am not a Christian and do not know much about your God and practices, I know that your God would never condone such senseless murder!! You all will suffer in the burning fires in hell, forever haunted by the soul of the man you brutally killed."

As Tessa said this, she began fighting her father again, trying to escape him. She didn't know what to do once she got away from him. All she did know was that she was angry and wanted to make someone pay for what they did to Lenny. Her father went to resituate his grasp, loosening his grip for just a second, and Tessa took that as her chance to escape. She twisted away from her father and started to run toward Hannah. Hannah was standing not 15 feet in front of her. At this point, she was turned away from Tessa talking to her husband. Tessa reached Hannah in about 5 seconds, and before Hannah could react, Tessa drew back her hand and slapped Hannah so hard that she knocked her to the ground. She looked back up at Tessa with shock in her eyes. Frank ran over to Tessa and grabbed her hand before she could strike Hannah again.

"Tessa, no! We are unlike these people; do not stoop to their level." "Father, they killed Lenny. They must pay for this injustice!" "Sweets, don't worry, they will. Karma will be their justice, if not in this life, then in the next, do not worry." "That is not enough, father! They have come here accusing me of things that are not true and then used this lie to justify this murder. They cannot get away with this." Tessa and her father continued to go back and forth about what they had done when Hannah stood up, brushed herself off, and gestured for one of the congregation to come over to her. "Sweets, please calm down. We need to get you out of here before any more blood is shed. They are not done here. They have not gotten what they came for yet."

Before Contessa could respond, there was a loud BOOM. Tessa turned around to find Hannah with an evil smile. A man beside her with a gun pointed at them, smoke pouring out of the gun. She did not understand what was happening when she turned back to her father and saw him with his hands against his stomach, blood seeping out between his fingers. "NO!" Tessa screamed. Her father looked shocked at first, and then a rage that Tessa had never seen on him before took over. He let out a loud cry, almost like a battle cry, and charged the man with the gun. Before he had a chance to pull the trigger again, Frank tackled the assailant to the ground. "Grace, grab Contessa and run!!!" Before Tessa could argue, she felt a tug at her hand and turned to find her mom pulling her toward the woods. She tried to fight, but she was still so weak from the pink liquor and the events that had just unfolded that she stopped resisting and let her mother pull her along.

They ran straight for the woods. Tessa heard another loud pop and turned around just in time to see her father drop to his knees. The blood in her veins ran cold. She tried to make her mom stop running, but she wouldn't. They got to the edge of the woods when Tessa ripped her hand from her mom's, stopped, and stared at the plantation that she once had amazing memories of. In the yard that she grew up playing in was now a battle scene.

The coven members had their hands in the air, with different colors shooting from their fingers, fire, frost, and lightning flying toward the church congregation. They were firing bullets back at their attackers. Tessa could not believe the sight she was seeing. All this because she fell in love with the preacher's son; she just couldn't wrap her mind around it. The coven members also began to move towards the woods, trying to take cover within the trees, blending into the darkness, making it harder for the congregation to hit them.

Grace grabbed her hand again and began to pull her into the shade of the trees. Hannah and the rest were now taking shelter behind their cars. They returned fire into the black abyss in front of them. Finally, they were in the woods, the low-hanging branches hitting them in the face and arms, making little cuts wherever they hit. "Stop, Mom, please slow down," Contessa yelled. "We can't," her mother responded as she dragged them deeper into the cover of the trees. Suddenly, her mother's foot hit something, sending both of them tumbling down a hill until, finally, a small clearing stopped their descent.

Getting to their feet, Tessa felt a shooting pain go down her arm. "Mom, I'm hurt," she lifted her arm up, and from her elbow to her hand, it just hung there, almost like it was filled with jelly. Before her mom could do anything to help her, they heard the barking of dogs and the rustling of bushes. "Tessa, move," her mother said as they both moved over behind an old, twisted tree, whose trunk and branches had almost formed a cave. Tessa picked up a big branch she had found, preparing herself for battle. The footsteps were getting closer, and so was the growling. Finally, there was a pack of snarling dogs in front of them.

Her mother pushed her back and stuck her hand out, mumbling something under her breath. Electricity began to spark from her fingers and then shot out, hitting the dog in the center of the pack. It knocked the dog back for a minute, but then it shook itself off and headed right back to the spot it was originally standing in. It reached out and grabbed Grace's dress with its teeth and began to shake it. "MOM!" Tessa said as tears began to roll down her cheeks. The villagers, hearing the commotion, were now at the top of the clearing. They made their way down to where they were hiding. "Think Contessa, think." She said to herself. Finally, she remembered what her father had done earlier. She raised her uninjured arm towards the sky and started mumbling the words she had heard her father say not hours before. Nothing. "Come on, Tessa, you're the daughter of Frank and Grace Montgomery. You are Contessa Ann Marie Montgomery, now do it, damn it." She said to herself. At that, she began to speak the words again, and blue sparks began to form around her fingers.

The sparks turned into flames, and she thrust her hand towards the dog, attacking her mother. It hit it with force and sent the dog flying into the air and throwing it against a tree. The flame then continued onwards towards the clearing where the villagers were standing. It wrapped around them, and then the dragonfly shot into the sky, knocking the people backward and lighting the night sky. At this, Tessa saw a man standing to the side with a gun pointing at her mother. She started to say something; she didn't know how she knew them, but it was almost instinctual. She continued muttering, almost chanting, and then a red bolt shot from her hand and hit the man with the gun right in the chest. He dropped the gun and just stood there, grabbing his chest. His eyes rolled into the back of his head, and then a red flame filled his eyes, and he imploded.

All this chaos and then nothing, silence. She listened closely and heard the rustling of the underbrush and the retreating footsteps of the villagers. Then she heard a howl, not from a dog, but something else. Suddenly, she heard the villagers screaming, not a scream of fear, but the screams of death. She heard several gunshots and then the thuds of bodies hitting the ground. Contessa and her mom sat there listening. Then, out of nowhere, two silver eyes were staring at them, almost like the moon had had chips removed and placed in the irises of these eyes. Grace got to her feet and instinctively faced this unknown creature, ready to fight and protect her daughter. "Listen here, I will kill you. Just go away," her mother warned. "What are you waiting for?" Her mother asked the mysterious creature.

It just sat there staring like a cat playing with its prey. "Mom, stop!" Contessa said, grabbing her mother's hand before she could do anything, "You saved us, didn't you?" Tessa knelt down and reached out to touch the wolf. As she touched his fur, she rubbed his back and then down one of his legs, feeling the hot stickiness of blood. "Mom, we have to help him, please!" "I don't know if I can, Tessa. I don't have anything with me, but I will try." Grace bent down next to her daughter, letting her hands hover over the spot where the animal was injured, speaking under her breath. The wolf lay down whimpering, and her mother pulled out a small silvery ball and let it drop to the floor. Then she stopped speaking, purple sparks wrapped around the dog's leg, and the wound closed up.

CHAPTER EIGHT
The shadows

Contessa and her mom were lying up against a tree, exhausted. Even though the chaos from the attack had died down, they were still hiding in an alcove of trees. Where a once bright full moon hung, lighting up the night sky was now covered by dark clouds and smoke from all the fire and gunshots that had been exchanged. The forest was now eerily quiet. Not a sound could be heard, and the only noise was that from the wind blowing between the trees. Tessa lay there trying to stay awake, fighting her heavy eyelids from closing. Still, all she could think about was her friends and family. What had happened to her father? Lexi? Celeste?

Every time she closed her eyes, she could see the image of her father on his knees and a gun in his face. Were they going to go back to see what happened? Was there anything to go back to? Her mind was racing as she kept fighting her body from shutting down. Finally, she couldn't fight anymore and let her eyes close. Her mind wandered into Queen Mab's realm, and she could have sworn that as she closed her eyes, she saw a shadowy figure standing just a few feet away, watching her and her mother. She even thought that she could feel something watching her. She couldn't do anything about it, though, because at that moment, her body gave up and passed out. Woooooooshhhhh, something blew across Grace's face, causing her to shiver. She abruptly opened her eyes and saw something fly by her; she quickly got up and looked around.

The wolf that Grace had healed was still lying at her feet, and when she got up, he popped his head up and stared at her. Grace continued to look around, her hair on end, "You stay here, wolf, and watch over my daughter. I'm going to see what that was." As Grace said this, she could have sworn that the wolf understood her because it looked like he nodded in agreement. Grace walked out of the alcove they had been hiding in. She started to walk into the rest of the forest. She stopped suddenly because the wind began to pick up, and when it did, she heard something say, "We can help you," it seemed to come up from the trees.

She took a deep breath and continued walking into the woods, kicking up leaves and dirt as she did, pushing low-bearing tree limbs out of her face. She had reached an incline when she could feel someone or something's eyes on her. She stopped and asked, "Who's there?" "Is she worthy enough?" said another voice that was carried by another gust of wind from her left. "I don't know," a completely different voice said behind her. Grace began frantically looking around, "ENOUGH!!! Show yourself God damn it!" Looking around her, she tried to remember every defensive spell she knew. "Calm, my child," another voice said from her right. "We are here to help you and your daughter, to get back everything you lost," the voice on her right said, "At a cost, of course." "What is this price," said Grace curiously. In unison, the voices responded, "In due time, my dear, in due time." This sent chills up and down Grace's body and shook her to her soul. Still not knowing exactly where these voices were coming from or to whom the voices belonged, she took a step back.

"No more games! SHOW YOURSELVES NOW!!" "Very well," all the voices said in unison. The wind picked up rapidly, blowing through the whole forest; shadowy figures swirled around the trees and all around her. They seemed to come from every direction, all coming together to form one body right before Grace. The first thing to appear was their feet, legs, hips, torso, neck, and head. When they all came together, they did not form a normal body. It wasn't a tangible or normal-looking body but all shadows.

Now, with this fully formed shadow man standing right before Grace, she was scared. She couldn't remember the last time she was terrified because she had always had the security of her magic. It was the only constant in her life since her parents died when she was just a little girl. All she knew was survival, so she took a deep breath and stepped toward the shadow man. As she did this, the clouds moved away from the moon, letting it shine on the clearing where they were standing, and that's when Grace really saw what the shadow man looked like.

She saw dozens of silver-lined faces and body parts trying to push through the body they were currently making up. Little screams were escaping all the mouths of the body. This caused Grace to gasp in fear at the horror she was facing, and she thought of Contessa, but she realized none of that mattered. Her path was revenge, and she would do whatever needed to be done to make that happen. "I will do whatever you want," Grace said confidently. "What we want is energy," said the voice coming from the face, "And souls," said one of the faces pushing out of the upper left arm.

"We will provide everything you need, which won't be difficult for you. It will be just like breathing." "Fine, anything you want. Now I must get back to my daughter before she wakes," Grace said. As she turned to walk away, the body spoke again, "Wait just a minute," and with those words came a bitterly cold wind. "You did not think we would do all of this without gaining some insurance, do you?" said one of the mouths from the torso. "What kind of insurance?" Grace said with a slight tremble as she tried to keep her composure. "You will sign a contract, and we will keep your soul until the debt is paid."

At those words, she thought about her soul. Did she really need it? For what, heaven? She was born damned, so that didn't matter. For love? Her friends and soul mate were dead, so she didn't need it for that either. Her daughter? The love for your daughter was more than just having a soul; it is almost instinctual, so she also didn't need it for that. With confidence lacing her words, she responded, "Where do I sign?"

The shadow raised up, outstretched his hand, and a piece of parchment and quill appeared out of thin air. With a flick of its wrist, the parchment unrolled. Grace reached for the quill and went to sign the paper when she realized there was no ink. "How am I supposed to sign this with no ink?" "Think, Grace, I know you are smart." She said the mouth on the face, which she realized was the main shadow, the one running things. She thought for a minute and finally realized what he meant, "Blood, you want me to sign in blood." "Good girl, I knew you were smart." She looked at him and then took the quill and jabbed the tip of her finger forcefully, letting the blood bubble up enough so that she could dip the quill in it.

Now she had her ink and went to sign the paper, but then she hesitated. "I have one more question. What do you want with the energy and the souls?" "We want the dark energy because we can't survive in this world without it, and the souls help to harness the energy and power. When we have enough souls, we will free yours." "I don't understand how the souls harness the energy?" "In short, the people you take the souls from are the ones that will be collecting the energy; they need to be soulless so that they can do what they need to get said energy. Do not worry, Grace. All will be clear soon."

At this, she shrugged and then signed. As soon as she wrote the last letter, the pen started to melt. As it did this, it flowed towards her body and made an outline around her. At first, it was painless, but then it started to feel like it was making a thousand cuts into her body. It felt like her skin was being ripped from her body, and she let out a blood-curdling scream. She dropped to her knees and then fell onto her side, curling up into a ball. Through the pain, she felt something soft brush up against her, and then, through the screams, she heard a low growling coming from somewhere in front of her. Unable to look and see what it was, she just tried to focus on anything besides the pain she was feeling. Suddenly, something hit her face, and a massive amount of wind started swirling around her. Her insides felt like they wanted to be outside her body; she felt like she had an out-of-body experience.

The pain reached a climax, which made her body twist in pain. She could feel something rip out of her, and then, just as quickly as the pain started, it was over. She didn't feel pain or wind and couldn't hear anything. She just lay there waiting to catch her breath, and then she felt that same thing rub up against her again, so she reached out her arm and opened her eyes to find the wolf standing there staring at her. "Didn't I tell you to stay with Contessa?" At this, the wolf shook his head rapidly and motioned. It was to tell her to lean on him to get up. Grace did as the wolf asked, or at least what she thought he was asking, and used him to help herself off the ground.

The wolf then approached Grace and motioned for her to follow him. They walked back to Contessa, and when they got to Contessa Grace saw her daughter cupping her arm wincing in pain so she kneeled beside her and mended her broken arm, then both the wolf and Grace laid down and fell back to sleep. The sun started to rise and slowly crept into the clearing where the wolf lay sleeping, his head on Contessa's leg. As the sun touched the wolf's back paw, his fur started to blow away, and its bones began to crack and form into toes, the heel, and then legs. His hips began to crack and twist from wolf hips to humans. As the sun fully enveloped the wolf, all his bones twisted and broke, changing, and finally, where once laid a wolf was now a naked human man. All the moving from him changing woke Contessa. She slowly lifted her head, and with sleep still in her eyes, she looked up just in time to see the butt of a naked man running away from her. She jumped up, ran over to her mom's side, and shook her rapidly.

"Mom, wake up now! There is a naked man in the woods; I think he was watching us while we slept." Grace jumped up with her hands full of purple sparks, ready for a fight. Grace looked around, seeing that the wolf was gone and where he lay was now a pile of fur. She started to relax and let the sparks dissipate from her fingers. "We are fine. It was a wolf. Now get ready. We have a lot of walking to do," Grace told Tessa. Contessa stood there for a moment, putting all this information together. Realization hit that the naked man had once been the wolf that had protected them so fiercely the night before. She started to collect her things and followed her mother out of the clearing. As they walked, Contessa noticed something different about her mother's demeanor that wasn't there the night before.

Still, she knew that that was ridiculous, so she let it slip from her mind and kept following her mother. "Where do you think the wolf went?" Said Contessa. "Who cares? We need not worry ourselves with that; what we need to worry about is how we will get out of these woods." For a long time, they just wandered through the woods blindly. Go left, go right, go straight, but never really going anywhere fast. Grace was about to give up as they walked, which wasn't in her nature. She was growing tired when something inside her started pulling at her. It tells her to make a left at the tree in front of them. When they reached the tree, they turned left, and smack hit something, making her fall back into Contessa. "Hey, watch it!" Contessa said. "I hit something, you stupid girl!" "You hit someone, and that someone is me," said the voice in front of them.

Then, the ground started shaking, and six rocks floated around them. Contessa looked down and saw the tree's roots protruding from the ground. "Mom, is this you?" said Contessa, never seeing this kind of power before from anyone. "Wait, calm down. It's me, the wolf. I saved you, remember?" When the words hit Grace's ears, it made her relax, and the earth stopped shaking. The six rocks hit the ground hard and split into two. "My name is Kalvin. I was running from my pack. No need to bore you with details, but I ran and ended up here in these woods, and I think we can help each other," said Kalvin. "How?" asked Grace, standing there eying him. "Well, first, I can get you out of here. He said you said you have never been in these woods." Grace said. "Well, my ears tell me a river is five miles to the left, and my nose tells me to the right two miles that way is a nice fat deer. So, you choose where you want to go."

Grace sat there, and then her gut told her to go to the river. "Okay, wolf, take us to the river," said Grace. And he turned, and the three started walking towards the river. When they reached the river, the three dropped to their knees and started cupping the water and drinking it, splashing it in their faces like they had walked through the desert for days. Then Contessa moved her feet out from under her and saw her feet and saw she had lost her slipper and then the other one and a hole in it. "Now what?" Asked Contessa with a puzzled, exhausted look on her face. "I still don't know, so stop asking me," said her mother, with an intense stern tone to her voice. With this angry feeling boiling up inside her, she grabbed her ballet slipper.

She ripped it off, threw it into the water, slipped it into the water with a plunge, and looked at the sky, leaning back into her arms and soaking in the sun's warmth. Toot came a sound. "Look, it's a boat," said Kalvin. Contessa then looked from the sky to the boat out on the river. It was a riverboat, white with a red tail. They got to their feet. "What do we do?" Asked Contessa. "Get its attention," said her mother. With that, they all jumped up and waved their hands, and the boat started to change course towards them.

When the boat came up beside them, they read on the side of the boat Redfin Ray's river boat cruises. Then, a group of men lowered a wood plank to bridge the gap between land and water. "Are you all alright? Asked the captain, a tall, slender man with a scruffy beard. "No, we have been stuck in the woods all night," which was apparent by their look. We were chased by wolves and were cold, hungry, and tired. Can you please help us?" "My word, child, come aboard, please. I will help you. Get some blankets and food, and you escort them to the dining hall."

The three of them walked onto the plank of wood across it and ended up on the boat, then the crew member directed them towards the dining hall. When they reached the dining hall, they sat around the table and were handed blankets, and out came a chief with food that he placed in front of them. In walked the captain. "Where are you three headed? Asked the captain. "I don't know," said Grace. "Were you headed to New Orleans to pick up another set of people for the cruise?" Grace sat and pondered this and waited to be told what to do.

Then it came, clenching her stomach as it came, and she said, "Well, I guess New Orleans is as good a place as any to start. Okay, raise the plank and tell the bridge full steam ahead." Then the crew member said, "Yes, captain," and ran out of the room. The three of them sat there eating like lions, ripping into their food with no fork, food just dripping from their mouths.

Contessa wiped her face with her arm and pushed the plate away, asking the chief where the bathroom was, then got up and walked out of the room. "Now you listen here, you wolf; whatever happened in those woods with that thing, you hush up about it. Don't say a word to Contessa. You hear me?" "Calm down, Madam. Your secret's safe with me. All I ask is that you protect me, and I want to come with you if you agree that we are in this together."

Humm, she thought. Madam had a ring to it and a sense of power in the name. Contessa returned, and they sat in silence until they reached the harbor dock in New Orleans. The captain came into the dining hall and told them they had docked and may leave the boat anytime. The three of them got out of their chairs and thanked the captain for their hospitality. They then walked out of the dining hall onto the deck, down the plank onto the dock.

CHAPTER NINE
The woods

James and Celeste emerged from the barn with three horses racing towards Frank. As they approached, they watched as Frank lowered his friend from the tree, laid Lenny down on the ground, rose to his feet, and stood over his friend, outstretching his hand. "Let your spirit soar," Frank said as the sparks left his hand and covered Lenny's body. A gust of wind blew, and Lenny's body drifted away in the wind, and he was no more. Frank wiped a tear from his eye and mounted a horse. "Let's save who we can," Frank told his two companions.

They raced deeper into the woods and helped fellow coven members conquer their attackers. Frank used his magic to launch big tree branches at the villages. Celeste set one on fire with hers, and James shot them dead as they passed. Screams of spells and gunfire were heard in the background. Frank fought off the advancing villagers from his left and right with the faint sound of the hounds in the background. Flinging sparks at as many as he could, which finally seemed to be working since they ran into the night. "Everyone who can hear me, some of you care for the wounded, and the rest of us will advance. look for my wife and daughter; we don't rest until they're found," said Frank, catching his breath in between words. "Let's ride!" he continued. The three raced passed a woman healing the others, and a few men joined them at either side.

They continued the search. "Mr. Frank, we should follow the dogs. They got baby girl's scent. I just know that is where we should be heading," said Celeste. "I agree with her. It is all my mother wanted. She is the target," said James. "Alright then, we will head east where the barking seems to be headed. Let the stars be our guide," said Frank. Woof... Woof came the sounds that broke the silence of the evening. They must be close," said Frank. "The Fuck?!" James screamed as he started to shake one of the hounds gnawing on his leg.

He could feel the flesh of his calf being split apart. POP!!!!! The sound was so loud it startled the hound, and it let go of James' leg POP!!!! Another loud blow made the hound whimper in fear, running into the woods. "Let me look at your leg, boy," said Frank. "It is fine. We have to find Contessa," said James in a thunderous and assertive voice. "Don't be stupid. You're no good to her if you bleed out in the woods, so give me your leg," said Frank. "Fine!" James said in protest, lifting his leg.

Frank moved close to him, propping James' leg up on his thigh, knowing right away the wound was deep. "This is going to sting. Dismount so I can hold you down, and Celest can mend your wounds," said Frank. Frank and Celeste dismounted, walking over to James and helping him down. I don't have much stuff to make it feel a little less painful said Celeste. Frank helped James to the ground. Celeste handed him a small vile that had a little liquid in it. He took it and downed it one gulp. Frank turned him over on his chest and sat on him. Well, Celeste laid her fingertips on his calf at the start of the opening, taking a deep breath.

Purple mist left her fingers lingering over the wound, seeping into it, closing it tight. Behind it, James bites his lip not to scream and give away their location. "This will have to do. You will be able to ride, but not much else. Skin closes easier than muscle repairs," said Celeste as she rose to her feet and mounted her horse. Frank got James on his feet and back on his horse, and they continued to ride. Heading in the direction the hounds came from, they came to an empty clearing, looking around but not seeing a soul in sight. "They could be anywhere," said James. "Yes, but they were here. I can feel the presence of strong magic surrounding us," said Frank. "How can you tell?" Asked James. "Baby magic finds magic; it just does," said Celest with a tired look in her eyes. "Celeste, grab my hand," said Frank. "We seek a lost friend who is nowhere to be found. Show us their path and make their footprints take us to them. Bless it be."

With the words they spoke, a mist came into the clearing. In front of them, the mist split apart, creating several figures, one that Frank knew was his wife. Still, there was a figure she was talking to. At the edge of the clearing were a dog and a body. They were curled up on the floor, leaning against a tree. "That must be baby girl," said Celeste. They watched the events fold out. Grace on the ground, a little creature now appearing next to her, then it and the other figure no longer there. Now, she talks to the dog and wakes up Contessa. They both leave the clearing. "Let's go follow them," said Frank. They all moved out of the clearing, making their way to the end of the road.

They ended up at the river, where they saw the mist take them on the steamboat and vanish. "Damn it, the path runs cold," said James. "Calm down. It may take us time. Still, we at least now know they are safe. Let's regroup at the plantation and talk to the rest of the cove. Eat, drink, and sleep should be our priority," said Frank. "I agree it is at least going to take the rest of the morning to get home, and then we have to find someplace to go until we can rebuild," said Celeste. "We're safe now in Blackwood. No one remembers you. We're safe until we're not. The spell I did is not strong, so at any moment, their memories can return to them, so, for now, the plantation, but afterward, we must find a new home," said Frank. Without another word, they rode through the woods again. Not stopping until they saw the rubble of the plantation and what was left of a joyous celebration.

CHAPTER TEN
Moving on up

They walked down the wooden dock and passed the local fishermen cleaning their daily catch, cats pawing at the fish heads that fell to the ground, and seagulls circling above. They kept walking towards the end of the harbor and entered the first place. On the left, it was a bar. The bar was nearly empty, with twelve round tables with local fishermen drinking and playing cards. There was a bartender serving drinks and a man playing the piano accompanied by a saxophone player. "What are you drinking, honey?" Asked the bartender, a tall man with wild brown hair and an unkept beard; he had brown linen pants and an oversized t-shirt. Behind him were a glass mirror and rows of bottles filled with liquor.

Grace looked at him and said, "We have no money. We just want to find a place to stay, work, and clean clothes." "Wow, and I thought my story was sad. Well, here, sit and let me get you something on the house." The man grabbed three glasses from under the bar, reached behind him, grabbed the bottle, and poured the brown liquid into the glasses. Pushing it towards them. "Name's Monty, what is yours, sugar?" Asked Monty. "Excuse me? How dare you speak to me like a street whore!" She spat at Monty. "Wooo, sorry, Madame," said Monty. Madame Grace thought to herself, sounds like a boss of a woman with power, and then nodded at Monty as if to say okay, I'm fine with that.

"Let's start over. My name is Monty. I came here from New York City. I came here after my father, a hedge fund manager, tried to marry me off to his boss' daughter, Bree. I dated her for a while, but she was snotty, too prissy, and too proper, so I waited till my trust fund kicked in and left the bitch. I got to the train station, taking the first train out, not caring where it went. I just knew I would be on it, and after some time, I winded up here until the next adventure comes my way. Now, what is your story? Who are your companions?" Asked Monty. "This is my daughter Contessa, and this is Kalvin," Grace said, waving her hand in their direction with a could-care-less look on her face. "Okay, why do you look like you got hit with the ugly stick and beat mercifully?" "Excuse me," said Grace, with Kalvin standing ready for a fight.

"Calm down. I am just saying, look at yourselves. You have no shoes," pointing at Contessa. "You, boy, look like a cat got the best of you," pointing at his claw-marked shirt. "And you, Madame, your hair reminds me of sunflowers. It is going in all directions to stay in the sun." At this, instinctively, Grace grabbed her hair, and a look of sadness started to come over, but she kept her composure. "So, tell me what your story is," repeated Monty. "Well, we were chased out of our home, which was burned down. By the way, my husband is dead. We slept in the woods since the dogs and villagers chased us, and now we are here," said Grace as she told their story. Kalvin sat back down and grabbed his drink, took a sip, and placed it back down on the bar.

Contessa sat there in silence, not drinking but staring at this man who, for no uncertain reason, frazzled her mother's feather. This was amusing and interesting at the same time because no one dared speak to her like this because they all knew what her mother was capable of, she thought to herself. "Well, that is depressing. Well, let me see if you are…" Monty said. Monty continued to speak and point to a man in the corner. "Mr. Johnson is looking for a live-in maid if that interests you. I could use a waitress and a bar back for the two of you," Said Monty, looking at Contessa and Kalvin. "Well, we are looking for something more fitted to our social class," said Grace with a matter-of-fact tone to her voice. Okay, by the way, what is that because the only place you look like you're going is behind back to the dumpster, " said Monty. "You know what, we're leaving!" She got up and knocked over the bar stool as she did. "Let's go!"

Contessa and Kalvin got up and followed Grace, approaching the door. Grace stopped and saw a sign: COME TO THE FRENCH QUARTER WHERE NEW OPPORTUNITY AWAITS. After reading the sign, Grace turned to Monty and said, "We are going to go from tourists to the top there in the French Quarter while you will be here slinging back drinks, ha-ha," she chuckled as she walked out of the bar. "Mom, how are we going to get there?" She said, "Patience, my dear, let Mama worry about that." Contessa looked at Kalvin with a concerned look on her face.

Monty stared past them and pondered for a second, then suddenly jumped over the counter and looked at his boss, who had just walked in. "I quit! Wait up," said Monty as he ran after them. Monty pushed through the doors and stopped in front of them. "How are you going to get there?" asked Monty. "Well, we are going to walk or hitch a ride with some nice people," said Grace. "Or you could let me drive you, but on one condition. That you let me stick with you guys," said Monty. "Why would you do that when you said pretty much, we look homeless?" Asked Grace. "Well, Madame, you intrigue me, and I believe I could start my next adventure if I go with you. So, what do you say? I make a mean drink and am great with customers," said Monty. "Fine, where is your car?" asked Grace on the side of the building. "Monty, follow me," he said with a smile, and they did just that. "See, Contessa, you always make men feel like they're in charge. Always remember life is a game, and I will teach you the rules."

They reached Monty's Model T and headed to the French Quarter. Leaving this small town, passing a lot of grass along the countryside, they reached the French Quarter. Monty pulled to the side of the road, turned off the engine, and told everyone to get out and start here. "Where is here?" Asked Kalvin. "My friend Deedee's restaurant has the best gumbo in town. She will know where we can find a place to live and where to get work." They entered the restaurant, and Monty saw his friend Deedee behind the counter. A short, pudgy black woman with black hair in a bun waving a spoon at a patron.

"How dare you bring your ass in here talking about my gumbo. I put my blood, sweat, and tears in this here gumbo, and if you would get your head out of that paper and start eating the gumbo, it would not be so cold, dumb ass. Now, eat that gumbo!" Deedee said. Then Deedee grabbed the book and threw it across the room. The man said, "I want to speak to the manager." "You're looking at her," said Deedee. "Who is above you?" Asked the man. "Jesus, and he don't want to talk to you, stupid," said Deedee.

The man threw the bowl on the floor, and Deedee turned red. She walked around the counter and started hitting the man with the wooden spoon. Monty stopped Deedee, grabbed the spoon out of her hand, and held her back as the man ran out. He passed Contessa, her mother, and Kalvin and headed out the door. "Don't ever come back, you hear? Deedee yelled after the man. "You okay? now can I let you go?" said Monty. "Yes, I'm fine. Sorry you folks had to see me like that. I just feel a way about my food, and as long as you like it, I can like you. Sit and let me get you a bowl for the trouble," said Deedee. "Who is your friend Monty? "We are not his friends," said Grace. They all sat down, and Deedee stepped over the pile of gumbo. Grace asked if there was a business venture that they could do that was not considered common work. "Sure; what do you want to do?" Asked Deedee. "I don't know," said Grace.

Deedee thought for a second and then said, "Oh wait, would you like to own a hotel? It is old, and boy was it a sight to see when it was at its prime, but since the rich folks moved here to the center of the French Quarter, it became obsolete. People just started to go elsewhere, and it closed. I know the realtor. I know you can get it for real cheap. I could be your chef and Monty, your bartender. The boy could do maintenance, the girl could be a maid, and you could run it."

"Don't you have the restaurant to worry about?" Asked Grace. "Well, it runs itself, and let's be honest, my sister Deloris could run it. She has my recipes and knows what to do. What do you all say? "Then Grace waited until that feeling said it was a good idea, and a voice came. The hotel is a good idea. It will help give us great energy, and Grace asked herself why. "We will let you know. Just fix the place up, and all will be revealed." "Okay, let's do it. Deedee, call your sister," said Grace.

Then Deedee got up, ran to the phone, picked it up, and dialed. All Grace heard was, "Hello," and "See you here in ten minutes," then Deedee hung up the phone. "Let's go!" Deedee shouted at the group. "Watch the restaurant!" Deedee shouted toward the kitchen. A woman's voice from the kitchen said, "Okay!" "Let's go. No time to waste," Deedee said again. They got up from their chairs and headed out the door. When they were out on the street, Deedee shoved them in the car. "We're going to Majestic Avenue. The Realtor will meet us there. Chop-chop Monty; we're burning daylight," Deedee said. "Okay, I am going!" Said, Monty. Away they went. The car turned down A street and made its way toward the edge of the French Quarter.

The Madame, Contessa and the Dollhouse

When the car reached the hotel and Monty turned off the engine, they all got out of the car. Wow, mom!" Contessa said as she exited the car and looked up at a three-story brick building with iron balconies and boards on the windows. "Hello, my name is Reed Johnson, and this is the Old Mill Hotel. It's called that because it was once a mill and then converted into a hotel by Mr. Clark and his brother." Grace did another round of introductions; then Reed brought them inside. They walked through the doors and saw a grand staircase with dirty red carpeting and a broken banister. On the left was the front desk with keys hanging on the wall with a door next to it. Then Contessa went right through the door on the right. Kalvin followed her, and they walked into the lounge. It had a stage, a bar, and a door that led to the kitchen.

The chairs were broken, and there was dirt everywhere. "Aww!" Screamed Contessa as something furry rubbed up against her leg. "It is just a rat. You know, for a witch, you're pretty jumpy. You remember? You do have powers," said Kalvin. "I know that, but I am not very good. I have only been in training for a few weeks," said Contessa. "Okay, I will protect you until you can protect yourself. The hotel has three stories, twelve bedrooms, a lounge, kitchen, office, and basement with a guest cottage out back. The seller is asking for one hundred thousand dollars, but just to let you know, there is nothing but fortune tellers, witch doctors, and women of the night around here. It will be an uphill battle to get this place to where it once was, but if you can, it will be amazing," said Reed. "Well, what do you think? We don't have that kind of money."

"Hello, yes, we do. I mean, I will lend you the money. You can pay me back, and as long as you promise me room and board, you and I can become partners. So, what do you say, Madame?" said Monty. "Yeah, mom, let's do it," said Contessa. "Fine, okay, Monty, you have a deal." Monty turned to Mr. Reed and told them they had a deal. "We will go to the office and sign the paperwork and then give you your money," said Monty. The men shook hands, and Monty said to the group that he would be back, and they would get started on the renovations.

CHAPTER ELEVEN
The remodel

"Ha!" said Grace as Monty and Reed walked out of the door. "Waiting for you, alright, you three, let's make magic." Grace clapped her hands with a determined tone in her voice. "Contessa, go find the maid's cart and clean some rooms. Deedee the kitchen. Kalvin, look into the elevator, and I will do the office and front lobby." Then everyone turned and went to work. "Remember, we need to open soon. We won't rest until this place is spotless." Kalvin and Contessa waited for Deedee to enter the kitchen and walked back toward Grace. "We could be done with a wave of a hand. Why are we scrubbing floors?"

Her mother looked at her with a stern look. "I have already been burned once this week. I don't need to touch a stove twice to know it is hot." Now, with such an angry, harsh tone to her voice, "Baby, we have to live in the shadows so we don't end up strung to a tree or burned alive. Besides, we don't know if Monty or Deedee will keep our secret. So, for now, no magic or transformation in front of them. So, we can do it to fix the elevator as long as she is in the kitchen." Grace nodded. "Also, I will work on a blinding spell, so when they see magic, they won't think it's magic," said Grace. Then Kalvin and Contessa looked at the kitchen door. Kalvin looked at Contessa and said he would watch the door so she could zap the elevator into working. Contessa nodded her head and walked over to the elevator.

Grace walked behind the front desk, and Contessa raised both of her hands. She said the word "fix amatotas," Blue and green sparks came out of her hands and made their way into the elevator. It was like the elevator was absorbing the magic like your ears absorb sound. the wires looked like an accordion and moved back into place. The panel on the floor now floated into the air and concealed the wires. Four small screws levitated and screwed the panel securely into place. The elevator light turned on when the blue and green sparks were no more. Then Contessa turned on her heel and walked to the other side of the staircase. She opened the door to grab the maid's cart, walked into the elevator, closed the iron safety gate, and hit the button for the second floor.

Kalvin walked across the lobby, moving without noise. He walked with such grace to the lounge to start cleaning. Now alone, Grace sat behind the front desk. Then she went to the door, grabbed the knob, and turned the knob pushing open the door and walking into her office. There was a desk with an eggplant-colored chair, a bookcase, a picture of a man in a black suit, and a safe. Two windows boarded up floor-length drapes, and the wallpaper was peeling. The wood floors were soaked and had a pee smell coming from everywhere, so she raised her hands before she walked any farther. She said, "Claeanorous!" The wallpaper seamlessly stuck itself back to the wall. The dust and dirt started coming to the center of the room. The boards flew out onto the wall, and the glass sewed itself together. When it was done, it looked brand new. Water started to come out of the wood. Grace threw it out the window with the wave of her hand. And everything that was once old and dirty was brand new.

Grace walked over to her desk, pushed the chair, and sat down. She opened the top drawer. Looking inside was a black book that said guest, and she opened it. The first name read Agatha Clark, which was to Grace, indicating that she must be Mr. Clark's wife, which was sweet. As she read the guest book, the temperature started to drop, and the black emptiness from the shadowy corners started to absorb the room. "Underneath the bookcase," said the voices that came from the shadows, which made Grace jump up and look around for the source of the voices.

"Move the bookcase now," said the shadows, so Grace moved out from around her desk and raised her hand. Without a word, she moved her hand from left to right, which made the bookcase move to reveal a round, golden ring embedded into the floor. Grace walked over to the ring, bent down, and the floor separated and revealed a staircase. Before she could step down onto the staircase, the darkness of the shadows moved down the staircase. When the feeling passed, she stepped down and descended to the cellar. When she was at the bottom of the stairs, she saw the last of a man appear just like before in the woods. Around the shadow man were stone walls with lanterns on them. Bird cages on the far wall, a desk and chair in front of them, and an empty spot in the corner. Grace thought to herself a cauldron would look good there, and the shelves above it could hold the ingredients and potions and a fireplace behind the shadow. "Madame," said the voice from the silver lips out of the shadow's face, pushing out of the shadow's face.

"You will open this hotel as a brothel. You will hire nine girls and boys to collect their souls. With their nightly duties, we will collect the dark energy, and you will shower them with gifts, food, and a place to stay. Therefore, they will work for you as you work for us." Then, nine hanging dolls were swinging lifelessly in the air. "Take them, and we will tell you what happens next when it is time. If you collect the dark energy from the patrons for us, we can soon rise to power, and you can regain your soul. Hurry and get this place fully operational by week's end."

With a quiver in her voice, standing in the darkness next to the stairs, Grace asked how she would pay for staff. The silver face protruding from the left arm said, "Madame, we will take care of that. You can trust Monty and Deedee. Remember this if nothing else. Sometimes, secrets are more powerful than money when buying someone's loyalty. You find out their secrets, and you can make them do anything. Now go and do what I asked you."

Then, the shadows flew out from the center of itself and through the walls, dropping the nine dolls. Then Grace walked over, bent to pick them up, got up with the dolls in hand, and put them on the shelf on the wall. She then turned and walked up the stairs. Now back in her office, she shut the door, put the bookcase back, opened the door, and went back into the lobby. Then, she made her way to the kitchen. When she got in there, she saw Deedee scrubbing the countertop. "I wish there was coffee," said Grace. Deedee, looking up, said, "I will put on a pot. I found some leftover stuff in the pantry." She dropped the rag, entered the pantry, and returned with a brown sack and pot.

Deedee put the pot under the faucet and turned on the water. She grabbed the pot with one hand and turned the faucet with the other. She put the pot on the stove and started brewing the coffee. Grace moved over towards Deedee, who was now grabbing two chipped mugs and grabbed the pot off the stove, pouring the coffee into the chipped mugs. Grace then put her hand over Deedee's mug, said a truth spell over the cup, and grabbed her. Leaning onto the countertop and waiting for Deedee to take a sip of her coffee. When she did, Grace asked Deedee to tell her about herself. Deedee, taking another sip, said that she and Deloris, her younger sister, worked for a couple up north and had a happy life. She cooked, and her sister cleaned.

The couple was older and had no children but were happy. Then things weren't so happy. Deedee's voice went soft and had a sorrow to it. see, the house was way too big for two people. So, they occupied their time apart, her on committees and him always hunting, so the misses was out. I was cooking, and Deloris was upstairs cleaning. The man came home and went upstairs. "See, my sister is pretty. Men notice her all the time. So, she was in the master bedroom making the bed. He had a few. He forced himself on top of her, and when he finished, he came down the stairs first. Then Deloris came downstairs. I asked her what was wrong, and she said nothing." Now, Grace came over to Deedee to comfort her, placing her arms around her. Deedee pushed away from grace. "Madame, I am not done." Looking half intrigued and half filled with sorrow for Deloris, Grace said for her to go on.

"Well, a week later, Deloris woke up in cold sweats, and I asked her what happened. She first told me how everything started out innocently through the tears and sobbing. He grabbed a shirt and then walked toward the bathroom. So, I was going to excuse myself and start to leave, and he stopped her. He looked her over like a lion stalking its prey; then his hand caressed her face. She told him no, but he didn't care. His hands then went towards her shirt and, with force, ripped it open. He said if she screamed, he would grab his shotgun and kill your sister dead right in front of her. He then threw her on the bed and had his way with her. I hugged my sister and let her cry." "I am so sorry," said Grace.

"Wait, there's more. With rage boiling up inside me, I put my sister to bed and went to bed myself. Then, the next morning, I went to work, and the lady of the house returned. It just happened to be his birthday, so I made him an extra special chocolate cake. That night I served the couple and all their friends. Laughing, his best friend gave him a "That's a boy" speech, so I served the cake to all of them, and they left, went home, and I cleaned up. I waited till I saw the bedroom light go out and went to the hall closet where I stashed a sac. I walked into his study and cleaned him out, then slipped into their bedroom, quiet as a church mouse. I cleaned out all her expensive jewelry, left the house, and went to put the loot in the car. Then I went back in and grabbed my sister, pulled her out of bed, covering her mouth so she would not wake them up. We crept through the house, and I got her into the car.

"We then went back into the house, pouring the oil from the oil lamps, and lit a match in his study, throwing a few books at the fire. We left the house, got into the car, and kept driving into the night. We did not stop until we got here in the French Quarter." While she spoke, a black string of grim energy moved out and away from her. something Grace had never seen before. But she quickly realized when she saw that the blackness leaving Deedee made its way to where the light did not reach that it was the dark energy that the shadows wanted. Grace said, "I will keep you and your sister's secrets if you can keep one of mine. I am not ordinary. I am a witch, and so is Contessa. Kalvin is a wolf. You don't cross us. You always have a home here, and the four of us will keep you safe now," said Grace. "Deedee, let's get this place ready to open," continued Grace.

Then Grace clapped her hands, and Deedee saw the rag moving by itself in front of her. The mop in the corner went to work with no help from anyone. "I will keep your secrets as long as no harm comes to Deloris or myself." "Madame, I swear it." She hugged Grace, and Grace turned away and walked out of the kitchen. She then went across the lobby and into the lounge. "Kalvin, where are we?" asked Grace. "Well, Madame, some of the tables are broken along with the chairs. The mirror is cracked, and I must fix and tune the piano." "Okay, stand back!" said Grace. She clapped her hands once more. Kalvin raced towards the entrance of the lounge. Grace told Kalvin that Deedee knows about us, can't, and won't say anything.

So, Kalvin turned around, not commenting on what he heard and saw. Behind the bar, the mirror sewed itself back together. The chairs stood right side up, sliding themselves under the tables. Once on their sides, the tables were upright, ready for people to use them, and at the far end of the lounge came an upbeat, jazzy sound from the now-working piano. "Go and help Contessa, and you two clean up. Take a bath or something. Monty will be back soon." Kalvin walked out of the lounge and ran up the two flights of stairs. Contessa yelled, "Kalvin up here!" She yelled back, and Kalvin walked to the second set of stairs. On the way up, he passed some old pictures of the mill when it was in its prime on its first day of operation. But now a relic.

When he reached the top of the stairs, he watched Contessa go into the farthest room at the end of the hallway and raced to catch up with her. "Hey, your mom said we need to clean up because we're going soon." Contessa nodded, and Kalvin peeked around the room. There was a bed, desk, chair closet, bathroom, and a door leading out to the balcony. Contessa said this will be my room, turning to look at Kalvin. All it needs is a mirror, and it will be good, so open the door to the balcony and stand back. Kalvin did what was asked. He Walked across the room and opened the balcony door. Allowing the brisk cold air to enter the room, she raised her hands like her mother, took a deep breath, and said, "Cleomise!" The room started to clean itself, dust being swept away with the cold wind. Then, the room looked as good as new. Then Contessa went to the bathroom, turned on the sink, and cupped her hands, letting the cold water fill up in her hand.

The Madame, Contessa and the Dollhouse

She splashed her face, reaping it several times, then took the black silk ribbon out of her hair and straightened it, pulling it back and retying it using the same black ribbon. "Maybe we can go into town and get some new clothes." She examined herself, looked at the torn black dress, felt the cold tile against her feet, and realized she still had no shoes. Kalvin peaked his head into the bathroom and said maybe let's go downstairs and ask everyone if they want to join us. Kalvin went out of Contessa's room, and Contessa followed, and she suggested they take the elevator. As she was already pushing the button for the elevator to open, they both stepped in. Contessa pushed the 'G' on the panel, and the doors closed. When the elevator opened, the two of them stepped into the lobby.

The others were standing by the front desk. "Madame, here it is. The deed to the hotel now makes you the sole owner and me a private investor," said Monty. He gave the deed to Grace, and Grace took it and walked back into the office. She put the deed into the safe, then returned a moment later. "Let's go back into the lobby. Now, we need to go into town to find some new clothes and look for some young girls to put on staff," said Grace. "I need new shoes," said Contessa. "I need to go to my restaurant and get some of the vendors' numbers to supply us with food and find a liquor supplier," said Deedee. "Well, let's go!" Said Monty. The group walked out of the hotel, and Monty said, "Let's go, Deedee, waving her over to follow him to the car. He got in, and Deedee did a few seconds later. He then turned on the car and sped off. "Where do we go now, mom?" Asked Contessa. Then she turned to look over at her daughter.

In the corner behind her, a hand appeared out of the shadows. It came from the corner of the building where no light touched it and pointed for her to go south. So, she looked at her and told her daughter to follow her. Contessa and Kalvin followed her. The three took a right, two lefts, and a right and ended up on a busy street of people getting last-minute items for Thanksgiving next week. "Mama, look a shop for Kalvin, and there is a dress shop for us," said Contessa, looking at her mother like Christmas day had come early. Grace looked at her with that irritated look she always had when Contessa bothered her with childish things. "Here, Kalvin." Grace reached into her dress, between her dress and left breast, and pulled out some money. Never give away all your secrets to a man, Contessa," said Grace, handing it to Kalvin. "Get a few suits and vest, a clean shave, and we will meet back here in two hours."

Kalvin took the money from Grace and ran off between the people on the busy street and into the shop-marked barber. "Come along, Contessa, let's not dilly dawdle. Contessa picked up her pace to fall in line with her mother, who moved through the crowd with Grace; unmoved by the street vendors and fortune tellers who saw fortune and love in her future, she kept following her mother into the dress shop with the lavender ball gown with a bow hanging on its side. Ring went the bell. When the door opened, the two of them stepped in. "Hello!" came a high shrill from a woman's voice. "Welcome to my shop." A tall, thin redhead pushed through the curtains draping the back room's doorway. "My name is Theresa. Let me know. Oh, my word, I don't want any trouble." She looked horrified at the two women standing before her.

Grace's hair was knotted, and she had tears in her dress, but she had a clean face. Contessa was with a torn dress and dirty hair pushed back into a bun with no shoes. "We wish you no harm," said Grace. "If you don't have money, get out. There is enough crime in this town, and I will not be another victim. Do you hear me?" Reaching towards the sheers on the front desk. "Wait, here it is!" She quickly pulled money out of her breast and waved it. Treasa then moved away from the shears. "Well, that's a different story. Please forgive me. Two shops just yesterday were hit," Treasa said, more relaxed and smiling. "Now go ahead, look around. "I will be here at the desk doing paperwork," Treasa said as she walked to the back of the shop.

She went around the counter, sat down, and went to the window for the lavender dress, and her mother walked to the other side of the shop. Ring, ring the bell went, and SLAM went the front door after a few seconds. Some ruffling came from behind Grace and the shuffling of the clothes rack. "Oh my, who is there? Hello." Teresa got up. Grace turned around, separated the clothes, and saw three dirty young black girls, the oldest holding two loaves of bread in her hands with a pleading look in her eyes for help. Grace had that feeling in her stomach, and behind the girls was the same stream of blackness leaving their bodies in a dark corner between the cracks where no light could reach. Ring went the bell on the door again, this time a short fat man with a beard, bald head, and gray suit with two police officers behind him.

"Mrs. Theresa had somebody come in the store moments ago. The baker down the block had bread stolen from him. He didn't get a good look, but we were close, so we gave chase and lost the thief in the crowd," the mayor said, sweat beading down his forehead despite the cold weather outside. "Why no, Mr. Mayor, just me and these two ladies," said Theresa, pointing to Grace and Contessa, blushing at the mayor and battering her eyes at him. "Hello, my name is Madame Grace, and I own the old mill hotel. My daughter works there as a maid, and we have a few other staff members helping," said Grace, moving from behind the clothes rack. She reached out her hand, and the mayor grabbed it and kissed it. "Nice to meet you ladies. I hope the quarter is prosperous for you. Good day, we have a thief to catch. Gentlemen, let's go," said the mayor as he grabbed the doorknob and opened the door with a ring.

The two officers walked out, and the mayor followed and shut the door behind them. "Theresa, can you see if you have the lavender dress in my daughter's size in the back?" "Let me go check, dear," said Theresa, walking to the back of the store and through the curtains. Grace returned to the rack's clothes and looked down at the girls. Contessa keeps her busy, gesturing her head back towards the back room. "Give me that, you stupid girl!" snatching the two loaves from her. "Now get out here and stand up now!" The three girls stood up, all very tall. "Why are you stealing?" "We grew up orphans, and we only have each other, so I promised they would never go hungry and always have a roof over their heads. So, I took the bread to keep my promise."

Grace looked at them and shook her head in disgust with them. With the harsh tone of her voice and the scowling look on her face, Grace said, "You stupid girl, you can't keep a promise if you're dead. Now you have only a moment to decide." "Decide what?" asked the oldest, stepping in front of her sisters in a protective motion. "Don't you ever interrupt me again!" Grace said, moving her face to the girls. "To choose a life off the streets with a job and room and board or chose to be nothing but a street rat. The only catch is you must never disobey me and always do what you're asked without question. Do we have a deal?" Grace said, moving back away from the girl.

The girls turned and looked at each other. "Let's do it," said the youngest. "Fine." Look, lady, "You can call me Madame and nothing else. Now, first off, what is your name?" "I'm Alexandria. I am twenty-four; these are my sisters," first pointing to her sister next to her. "Brooke is nineteen, and next to Brooke is Lindsey. She is twenty-two. Please don't turn us in said, Lindsey." "We'll do what you asked," said Brooke. Contessa, go to the door and open it now," said Grace. Contessa moved through the clothes quickly and grabbed the knob. She opened the door. Ding-dong went the bell. "Hello," said Theresa from the back, coming through the curtain. "Hello," repeated Theresa. "These are my nieces, and they will need dresses for them as well," said Grace. "Girls say hello, don't be rude," said Grace. "Hello," said the girls in unison. "Now go start looking. We have a lot to do," said Grace.

As the girls started looking, Grace looked at them. Lindsey was a tall, chicken-legged girl with short, straight black hair with a beautiful face. Alexandria was the oldest but a little shorter than her sister. She had wild curly hair but was very busty. Brooke was right up there with her sisters with long, black, straight hair, all three of them having potential. Grace returns to their eyes, so striking they don't look real. Theresa, we'll take one outfit a piece, and hurry, ladies, we must go." Theresa, you see what we like. can you pick out a few more dresses? Can you deliver these dresses to the hotel, pick out a few more, and bring those to Grace?"

Grace was handing her a huge wad of cash and walking towards the door and opened it. "Yes, Madame," Theresa said as the girls went out the door. "Goodbye, Theresa," said Grace as she walked through the door and shut it behind her. "Can we eat, mom?" said Contessa. "Sure, let's find Kalvin and go eat, Contessa. Looking passed her mother, she saw a crowd gathering and becoming very loud.

Contessa, out of curiosity, pushed passed her mother, moving with the people. She then pushed her way through the center of the ruckus. In front of her was the mayor, and two cops turned to her and cornered someone. The mayor asked for the bread, and when the mayor stepped to his left. Contessa saw Kalvin's anger showing on his face. Backed into a corner, ready to defend himself. Fear built up in Contessa, turning every shade of white. "Think," Contessa spoke in a soft whisper to herself. She stepped forward and snapped her fingers close to the mayor's butt, and two silver sparks shocked him, sending a bolt of electricity through him.

Contessa moved in between him and the sheriff, and Contessa turned to face them. "Mr. Mayor Kalvin didn't steal anything. He works for my mother and has money on him. He does not need to steal." Contessa felt the heat coming off Kalvin and a cold chill blowing past her. Grace now pushed through the crowd with the girls. "Mr. Mayor, you who?" said Grace. The mayor turned to look at her. "Listen, I can put two and two together and see what is going on now. Kalvin dug drawn-out claws into his palm, making them bleed. Still, Grace kept calm. "Let me pay for the bread." She pulled more money out of the space between her breast and dress and handed it to him. To show good faith, come with your two officers and stay at the hotel on the house, Okay?" said Grace. The mayor bit his lip and took the money. "Thank you, Madame, we will take you up on your offer; good day to you all now." the mayor turned to the crowd. "Go on now, nothing to see here."

The crowd parted at his words. "That's BULLSHIT! He can't just get away with accusing me?" His nostrils flared. Grace and the girls moved to Contessa and Kalvin. "You!" Grace looked at Kalvin angrily. "Let's go now. Thanks to you, we have drawn too much attention to ourselves. Back to the hotel dog. Just to inform you, to win the war, you must sometimes lose the battle," said Grace. She turned to walk down the street, and the sisters followed her. Walking towards the hotel. "Thanks, Contessa, for defending me." Kalvin's claws retraced the wounds and closed up. Just the red sticky blood left on his hands. "Of course, no problem. Let's go before she gets furious." The two walked side-by-side in the direction of the hotel, picking up the pace to catch up with the others.

CHAPTER TWELVE
The Nine

Madame Grace was standing out front when Contessa, Kalvin, and the girls arrived at the hotel. She said to Contessa, "It looks, kind of looks drier." "Yes," said Contessa, looking at the building in front of her. The awning was torn, boarded-up windows, and the front yard was dead. Nothing grew there. "Well, just wait. It will be amazing when Kalvin takes the boards off the window and fixes the awning and yard, plus a little paint." You are excited. She looked at her mother, gleaming for the first time since she saw her mother and father dance the night of the solstice, shuttering away at the thought of the horrible events after that. "No," said Madame Grace. "He can start all of that tomorrow. I have another task for Kalvin tonight, continued Grace.

Kalvin just nodded, waving the girls to follow him. "Kalvin, run along, take the girls inside, and get them settled. Meet me in my office in fifteen minutes," Madame Grace called to him. This left Madame Grace and Contessa on the street alone. Nobody in either direction was normal this time of day because normal business hours are around ten-thirty or so and go well into the morning. "Dear, I'm going to teach you a spell. Raise your left hand out and point them at the hotel and repeat after me," said Madame Grace, nodding her head and waiting for further instructions. "Decomortosis!" said Grace. Contessa repeated what her mother had said.

When the "s" left Contessa's mouth, blue and green sparks shot from her hand at the hotel, and then the wood boarding the windows began to rattle. Nails flew from the wood, leaving splinters behind, floating above the ground, then dropped to the ground with a thud, bouncing once lying lifeless. Shards of glass rose like wingless birds, flew towards the windows, and the glass wove itself back together. Last, the Old Mill hotel sign Lit up the night sky. "Know that is a hotel. I will make Kalvin a list of stuff to pick up tomorrow. Let's get ready for dinner. We have a lot of work to do before we open," said Grace. Then Grace and Contessa went into the hotel. Monty was talking to the girls. Deedee came out of the bar, crossing the lobby with a plate full of sandwiches and a pitcher of lemonade.

Contessa walked ahead of her mother across the lobby. She grabbed a sandwich on the way to the staircase, climbed the stairs, turned around, and sat on the bottom step. Madame, would you like a sandwich asked Deedee without saying a word. She reached out her hand and wrapped her bony finger around one of the sandwiches, then Deedee turned and walked to the front desk and placed the plate and pitcher down on the desk. "Now, ladies, you will be working here. I will clothe you, feed you, and put a roof over your head. You do what I ask, and you will never be turned into the authorities, " agreed Grace. The three girls looked at each other, Brooke now with pleading eyes at her two older sisters. "Please, Alexandria, I'm tired of running and wondering where their next meal will come from."

Listening to Brooke's plea, Lindsey looked at her older sister with the same pleading eyes. "Okay, Madame, we promise. No lip from any of us if you keep your word and question what we will be doing here," said Alexandria. "Okay, then you three can take the guest cottage in the back. Deedee, you take the bedroom behind the kitchen, and Monty, who is this?" Madame Grace said after staring down this five-foot-four-inch man with ginger hair and a pudgy gut. "This is Reed; he is Mr. Johnson's co-worker and heard what we were doing and decided to join us. Monty finished. "Whatever!" said Madame Grace. You and Reed stay in the super's room under the stairs. Contessa and Kalvin upstairs. Now, finish eating, wash up, and get into bed early.

We're opening next Friday, and Brooke, you're working in the kitchen. Lindsey, you will be a cocktail waitress, and Alexandria, you're on house cleaning duties with Contessa." All the girls nodded in acceptance of their roles. "Kalvin, I need to see you in my office now," Madame Grace said as she walked across the lobby, Kalvin at her heels, moving around the desk and through the door. "Close the door behind you!" said Grace to Kalvin, and he did so. He then turned to face Grace, watching her move behind her desk and sit in the eggplant chair. "Kalvin, we need some staff to appease the shadows. Come sit down," said Grace. Kalvin walked to the claw-footed chair and slumped down into it. Grace then continued speaking in her calm voice, asking Kalvin to retrieve them. "How, Madame?" Asked Kalvin.

Grace then reached out her bony hand, placing it on top of her desk, and whispered a few words, with smoke spewing from underneath her hand. She then raised her hand. As the smoke cleared, a deck of black cards as big as her hand appeared out of thin air. Kalvin just sat in silence and stared at the cards without saying a word. The nine cards before you. As she moved her hand away, she said, "From the cards before me, I have nine cards." Grace spread them out in front of him as she spoke. They're magical when you get close to someone who would be a good fit for the hotel. Grace now grabbed a card and handed it to Kalvin. Before she could explain how they worked, Kalvin took the card, examining it.

At first, Kalvin thought the card was nothing out of the ordinary. It was black with a crimson-red border and a red Marinette doll on one side of the card. When you get close to the right person, the doll will move. First, it's strings, then when you're standing next to the person, it will make the doll fully animated." Half listening to Grace, Kalvin looked up from the card and said it would be done. He reached out his hand and scooped up the cards from the desk, got up from the chair with ease, and stuffed the cards in the inside pocket of his jacket. "Wait, there are some rules, and I made the cards to obey them first. One, no locals that will draw attention to us. two, don't draw attention to yourself. I don't want another incident like the one this afternoon." "Three, just hand them the card; it will help them find their way to the hotel. That's it. Go, you need to start tonight," said Madame Grace.

Kalvin nodded, turned, and quickly left her office, closing the door behind him. He grabbed his key that hung on the wall with the number ten etched into it, walked around the desk, and headed upstairs. When he reached the third floor, he walked to the end of the hallway. He turned left to the door marked ten, placing the key into the lock and turning it. He then pulled it out, turned the knob, walked into the room, and shut the door behind him. The setup was the same as Contessa's room: bathroom, bed, balcony, closet, and wood floors, but clean. Then Kalvin laughed, thinking how Contessa must have found a rag and some running water and decided to start cleaning.

Kalvin then took off his shirt, threw it on the floor, headed to the bathroom, reached into the tub, and turned on the water, taking a rag and feeding it into the drain so the tub would fill up. Then he took off his pants and underwear. He let them drop to the floor, stepping out of them and kicking them both to the corner of the bathroom. A knock came at the door. "Who is it?" asked Kalvin as he shouted from the bathroom. "It's Alexandria!" came the voice from the hallway. "What do you want?" he asked. "May I come in?" she asked. "Sure," said Kalvin, peeking his head out of the bathroom. Alexandria stepped into his room. "Madame said you will need some towels and soap to help you clean up for tonight," said Alexandria. Kalvin thanked her, stepping out of the bathroom to grab the towel and soap. Alexandria started to blush at him. His body was chiseled like a granite statue. Then she threw the towel and soap at Kalvin, apologizing for the intrusion.

Before Kalvin could say anything, Alexandria ran out of the room. Kalvin moved towards the bathroom door, grabbed the knob, then ran past his bed, catching the bedroom door before it closed. He peered out into the hallway, screaming her name and watching her as she ran down the stairs. Then he slammed the door shut, banging on the back of the door, and then turned to head back to the bath. After his bath, he finished getting ready, grabbed his jacket, and walked out of the room and down a flight of stairs on the second floor. He passed the girls. Brooke and Lindsey giggled while Alexandria was blushing, telling them to stop. Kalvin smiled and continued down the second flight across the lobby and out into the streets. He passed the local working girls who offered their services, which he declined and kept walking. He kept walking to the heart of the French Quarter.

Bourbon Street, where tourists would go to forget their troubles and drink the night away. When Kalvin got to Bourbon Street, it was packed, and wasting no time, he went into the first bar on the street called The Witch Doctor. He pushed through the crowd and grabbed a table in the back, remembering Madame Grace's rules. "What you having, honey?" asked the cocktail waitress dressed like a doctor. "I will have a scotch, straight." She walked away, and Kalvin watched her go. Kalvin then scanned the crowd, watching people dance. A group enjoyed a round at the bar. Then, the waitress put his drink on the table and walked away. Then, in his jacket pocket, cards began to shake, remembering the cards that would help him find his mark. He reached into his pocket, pulled out a card, and put it in the air, hoping it would help.

He moved it in front of the group, dancing in the corner nothing, then moved the card to the group by the bar nothing. He moved the card towards the door in nothing once again. Then, when he moved the card back towards the bar, the legs of the marionette doll moved. So, Kalvin got up and went towards the bar. When he got to the bar, he noticed that the marionette doll's arm had moved. Then Kalvin stood in behind a young woman, reached around her, dropped the card on the bar top, and left out of the bar.

The woman turned around and watched as he walked away. Then she looked back at the card and examined it like watching a movie. It was magical when she reached out and picked up the card. Darkness rose from the card, which made the young woman jump. Still, the cloud of smoke entered her mouth and nostrils. She then turned around, walking out of the bar and onto the crowded street. She pushed through the tourists and walked around the corner.

After a while, she passed Kalvin, who did not recognize her. Not believing it was her, he saw her stop in front of the hotel, just standing there waiting for further instructions. "Hello," said Kalvin. The young woman jumped back in fear. "It is okay. I work here at the hotel. Can you tell me what your name is?" "My name is Ceci Dupree. Can you help me, please? I don't know how I got here." "Well, my name is Kalvin; like I said, I work here, and if you come inside, I think I can help." Ceci looked at him, then at the hotel, shaking her head, and Kalvin gestured to follow him. "What brings you to New Orleans?" asked Kalvin.

Ceci responded, "I just ran away from home. It was a bad situation. My daddy's a drunk, and I'm tired of being at the end of his fist. So, I took his car in the middle of the night and drove it till it ran out of gas; then I walked for a while and hitch-hiked and ended up in the quarter. "Kalvin, who is this?" asked Madame Grace. "This is Ceci, and she needs help." Kalvin motioned with his eyes at the card in her hands, and Madame Grace perked right up. "Welcome, child; let's go into my office. Let's see what we can do for you." They followed her to the office, Kalvin shutting the door behind him. "Sit, Ceci," said Madame Grace; Ceci sat across from her, and Kalvin stood behind Madame Grace, leaning against the wall.

Ceci watched Madame Grace, sitting in her chair, all primed and proper, with an eerie feel to her. This put Ceci on edge. So, Ceci said, "You could help me." "Ceci, what are you looking for?" asked Madame Grace. "I'm looking for a place to stay, maybe a job. I can do anything. I learn fast, and please just give me a chance. Please," Ceci replied. "Well, we are just getting started, and this job is not for everyone. But if you make the cut, you can earn three square meals a day, clothes on your back and a roof over your head, and the extra perk that if a patron finds favor with you, they can give you money and presents," said Grace. Ceci straightened up, intrigued by the idea of a gift, especially since the last gift she got was a black eye from her dad's left fist instead of his right fist. "Lady, I can do anything you ask of me, I swear," said Ceci. With a sour look, Grace leaned forward and said to Kalvin, "You can go. Now! Get out of my sight!"

Without a word, Kalvin walks behind the desk, grabs Ceci, forces her from her chair, and then starts showing her the door. Ceci starts pleading with Kalvin to stay. Ceci, scrambling to fix the situation, said, "I would do anything. I need help." "Wait, Kalvin," said Grace. Kalvin then stopped and released his grip on Ceci. "Look here, little girl; first, you will only address me as Madame Grace. Then, second, you will drop the attitude. And last, do anything I ask of you without question. If you can do all that, I will look past your lack of home training," said Grace.

Ceci then looked at Grace and bit her lip after letting out a breath of air and letting Madame Grace know she agreed to the terms. "Great, well then, I need you to sign the contract. Ceci was about to ask what this contract was but saw her face and knew if she objected, she would not get a second chance. She instead asked where to sign. Then Grace moved past them and went and stood in front of the bookcase, raising her bony fingers and moving them back and forth like before.

Purple and green sparks shoot from her fingers. The bookcase moved and revealed the golden handle embedded into the floor, and Grace moved her fingers back and forth again. The floor separated, revealing the staircase. "Follow me," Grace said and headed down the staircase. She watched the black shadows move in front of her, lining the walls and descending into the staircase. Gracefully feeling their presence, she moved further down into the basement. At the end of the staircase, Grace noticed the room looked the same except for the cauldron in the corner.

There was a caldron in the corner boiling, and the shadows and all their faces stared at them, which made Ceci jump back into Kalvin. He caught her and held her, fighting to get back upstairs, but it was no use against his werewolf strength. Madame Grace turned around, throwing sparks from her hand and the sparks moving around them, closing the floor back up. "Stop, Ceci; if you do this, she will protect you if your father ever comes looking for you," said Kalvin. She stopped fighting, turning with tears in her eyes and fear showing all over her face. "Stop fighting, Ceci. She can help. She can protect you from your father if he ever comes looking for you." She then looked at Madame Grace and asked if this was true. "Yes, my child, I will protect you with my life. He will never put a hand on you again."

Ceci relaxed and was okay with this. She was at ease with whatever was about to come. "Now, stand before the desk, and we will start. Do you have a pen?" said Ceci. Madame Grace was pleased with this and walked towards the shadowy figure with faces protruding from it, and in its outstretched hand appeared a parchment and quill. Madame Grace took them, turned, walked back to her desk, and sat down. "Give me your hand," she said to Ceci, and Ceci did as she was told, outstretching her hand. Madame Grace opened her desk drawer and pulled out a silver letter opener. "WAIT!" said the voices from the shadow in the corner. "Come, dog. Take this veil and make a circle with the powder around the girl; NOW!"

Kalvin immediately went over to the shadows, grabbed the vile, popped the cork, and let it fall to the ground. He then turned it on its side and walked in a circle, letting it fall from the vile onto the floor. When the last drop of powder left the vial, he put it into his pocket and stood waiting for further instructions. "Give me your hand," said Madame Grace, staring at Ceci, who watched Kalvin moving around her. "Give me your hand," she said again and snatched Ceci's hand. This snapped her back to reality, and she stared at her hand, watching the letter opener pierce her skin and her blood swarming the tip of the blade flowing down her finger onto the desk. Then, Madame Grace put down the letter opener and picked up the quill. "Dog, I need you to get me a few drops of blood for the potion brewing in the cauldron. Collect some and add it to the cauldron.

Kalvin pulled the vial out of his pocket, putting it under Ceci's bleeding finger, letting the red liquid drip into the vial. Then Kalvin took it to the cauldron and tossed it in. Then crimson-red smoke filled the air. When it cleared, a small wooden Marionette doll appeared. It had no face. It was lifeless, and its strings were half submerged. Grab it and put it in the circle with the girl. Kalvin picked up the doll and walked over to the circle; fearing what would happen if he got too close, he kept his distance and threw it into the circle. The doll landed in the circle with a thud. Then Grace dipped the quill into the blood as if it were ink, handing the quill to Ceci. Then she rolled out the parchment and told Ceci to sign next to the X. When quill touched the parchment, the blood-soaked the paper with the words, Ceci Dupree.

When she finished, she dropped the pen and felt weird, with a little pain at first. Then it became so intense she jolted back, falling on the floor. She crawled to the corner of the circle, trying to escape the pain intensifying, reminding him of the night Grace made her deal with the shadows in the forest. Then, watched the outline of Ceci rise out of her while Ceci lay curled up on the floor now, her soul trying to make a run for it but kept hitting the invisible wall. Then it brushed against the doll, and it started to move. flipping over and sitting straight up. It started to pull Ceci's soul into itself until it was gone.

Then, the once faceless marionette doll had a mouth appear. Then, the same brown eyes as Ceci and hair grew out of the top of its head. It had the same haircut as Ceci, and the doll started walking around. It tried to escape the shadow, moving toward the circle, kicking away the powder with its foot. The shadows bent down to pick up the strings of the doll, wrapping its hand around the control bar, and then Ceci came to life. Standing up, moving like her puppet counterpart moved. "Madame Grace, come take the strings," said the shadows. Madame Grace walked around the desk and reached out her hand, taking the control bar from the shadows, shivering when her fingers brushed its hand. "You are now in control and will have no trouble getting what we need. The faster you get the dark energy for us, the faster you get your own soul back. I will remove the strings, giving the girl free range of her body. Still, as long as her soul remains trapped in the puppet, you will have the final say of what she does even without the strings."

The shadows waved their hand threw the strings, and they disappeared into thin air. "Now pick up the puppet, lock it in the cage, and get to bed. Both of you have a lot to do. Kalvin, take Ceci upstairs and put her to bed. See you tomorrow," said Madame Grace. While talking, she sent more sparks shooting up the stairs to open the door, and Kalvin grabbed Ceci's hand and walked up the stairs. Then, the shadows watched Madame Grace open the cage, throw the puppet in, and lock it. Madame Grace watched the doll get up and run towards the door. The doll stretched its little hand out, trying to grab Madame Grace, but it was unsuccessful. Then, Madame Grace turned away from the cage and watched the shadows escape through the cracks in the wall. When she was the only one left, she just walked upstairs and called it a night.

CHAPTER THIRTEEN
Found Love

BAM!!!! Went the books, maps, and cauldron hitting the library wall. "I thought I was marrying into a powerful family with spells that could let a person do what they wanted. It has been five years and nothing." "Calm down, baby. I know you're frustrated, but it will all work out. But I feel that something is counseling them, and I can't figure out what it could be," said Celeste. "We just have to be smarter than the bastard keeping them, and we know it is not human," Celeste said as she walked over to put an arm around James.

"Then let's change our strategy. We keep looking at the obvious. It is a human playing with magic instead of someone more intelligent than that! I need a break, and I still have to keep up appearances with my parents until we make our big escape," James said in more of a shout than anything as he walked over to the chair and picked up his coat. He put it on and headed out of the library. Celeste remained in the library looking at last night's dinner plates, which were barely touched. Then she bent down to pick up another mess made by Frank and James that was becoming more often with each passing year. In the rubble was a picture of her beloved home with every member of the cove. Remembering ones that had been lost, which now stands at only fifteen members of the forty-five that it once had.

Lexi and her parents are among the survivors, which she wishes she could tell Baby Girl. Their plan to leave fell through. Frank could not bear to leave. He told the coven that the pain of walking away was too much. So, the cove surrounded the ashes of the house and did a repairing spell and ceremony. They made the ashes of the plantation rise from where they lay and look like rain going backward in a topsy-turvy universe. The only change to the property was that the remaining families of the coven lived on the property. This was in case the people of Blackwood ever got their memories back. They could have each other fight back sooner than the night of the solstice. Still, the townsfolk remain oblivious to that night, waking up the next day back in their beds and going about their daily lives.

In contrast, the people who lost everything held funerals and made a family tree out of the one Lenny swung from that night. "Aww!" As Frank and some other man walked into the library, Celeste screamed back to reality. "Sorry, Celest, I did not know you were here." "Yeah, I figured I would clean up between meetings, but I will get out of your way so you can work." As Celeste rose from the ground, Frank told her they would be a while. He would help her clean the office later that the men were a part of the latest search party, and out the door, Frank went to continue the hunt for his wife and daughter. "So, what did you discover, Lex?" Frank spoke to the tall, lengthy man as he walked on the edges of the pile of last night's research pile. He makes his way to his chair, looking up at the man, seeing the toll it is taking on his coven, but knows it must be done.

"I think we have exhausted everything, but I had my wife go deep into the vial to ask the ancestors for their help. Now I'm just waiting for her to come to so that maybe there is something that they know that can help us," Dawson said as he stretched out his arms, slumping into the chair opposite Frank. "So that is it?" Frank was short with Dawson at that point. We might as well hold a vigil for them. He huffed as he balled his fists, hitting them on his desk. "Calm yourself. We will find them. We love them. The coven has lost so much, and this is the hope that keeps us going. In between the day-to-day life, we have not done the traditions or ceremonies we once held dear." Dawson spoke as he laid his hand on his leader's fist. "We need a distraction. Something that will bring a breath of fresh air."

"What do you have in mind?" Frank asked, a little calmer as he inhaled a shallow breath. "Well, we don't have a lot of young members. So, either we must recruit some people, or the ladies of the coven need to increase the fertility statues on the grounds." He laughed, and Frank got up from his desk. Trying to go over the fifteen names of the people he had sworn to protect. Two of them were his wife and daughter, only three other than Contessa in their twenties, and Contessa and Lexi were the only girls. In contrast, Quintin was the only male. No baby has been born into the family in five years. How could I have missed this? We, a once prominent coven, are going extinct. He flung his hand out, causing an overbearing fire to roar out of the fireplace. "Calm yourself, Frank; we will get everything as right as rain.

Lexi patted Frank on the back. "I'm here to help." "Aw-wwwwww!" by the angel came screams of joy and jumping from the foyer. "What is it, women?" Frank's voice filled the space between screams walking out into the foyer. Behind the final word leaving his lips, he saw Celeste and a short woman with a messy bun and sun dress hugging and jumping together. "I will ask again. Why are we shouting and jumping?" Celeste let go of Annie and then turned to the men. "She found baby girl," Celeste said with so much joy and happiness that the house came to life.

The walls seemed to glimpse, the flowers bloomed, and electricity went through the house that radiated to the rest of the plantation. "How, my love? What did the ancestors say it was?" Said Dawson, rushing to his wife's side. "One which I was shocked to speak to because she has never participated in any rituals or conversations during reading with Grace Annabel, Grace's mama." Frank stepped back. "What did she say?" He stepped forward. "Well, at first, she had some not-so-nice words to say about Grace and you but loved watching her grandbaby. She spoke joyfully at her fellow coven members." "Get to the good stuff," nudged Celeste. "Well, she said her daughter has always had a shadow following her, which she did not see but a few times. She brushed it off as some passing spirit or whatever. Not knowing that she always had a firm grip on her little girl with boundary spells and protection talisman on her at all times. Until right when she met you that day, you visiting the village seemed odd because everything until that moment she saw coming."

The Madame, Contessa and the Dollhouse

Annie could barely contain herself speaking at a speed faster than her thoughts and memories of the conversation could form. "So, when you whisked her away, she went to work looking into the in-between things that were nothing to worry about. The small stuff. When she got close, she died a mysterious death. But, with a lot of time on her hands being unalive, she discovered the shadows that had their grip on her from before she was even a thought in her mind. Wielding their will, playing a long game that, from what she can see, was put into motion the night of Contessa's birthday party."

Annie finished breathing in, catching her breath, and hugging Frank. "Well, tell us, my love, where are they?" Her husband gleamed at her, so proud of his wife, who cracked the case and helped get them one step closer to making their family whole. "They're in the French Quarter, but where in the Quarter? Why is their whereabouts so unclear?" She got frustrated at the fact that I told her you were a good man and not the white devil cracker she thinks you are, so she ran out on me, but I do think maybe you can get more out of her, Celeste, since she loves and misses you dearly. Your mother and father say hi, by the way, and wish you would have remarried and made lots of babies, but that is beside the point," Annie said, waving her hand away from that train of thought. "So, now, what do we do?" Asked Dawson. "We come up with a game plan. We start with you, Celest. You and Annie gather the women of the coven and convince my wonderful mother-in-law to tell us everything. Then I will get a message to James and devise a game plan."

Frank, smiling from ear to ear, stood tall and looked more alive than he had in a really long time. "Well, sir, I can head out tonight, get some people on the ground, and report back," Dawson said. "Good idea." Celeste chimed in. "And make sure you report back on Baby girl, and don't you dare leave any detail out!" she threatened him with a smile. "Okay, well, everyone has their orders. Get out there, and let's bring my wife and daughter home!" Frank said, and then he stood in the foyer. Well, the others, one by one, hugged him. Celeste hugged him tighter than the others. She turned to Annie and grabbed her arm as Frank watched the three of them walk out the door. As it closed behind him, Frank went to his office, walked over to the French doors, twisted the handle opened out to the porch sending a message thru the wind so James knew to hurry back that good news was waiting when he arrived.

CHAPTER FOURTEEN
Nightly Run

"Come in," said Madame Grace. Monty and Reed entered through her office door. "Close it behind you," Madame Grace spoke in her most irritated tone. "Yes, Madame, what can we do you for on this fine evening?" Monty said, watching Madame Grace fixated on her paperwork. "Don't need the pleasantries tonight. I need you and Reed to go and make a run. We are low on whiskey," Madame Grace spoke. She peered up from her paperwork once in a while. She checked that the two were getting what she was saying. Grace put her quill down, got up from her chair, and started adjusting all the lights in the room. She wanted to ensure there was no way the shadows could come in and eavesdrop on the next part of the conversation.

Even though she believed they were busy collecting the night's energy from the dolls' rooms. "I need you to find some information for me," Madame Grace said. "What kind of information?" Monty said, stepping towards her. "You said that you have a supplier that comes out of Mississippi," she spoke to Monty, examining his facial expressions. "And I want to know what has happened to my family." Madame Grace coughed and cleared her throat. Were there any survivors the night I and my daughter left?" Madame Grace fell silent, waiting for a response. "Why, after all this time, would you want to know that after all these years?" Reed chimed in from by the door.

"Well, because I want to fool. Mind your biscuits!" Madame Grace snapped at Reed. "Sorry, Madame," Reed said, cowardly into the background. "Can you do it?" Madame Grace spat at Monty. "Of course, I can. I know where he sells his stuff and can get some info, but you know it may not be tonight that you get an answer. I have never failed you. I will get the answers you seek," Monty told her, giving Madame Grace a charming smile. "Good; go now, and I will see you tomorrow before breakfast."

Monty tipped his hat to Madame Grace and turned towards the door. "Come on, old chap, we have a long drive in front of us," said Monty. As Reed stepped aside, the door swung open to let Monty lead the way. The two gentlemen walked from around the front desk through the lobby and into the kitchen. "Where are you two going?" said Deloris, looking up from her hand, Deedee's back turned away.

"I win!" came a gleeful squeal. "Yeah, where are you going? You did a run two days ago." Deedee questioned them. "We must get some extra stuff for the ball and Mardi Gra. The Madame asked us to make an extra run," Monty said but did not reveal the extra assignment Madame Grace sent them to. "Well, drive safe," Deedee said as she shuffled the cards. "Don't wait up. It will be a long night," said Reed, and out the back door, the two gentlemen went. After about two hours into the drive, Reed spoke up. "Where are we headed?" "We are headed to the edge of the bayou way past the city lights. My supplier, Buster, works all the way up to New York, and his last stop is here, so he comes here every couple of weeks after giving his high-value liquor to the fat cats in New York."

"Then he makes his way down here. He's one of those fellas who never settled down. No misses or children to speak of," Monty finished as they passed the marshes and the swamps. The cool night air surrounded them. The moonlight is the only light for miles. "Monty, I was thinking, Why did you give Madame Grace all that money for the hotel?" Said Reed. "Why would you ask something like that?" Monty asked. "I was just wondering. You're a smart business savvy man. You could have bought it and been in charge. Reed kept his eyes forward as he spoke.

With his left hand on the steering wheel, Monty brushed his hair back with his right hand. "Well, you're right. I'm a schmoozer, but I left that life. I was the one wining and dining those fat cats, but I don't want that. I like being out here on the road with you in these situations. I believe I could do more behind the scenes than there front and center. Monty took in the cold night air. He continued, "Also, Madame Grace has this fire in her to make it to the top of the ladder, which will keep me here where I like it. After she paid me back the loan, I still, even to this day, collect a check. So as long as she is in charge, I get to play and be free," Monty finished, and Reed slapped Monty's shoulder. "What about you, Reed? You were so successful and then just quit." Reed pondered this, though, for a moment. "Well, I don't know. My life was easy. I could just enjoy the company of any woman I wanted, and the money in the safe was always full. But I felt alone. A little like you. Always had to play a part. But then, when I saw all of you, I saw this weird, fucked up family I wanted to be a part of."

Reed continued, saying, "So, I closed up shop after I saw Madame Grace in the Quarter and spoke to her. She said I could work the bar with you and do the weekly runs. The rest is history." After the two swapped stories, they sat silently until they pulled into a side clearing. They stopped in front of a towering tree covered with moss and watched two gentlemen outlined in their headlights. Monty shut off the engine, and he and Reed got out of the truck. "Hey, Buster!" Reed shouted as the sound of a shotgun cocked in, breaking the silence of the silent night. Reed asked, "Is that buster?" "What are you doing here, Buster?" Shouted as he walked over to shake Monty's hand. "Hey, said Reed. Who is this?" "That is my partner. Reed, this is Buster; Buster, this is Reed."

After Monty introduced the two gentlemen, Buster said, "That is my associate. Don't let the gun scare you. That is mostly for the critters." Then Monty told Buster he would take everything off his hands. Buster smiled. "You mean I don't have to worry about gators tonight? "Well, damn!" Buster said, smiling ear to ear. The two shook hands, and Monty gave him the money. "Reed, help Buster's associate get everything into the car." "No problem, boss," Reed said as he shut his door and walked to the back of the truck to drop the bed. He pulled back the burlap cloth that lined the bed, then headed to the other man, taking one crate at a time to their truck. "Now, I needed to ask you about a group of people in Blackwood, Mississippi," Monty said. "Blackwood? Why would you want to talk about that place?" Buster asked inquisitively. "Well, my boss, the lady I work for, was at a party five years ago around October."

Monty spoke with very little detail, trying to fish what he could out of Buster. Knowing a big party would have had to get their liquor from somewhere. The biggest supplier to make runs through Mississippi would be Buster. Monty thought to himself the whole way over to this trip. "Maybe; it sounds familiar. Was it on a plantation?" Buster asked. "I think so," Monty replied. "It was the owner's little girl's birthday," Buster continued. "I believe so!" Monty impatiently said through gritted teeth. "Well, if it was that party, I made that night's run right before sunrise and left to head down here," Buster said. "So, what does she want to know?" Asked Buster.

Monty, shifting on the balls of his feet, arms crossed and chewing on a loose fingernail, spoke. "Well, there was some ruckus that night, and some of her friends got hurt. She was just racking her brain about what came about it and who started it. That is all, and I thought of you. Someone who travels through Blackwood would have to have heard something, being you kept your ear to the ground, trying to drum up new business," Monty finished, going back to chewing on his nail. Buster paced back and forth, running his finger through his hair. "Well, on my way back through Blackwood, I heard nothing. No one from town talking about any major event, so I assume nothing happened," Buster sighed. "Well, thanks for the info. I appreciate all your help," Monty said, reaching out his hand to shake Buster's. "Well, I could ask around if you want me to. It won't take long to get back there. I can tell you what I find out when I come back here in a week or two."

Buster smiled, and Monty said that would be appreciated. "Reed, let's get moving!" Monty shouted. As the truck bed slammed, the two gentlemen got into the truck and drove away. After some time had passed, Reed spoke. "What did Buster say?" "Well, he did not say much, except there was no mention of any disaster. Like nothing happened. But you and I both saw Madame Grace and Contessa. Something happened that night. It is just odd that there would have been no gossip about that night," Monty said as he scratched his head. The two rode in silence all the way home. When they pulled into the ally, Reed was dead to the world snoring away, and Madame Grace was standing in the doorway of the kitchen waiting for their arrival.

Monty got out of the truck, tipped his hat to Madame Grace, and said good morning as he stretched out his arms and gave out a big yawn. "Well, what did your guy say?" Madame Grace asked, ushering to speak. "Madame, he said nothing. He said when he went back through Blackwood, there was no gossip about the night in question," Monty said, kicking the truck to wake Reed, who sprung to life, yawned, and stretched, stepping out of the truck to greet Madame Grace. "Well, that is odd," Madame Grace said. "Madame, he assured me that he would ask about that night discreetly to some trusted people in his circle of associates," Monty said as Reed made his way to the bed of the truck to start unloading their bounty. "Good, when will we hear from him?" "In a week or two, he will send word so that we can meet, and I will relay the information to you then," Monty reassured her as he grabbed a crate of liquor from the bed of the truck.

Without a word, she disappeared into the hotel. "I assume we will not have a good day from the look on her face." Reed smirked and Monty gave him a look. "Well, we will keep our heads down until we can give her some good news. The two chuckled and took their crates into the kitchen.

CHAPTER FIFTEEN
The Messenger

Buster made his way back to Blackwood. He drove through the town center, waving at all the nice people. Only a few know what he actually did for a living. Buster passed all the shops until there was an open spot. He pulled off where he honked, waving at the lovely couple and their son to come over, knowing if anyone in this town knew anything, it would be them. "Hello, preacher, Mrs. Preacher James." "What can I do you for, Buster?" "Well, a strange question I got to ask you, but I know if anyone knew about it, it would be you, fine folks," said Buster with a devilish smile.

The preacher laughed, and his wife chuckled along. James listened with very little interest. "Go on, what is it?" asked the preacher. "Well, about five years ago, there was a party out at that fancy plantation run by the white man with the colored women." At this, James perked up and listened intently. "Yeah, the Montgomery plantation, I think," said the preacher with a kind of fog to him. "Yeah, well, a fellow that works down there in the French Quarter, said his boss, a lady, was wondering what all happened that night after she left. Said there was some kind of ruckus," Buster spoke nonchalantly. "Nope, don't think any ruckus has happened here for a long time. "Okay, well, maybe I will do my friend a favor and go ask them." "Alright, you have a good day," Buster said as he shook the preacher's hands.

The three backed away from the car, allowing Buster to drive off. "Mom, dad, I need to go see Tilly. Do you mind if I do lunch another time?" James asked in the most calming voice to not sound alarmed. "Sure baby, that will give me and your father time to run over some paperwork for the church said Hannah. "Thank you," James said as he kissed his mother and father and raced off in the direction of Tilly's house. He then circled back around to head to the Montgomery plantation as fast as he could. So, over the moon, swirling images in his head as he ran until he was all of a sudden surrounded by this cool gust of air that spoke to him. Telling him to get to the plantation as soon as he can. There is news waiting when he gets there.

The guest of wind swirled around him a few times, whispering the message softly into his ear, then drifted along. As it left, a gentle kiss swept across his cheek. James shook off the encounter, not ever knowing how he would get used to that. When James pulled himself together, he hopped onto the trolly, riding it out to the edge of town, running past the fields all the way to the edge of the Montgomery plantation, where he saw Buster's car. Inhaling some much-needed deep breaths, he continued his journey to the main house, where he saw Buster creeping around outside the door that led into Frank's office. James snuck up behind Buster, grabbing him by the scruff of his collar and pushing him into the door. Buster struggled a little, but James had him good. With James' free hand, he reached for the doorknob, opened it, and threw Buster into Frank's study.

"What in the hell, James? Who is this guy?" "This is Buster. He was asking my parents about you and the night of the party," James spat out, inhaling a few good breaths. Silence fell into the room, and James' heart beating was the only sound to be heard as Frank examined the guy who stood before him. "Explain yourself," said Frank harshly, his face scrunched up, waiting to see if Buster was friend or foe. "Well, sir, while I was down in New Orleans in the bayou, a man who buys some of my goods asked me about Blackwood and some party five years ago," Buster calmly explained things as he searched the room for an escape route if things went south. He said it was for his lady boss. She was at the party and, at the end of the night, left when some ruckus broke out.

Buster stood up more confident now that Frank's face softened at this. "Go on," Frank encouraged the man. "Well, he knew that my trade route runs through Blackwood, so he asked me. I told him after I left, I finished my route, which ended at the bayou, turned around, stopped here for some gas, and there was no gossip about anything from that night. I only remembered myself of that morning because I supplied the liquor for the party." Buster smiled and started watching as James and Frank mumbled about if it could be them. "It has to be. That is where they ended up, according to Grace's mother," Frank said, combing his fingers through his hair and James letting Buster's shirt collar go. He questioned this, knowing Grace's mother was dead and Frank calling James an idiot for continuing to forget who they were. "So, what do we do?" asked James.

Frank stopped talking about forming a plan when Lexi walked in from the foyer. "Whatever it is, I'm in. Whether you all want me there or not, she is my best friend, and I could not help her that night. However, I can help her now." She firmly said. Buster watched as the three argued, ready to slip out the door he was shoved into moments ago but raised his hand like a schoolboy waiting to be called on. "What is it, man?" Frank scoffed at Buster. "Well, I know where the fellow works. It is a hotel where people can go to enjoy themselves. Mostly gentleman," grinned Buster as to knowing what went on there when he visited the establishment a few times. "A whorehouse? My wife? No sir, you must be mistaken," said Frank, growing angry at these new discoveries. "Well, sir, my buyer did say his boss, which would mean if this were the lady you all seek, she is running the joint. Her name is Madame Grace."

As her name left his mouth, all Buster saw is Frank's shirt collar, suffocating him. "My sir, thank you for this wonderful news, but I need you to do me a favor," Frank spoke as he let Buster go, allowing him to collect himself. "Yes sir, what can I do you for?" "I need you not to mention this to anyone, for if you do, you will cease to exist!" Frank then went over to his desk drawer. He reached over to grab the key lying across the desk, put it into the lock, lifted up the piece of wood, and grabbed an envelope, handing it out to Buster. Buster grabbed the envelope. He opened the envelope, looking at the amount of money. He then looked back up at Frank and smiled. "Not a word," Frank said. "I will take it to my grave," said Buster.

Then he turned and smiled at Lexi and James. "Well, I guess I will be off," Buster said as he walked backward toward the door and was out of sight, leaving Frank, Lexi, and James. "So, what is the plan?" James said as he looked at Frank. Lexi flopped down in the office chair. "Well, we wait for Celeste, then we leave at first light to the Quarter," Frank said. "You do mean we like all of us, right?" Lexi asked in an I'm coming no matter what kind of way, so make sure you are aware tone. "Yes, all of us. Me, you, Celest, and James," said Frank. "Where are we going?" Said Celest from the doorway, making Frank look up.

James turned, and Lexi jumped. "Child, it is just me!" Celeste said, walking into the room. "We are headed to the French Quarter. It is where Grace and Contessa are at some whore house!" Frank spat in shock, thinking his wife would be caught dead there. "Especially with his child; makes sense from what I learned from Grace's mother. This dark demon thing needs the lustful energy of people to begin to substance itself into this world." Celest said, not rattled by Frank's temper, "Well then, James, go on home and get your stuff together. You're about to make your grand exit. Meet us at the cantina in two hours," Celest said, like a general in an army. "Lexi and I will get some clothes, books, and potions together, and we will leave tonight. Then we will be in the Quarter by tomorrow afternoon." Celest started shouting orders, grabbing James' arm and guiding him towards the door; then Lexi smiled. Waiting for Celest to lead the way to her post of what she will need to bring on this journey.

"What will I be doing, pray tell?" Frank said. "You, sir, will get up and go tell the coven to put Dawson in charge until you return, and let's go get Grace and baby girl," Celest said cocking her head at Frank, clapping at him to get a move on until he was out of his chair making his way into the foyer. "Don't worry, I'm coming for you, baby girl," Celest said as she looked at a picture of Contessa and her parents on Frank's desk.

James started running. It was late afternoon when he got home and whisked past the living room and up the stairs. Halfway up came his mother's voice. "James, can you come here for a moment?" James walked back down the stairs and lay up against the door frame. "Your father and I ran into Tilly in town today." His mother spoke to her as if she was hunting for a killer.

Giving her son the third degree, his father did not look up from his ceremony notes but kept an ear in the conversation. "Well, I ran to her house and to Jessica's. I gave up, then took a stroll in the park." Not giving too much info away, just trying to provide enough to satisfy his mother's inquisitive nature. James stared at his mother, trying to come up with the next lie before her next question was thrown at him. "Oh, okay, well, I told her to come by tonight so you two could chat." His mother said, "Well, actually, I will have to catch up with her tomorrow since I have that card game with the fellows." He smiled at his mother, starting to turn, speaking as he went. "So, I have to get ready." "Come back, James." His mother said sternly enough that James stopped in his tracks, turning back around on his heel.

"Yes, mama," James said. "Are you really going to hang with your mates or are you going back to the plantation?" his mother said sharply. "What do you mean plantation? Why would I ever go there?" James said, with a softer tone than his mother had given him. "Well, some of the parishioners watched you make your way out of town, heading toward the plantation. Your father and I came here and pondered why, on the day a man came into our town asking about the plantation, that our son would head that way. We started to remember things from that night. There it was. The Montgomery's daughter's birthday." James held his composure as his mother spoke. "And there were fireworks and commotion, but we can't remember much else."

James inhaled a deep breath and stared at his parents. "You're right, I did run to the plantation. But it was only to ask Mr. Montgomery if we could use his plantation for the wedding reception. When Buster talked about it, I just remembered the barn in the back where we could set up the dance floor and string some lights from the big oak. I was going to ask Tilly to come with me, but she was not home. Hence, I went myself since next month is the wedding." James said, then waited, watching his mother examine him, digesting this new information. She smiled at her son, adding a new lightness to the air. "Well, I thought you were thinking of the park, but that is neither here nor there since I'm just excited that you are taking the initiative. His mother beamed at him. His father was unmoved. "So, did you get to talk to the Montgomerys?" His mother inquired. "No, the maid said no one was home, so I will try again tomorrow," James said. "I will have to give them a buzz, maybe after dinner," his mother said as she got up to hug her son.

Then she wished him well in the game. James darted up the stairs, passed two doors in the hallway, and into the third door on the left. He slammed it behind him. He collapsed onto the door, collecting his thoughts and scanning his room, trying to remember what to do next. James then picked himself off of his door and walked over to his closet. He opened it, bent down, and collected a bag. He opened it up, looking at everything he had in there. A few shirts, underwear, socks, and money over in the side corner of the bag. Next to that was a small caliber handgun that James picked up sometime last year.

Worried when it was time to leave, fearing he would have to face his brothers, knowing with this, he would be prepared. James zipped up the bag, stood up, walked over to his window, opened it, and flung the bag out of the window. When the bag left, James closed the window and took off his shirt. He grabbed a fresh one from the closet, put it on, and flopped on the bed, trying to close his eyes just for a moment. The door opened up, making James shoot up. "Hey bro, mom says dinner in five minutes," said Mathew. "Okay, I will be there in a second," James said, staring at his brother. "Where are you going all dressed up?" Mathew said. "To a card game with the guys," James replied, annoyed at his brother disturbing his moment of peace. "Sure, you are," Mathew said as he grabbed his brother in a playful headlock, which made James fight back. As the two joked around with each other, James shot his head up and hit Mathew on the nose, making him stumble back as blood poured out of him. "Oh, Mathew, I'm so sorry," James said apologetically.

Mathew stammered back, gripping his nose, letting the room back into focus. Having swirling images of a night long past of him and his little brother quarreling. Holding him in the basement. "Wait, who is Contessa?" said Mathew, and James went from sympathetic to panic. Looking around the room, trying to find a weapon, cursing in his mind for disposing of the gun out of the window. He reached his hand out and grabbed the heavy brass clock that lay on his bedside table. He then made his way over to his brother, arm stretched out, and swung the heavy brass clock into the side of his brother's head. He watched his brother fall to the floor, leaned down, released the clock onto the floor, and checked his brother for some sign of life. He laid his brother on his back and pressed his ear to his chest, listening for the sound of his brother's beating heart, which was slowly and faintly thudding in his ear.

So, at this, he got up onto his feet, walked over to his bed, and pushed down his covers. He then turned down to hoist his brother into his bed, covering him so that he was as comfortable as he could. He picked up the brass clock off the floor, placed it back onto his side table, and reached for his dirty shirt to wipe the blood stain off the clock and remove some of the blood from his brother's face. After James did the best he could to make normalcy out of chaos, he made his way out of his room and down the hall. Trotting down the stairs, James stopped in his tracks as he heard his father's voice, making him turn and face his father. "Yes sir," James responded with a smile. "Dinner, now where is your brother?" His father asked James, which made him clear his throat so he could devise an excuse for why his brother was not down yet.

"We were wrestling, and I banged his nose. Hence, he had to change his shirt. I was running out to fetch the doctor to see if he could look at his nose. I would feel bad if I broke it so close to the wedding. Mom would have my hide." James spoke this half-truth to his father. His dad chuckled and assured his son he would distract his mother but demanded he make it quick. "Yes sir, thank you," said James. He hugged his father before he quietly slid out the front door. James, on the porch, breathed a sigh of relief. They did a light jog around to the side of the house. Halfway through the yard, James heard a voice. "James love, where are you going?" asked Tilly.

James stopped and kissed Tilly on the cheek. Used to this slight interaction to keep up appearances. "My love, sorry, I have to fetch the doctor. My brother has had an accident," James said. "Oh dear," Tilly covered her mouth. "No, my love, nothing serious, just head into the house, and I will see you soon." "Well, I will come with you. We can spend some time together," Tilly smiled at him. "No, dear," James said, taking in a deep breath and placing his hands on her arms. "My mom needs to be distracted because she doesn't know he busted his nose, and mom will have my head when she finds out I did it. Please help. She has some stuff involving the wedding to talk about." James spoke, pleading with his bride-to-be to just do this favor for him. She looked up into his eyes and smiled. "Sure, my love. Anything for you. Your mother will never know what is happening," said Tilly. He gave her one last kiss on the cheek, then watched as she entered the house.

Without another second to waste, he ran over to the bag he flung out the window, slung it over his shoulder, and ran out of the yard as fast as he could. Knowing time was of the essence, fearing at any second his brother would be discovered, James headed through town. He dodged between houses and alleyways, trying not to be spotted. In front of him was the Montgomery's town car, just lying in wait. Ready to take off at a moment's notice. James made his way to the car, popping open the back door and startling the occupants of the car. "Child, you best be careful! You would have been as good as dead if you weren't cautious," Celest said from the passenger seat, Frank in the driver's seat and Lexi beside him. "Sorry, but we are out of time."

CHAPTER SIXTEEN
Preparing For The Ball

"GET UP! GET UP!" yelled the voice in the hallway, along with the loud thud of the knock on Contessa's door. "I'm up!" she yelled back at the voice, taking her pillow and throwing it at the door. After that, Contessa pounded her fist and feet into her mattress. Eventually, she scooted her body to the edge of the bed and rolled up, letting her feet hit the cold wood floor. She got up, walked to her balcony, opened the door, and let the chilled air hit her face. Then, she turned her attention to her calendar to mark another day off. February twenty-fifth nineteen forty. Tomorrow will be our fifth year since we have our annual masquerade ball. That is two days till Mardi Gras, when the French Quarter will celebrate. The sheriff, the mayor, the committee, and anyone else my mother invites will be there, she thought as they arrived in the French Quarter.

Luckily, since then, the hotel has opened and has never been empty, and the staff has gotten into a rhythm. The staff has grown. We have Alexandria, Brooke, Lindsay, Monty, Reed (who quit his job and started making nightly runs with Monty to help keep the liquor flowing), Kalvin, and Deedee. Then you have the dolls who came to us for many different reasons, but their job is catering to the guest's needs. First was Ceci; then there was Amelia and Kat a while later. Then there were the twins Amy and Kristen, Miles and West, and our little bombshell Bailey. Yet despite all that, Madame Grace still wants one more doll.

Fighting with Kalvin, telling him to keep looking. Day after day, coming up empty-handed, Kalvin looked at the last card every time they left the hotel. Contessa knew she had to clean up and help escort last night's guest out before the ten o'clock checkout time. Her mother was very strict about it. So, she threw on her uniform and dragonfly necklace, and out the door she went. "Hey Contessa, you look like hell," said Kalvin as he passed her in the hall, arms filled with guest luggage. "Gee, thanks, I'm just tired. I delivered for my mother last night and returned late," said Contessa. "Move out of my way," said Miles. Stepping between them, Miles, a Caramel-skinned man, passed by her with only a towel and one hundred and fifty pounds of pure muscle.

This did not faze Contessa anymore because clothes were optional till five when dinner was served for the staff, and that was the only meal Madame Grace ate with them. "Hey, watch it!" Said Contessa. "Sorry, little one," said Miles. Kalvin, so unimpressed, passed Miles and walked down the stairs, bumping Miles with a piece of luggage as he passed him. Miles shook his head at him and turned his attention back to Contessa. "Sorry again, there was a gift left for me at the front desk, and I wanted to shove it in the Other's face at breakfast." He laughed as he turned, too excited with glee to bother himself with small talk and disappeared down the stairs. Contessa stood there until she heard the same voice that woke her up, attempting to do the same to people from the room three doors down from hers. Alexandria, the other housekeeper, was trying to get some laundry started before she ate breakfast. "If you don't get up, there is a bucket of cold icy water for you."

Then the door opened, and the mayor walked out. Alexandria stepped aside and pointed towards the stairs, indicating it was time to go. Still, an arm turned him around and kissed his cheek. It was none other than the hotel's bombshell Bailey, standing five feet tall with brown hazel eyes and shoulder-length hair. "See you at the ball," the mayor said, telling her he would have his assistant bring her dress and mask for the ball and headed down the stairs with a piece of pink boa trailing behind him. "You two get downstairs and go eat. We got stuff to do to get ready for the ball," said Alexandria. "Okay, wait here, Contessa. I want to get my robe," said Bailey, who turned and grabbed her robe, flung her arms through it, and grabbed Contessa's hand.

"What is your rush?" Contessa asked. "That bitch Kat has stolen my specially requested French toast just because the mayor is buying me my outfit and mask for the ball. That jealous bitch! But not today. I will hit a bitch; don't let her try me today. "HEY, DOLLS, BREAKFAST!" yelled Alexandria, opening a few more doors. All Alexandria heard until they got out of earshot. Alexandria then chuckled to herself, thinking that the dolls would eventually kill each other to win the top doll spot at the end of the month. The completion was something all the dolls competed for. The winner was the doll who took the most energy from their guest for the shadows. They received a prize at the end of the month. It differed from month to month. Bailey won last month and got a new dress. Lindsay knew all about it since she played mama to the dolls, being gentler with them. Madame Grace played their father's role and was stricter with them.

Then, the door next to the stairs opened, and West came out. A five-foot-six-inch Texan who just smiled at her. Behind him was a couple whom Alexandria recognized from the French Quarter's committee that she and Madame Grace attended every week, discussing business that benefits them more than the Quarter. Behind the husband came Kat with her emerald-green eyes and legs for miles, all made their way down the stairs. Alexandria headed down when she saw all the doors were open. She crossed the lobby and entered the bar looking at the group eating breakfast. Bailey and Kat were in their usual shouting match at the center of the table. Then, she saw Kat grab a piece of Bailey's French toast. She put it in her mouth, with syrup dripping from her face onto the table.

That is all Bailey needed to see. She reached over the table, snatched Kat's hair, dragged her across the table and onto the floor, bringing down food, plates and glasses, crashing all around them on the floor as bailey started hitting Kat. Then Kalvin and West were on top, trying to pull them apart. "Let her go!" said West. "No, that jealous BITCH has touched my stuff for the last time!" "ENOUGH!" said Madame Grace, and with her words, the scene in front of her froze. Nobody moved. They just listened to what came next. "You children disgusted me going back to your street rat ways. Now the rest of you clean up this mess, get upstairs, and clean the rest of this place. Breakfast is over! Kat and Bailey, you two are out of the top doll competition," said Madame Grace. She turned back to her office, slamming the door behind her. Amy walked past the pile of bodies on the floor and giggled as she passed her sister behind her.

THAT IS BULL SHIT!" said Brooke. Deedee and I slaved over a hot stove all morning to bring you a hot meal, and you all go and ruin it!" Brooke continued her rant. "Shut up!" said Kalvin. "You're such a drama queen. now lay off of it!" continued Kalvin. Alexandria chimed in, "All of you stop! Monty Reed and Kalvin, get ready for your errands. Miles and West, you pick up the glass. Brooke gets in the kitchen, Lindsay gets started on the inventory for the bar, Eric will be here with a delivery soon, and Contessa takes these into the kitchen and clean them up. That shiner needs to be gone before tonight. Now move! all of you!" said Alexandria. "There is not enough makeup in the world to cover that shiner up," chimed Miles, sitting at the bar in his white towel.

Kat quickly put her hands to her face and started turning red and mad. "That is my cue to leave you with this mess. You made this mess; you clean it up," said Miles, and he walked out of the bar. "Monty, Kalvin, let's go. We have work to do," said Reed. Kalvin got up and followed Reed and Monty out. Brooke went to the kitchen. Alexandria went back out of the bar and headed upstairs. West wrapped the dishes into the tablecloth and walked to the kitchen. "About time someone cleaned your clock," Lindsay said as she wiped down a bottle of whiskey from the bar. Kat just glared at her, and she just piped down. "Come on, you two. Into the kitchen, now," said Contessa. She snapped her fingers to the kitchen, and without a word, they obeyed. before Contessa followed, she stood at the entrance to the kitchen and raised her hands. "Cleanmounse!" She spoke.

Green sparks came from her hands and circled the room, then imploded on itself, and then the broken glass on the floor rose into the air, putting itself back together. The chairs became right side up, and the room was now destruction-free. Contessa went into the kitchen. Deedee was cutting up cucumbers while shouting at Brooke for her to write down all of the stuff she needed to get from the market for dinner tonight, plus some extra stuff for the ball. Kat was on the counter holding her face, and Bailey was washing her hands. Contessa walked over to Kat and started helping her. "You girls are just acting like fools. You need to be doing your part to help with the ball, not throwing each other across tables," said Deedee, waving her knife. "Get your act together, please. The Madame will not keep putting up with it," Deedee continued.

Contessa then put her hand on Kat's eye and whispered a few words, and Kat felt a cooling feeling on her face, then nothing. "All done, now go clean your room," said Contessa. I need flowers, Deedee. Brooke just kept writing. "Bailey, come here. Let me fix your hand," Contessa said. She repeated the same words she did with Kat, which made Bailey's bruised face clear up. She stretched her fingers a few times, and Contessa told her to head upstairs. Bailey walked out of the kitchen without a word. "It looks like we will need more table linens, and I think that if it goes quickly, I need you back soon. We have so much to do." Brooke shook her head, grabbed her coat and scarf, and opened the door, shivering when it hit her face. "Wait, why don't I go instead? Contessa spoke quickly, hoping to get out of the hotel.

"Brooke, you stay and help Deedee." Contessa continued while watching Brooke smile. "I hate the cold anyway," Brooke said. She did not argue and held up the list for Contessa. Contessa then walked to the door, put on her coat, shoes, gloves, and scarf, and grabbed the list before leaving. In the alley, there was no one around, so she walked around the hotel and walked to the market. When she got to the market, the crowd was large, and she walked in and out of shops, marking things off the list. Spirits were high, and people buzzed about the ball in two days. Smack! Contessa ran into someone and fell to the ground.

Contessa felt hands under her, scooping her up, and walked into the nearest shop. Ding rang the shop's bell. "Mrs. Theresa, can you clear this table? This young woman fell outside." "Yes, sheriff." She cleared the table, and he placed Contessa on it. "Please get me a towel for her head." Then Theresa walked to the back. Contessa regained consciousness. "I'm fine! I'm fine!" she said. "No, you hit your head, and you were out cold for a few moments there," said the Sheriff. "My name is Lucas. I am the Sheriff. Please wait." Contessa pushed on her arms to sit up and scooted over to the table's edge. She stood up, trying to push past the Sheriff. "Here you go," said Theresa, handing the towel to the deputy. "Please, I need to get going. My list is not done, and I have to finish it so we can prepare for the ball at the Old Mill Hotel. Everyone is waiting," said Contessa. "Please, can you grab Savannah from the back? I need her," said the Sheriff. "Savannah dear, please come out here," said Theresa. "Yes, oh Uncle Lucas, what's wrong?"

"Can you help me? This young lady fell after bumping into me, and I need you to go finish the list so I can take her home," said her uncle. "Sure, I will; what do you need?" said Savannah. Contessa outstretched the list to her without a word, and Savannah walked out the door. Before she closed the doors, her uncle told her she may have dropped some bags, and she closed the door behind her. "My car is around the corner. Let's go. I'm going to drive you home." They left the shop and walked around the corner. Lucas walked in front of her when they reached the car to open the door. Lucas then told the crowd to clear a path so he could leave, and they did. He got in the car and drove off. "Your niece seems nice," Contessa said. "Yeah, she is. It's been just her and me since my sister died," Lucas said. "Oh my, I'm so sorry to hear that," said Contessa.

As they approached the hotel, she saw Reed and Monty hauling a big crate into the hotel. They froze when they saw the police car and watched the deputy leave. "Hello, gentlemen," said Lucas. "Hello," said Kalvin, looking awkwardly at him. "Well, then, I have your coworker Contessa, who took a nasty fall in the market, and I have my niece finishing the list, so it doesn't stop business. I know the sheriff is looking forward to the ball and the mayor and would be displeased with me if I did not do whatever I could to help," said Lucas. Then Kalvin ran to the car to help Contessa out. She slapped him away, telling him she was fine and there was no need to fuss. "Well, if you got her, I would head back to pick up Savannah and get the stuff back to you," said Lucas.

"Thank you! Hey, why don't you be my date to the ball on Friday? My way of saying thank you, and if you want to, you can bring Savannah," said Contessa. "Okay, thank you, I will," Lucas said with a huge smile, tripping over his feet, trying to get back into his car, and driving off. Then, the four of them headed into the hotel. "Your mother would not like to hear you have a date," Kalvin said. "Well, if you don't tell her, she will not know until the party," Contessa said as she watched Reed and Monty. "Go take the crate to her mother's office shouted Kalvin. Contessa headed into the kitchen to tell the girls what had happened. "Please don't say anything to her," Contessa said to Kalvin as she grabbed his arm with pleading eyes.

Kalvin just nodded his head, took back his arm, and walked out of the kitchen. Contessa then went through the bar to the kitchen. A knock came on Madame Grace's door. "Who is it?" said Madame Grace. "It is Monty and Reed. We have your special delivery for you." "Come in, come in," said Madame Grace. Monty opened the door and walked through with Reed in tow. "Put it down here on my desk. Monty, open it, please!" Madame Grace snapped at them. Sitting before Madame Grace was a wooden crate that was knee-high in size and had a red FRAGILE sticker on all four sides. Monty opened the top, and inside was hay. Madame Grace reached her skeletal hand into the hay and pulled out one of the best champagnes this side of the Mississippi. Armand de Brignac. Very hard to get it, but she did. Fifteen bottles cost her one thousand dollars.

"Monty, you are the best. When you say you can deliver, you do deliver. And Reed, did you run into any trouble getting here?" "No, Madame, you know no one can catch me." He smirked at her, and she cocked a half-smile knowing it was true. She used his driving services to take her to clients and to give them what she had always given them. Anything they want for twice the price from when she was in Mississippi. "Leave me, both of you, and fetch me, Contessa." When Contessa's name left Madame Grace's mouth, Monty gave Reed a nod. Reed was about to open his mouth before Monty nudged him in the ribs. Both of them backed away towards the door. "Right away, Madame. Will get her in a jiffy," said Monty as he left the office.

Madame Grace pulled the bottles out and reached for the extra special boxes she had purchased. Along with the champagne were two medium-sized boxes wrapped in a crimson red bow and smiling, waiting to tell Contessa what was happening tonight. The ball was not only to celebrate Mardi Gras. It was to introduce her as a Madame in training. Even though Madame Grace loves being in charge, she can control a lot more from the shadows. She can get more of the darkness out of people if she hands the reins over to her daughter and gains enough energy from the people to get her soul back. Maybe even become equal with the shadows, both in standing and power. "Monty, what do we do?" They ran through the bar into the kitchen to tell Kalvin that Madame Grace had requested her daughter. The men pushed through the kitchen door and watched Brook and Deedee throwing meat into the pot of gumbo and Kalvin making tea for Contessa.

"Dang nabbit! Monty nearly got a knife to the head, scaring an old lady like that." "Not now, darling, we have a problem. Madame Grace wants Contessa to come to the office now," said Monty. "Okay, listen, don't panic. Contessa can handle herself. I will take the tea to her and ensure she is prepared. All of you stick to the schedule. Go get the crate from the office, finish setting up, make sure the piano is tuned, and I will make sure the dolls are on their best behavior." Kalvin put the teapot on a tray, along with the cream and sugar, then picked it up and moved past Monty and Reed straight up to Contessa's room. Bang-bang came a sound on Contessa's door. "Open up; my hands are full," said Kalvin.

With a wave of Contessa's hand, she opened the door. She never moved away from her bed as she leaned against the headboard and applied some cream to her ankle, which immediately started to look better. "That will never get old," said Kalvin, giving her that chiseled smile he only reserved for her. "Your mother wants you immediately," said Kalvin. "Really? For what? I have to get to the laundry." "The dolls will finish that," he said. "Yeah, that will work. Bailey and Kat will fold laundry and gossip like best friends." Contessa chuckled at the thought and smiled back at Kalvin. "Don't worry. I will make sure it's done, but you need to hurry up because the guest will be arriving soon." "Fine, fine, I will go. I'm right behind you," said Contessa. She took a deep breath, got up, and left the room. As she descended to her mother's office, she started to contemplate what her mother wanted from her to complete.

For the last five years, right before the guests arrive, she has always checked the reservations and books and called the girls at 8 pm for roll call and lineup. When Contessa reached her mother's office door, she hesitated but eventually knocked. "Come in," said Madame Grace. Contessa opened the door, stepped in, shut the door behind her, and stared at her mother. "Don't just stand there, Contessa. Honestly, you act as if I taught you nothing. You must walk into a room and just with your domineer command the room and have all eyes follow you. Now sit down," Madame Grace said.

With that, Contessa walked to one of the oversized purple chairs in front of her mother's desk. "Yes, mama, what can I do for you this evening?" said Contessa with arrogance in her tone. "Don't sass me. This is serious. Tomorrow, I will name you the successor of this hotel. I want to take a back seat to the hotel so I can think bigger than this hotel and start focusing on the entire French Quarter and the bayou and become queen of the Quarter," said Madame Grace. "But MAMA!" Panic was in Contessa's tone, knowing that she may let her down and, worst of all, not be a worthy advisory and make her father proud. "Please don't interrupt me." Madame Grace's tone was sharp with her words. "You will shadow me tonight, and on the night of the ball, I will name you co-Madame of the doll house, and then you will run day-to-day stuff, and I will run everything else," Madame Grace continued, then she looked down and remembered the present.

Madame Grace wrapped her bony fingers around the box and pushed it at Contessa. Contessa grabbed it and examined the white box with the crimson-red bow. "Well, open it," said Madame Grace. At that, Contessa grabbed the bow, pulled it off, and let it slip through her hands. It slowly fell through the floor, and she took the top off and flung it to the floor as a child would on Christmas day. Inside, she pushed aside the paper to reveal a beautiful venison masquerade ball mask. It was blue with black lace, and a dragonfly was embroidered into the lace, which made her smile and grab at her neck at the necklace that her father gave her. It had a mystery behind those hollow eyes where her eyes would be on Friday, sending a shiver into her in fear of what would become of her at that ball.

"Thank you, mama, it's beautiful." "I had it made by a special mask maker and thought it would give you a piece of your father that night. "Go. I have to start roll call," said Madame Grace. "Go get dressed in something nice. You're no longer the maid. I will find someone else to take your place, maybe even that ninth person we're looking for," said Madame Grace. Contessa walked out of the office, mask in hand, and ran up the stairs, passing Kalvin on the way. "Hey, what is the rush? Everything is done," Kalvin said, grabbing at Contessa's shoulder to slow her down. Trying to catch her breath, Contessa said, "My mother wants to announce me co-Madame at the ball." She eventually got out in between breaths.

"What? Are you kidding me? That is nuts. Why would she do that? She loves being in control," a shocked-faced Kalvin said. "Well, apparently, this hotel is too small for my mother to rule, so she has set her sights much bigger than this. So I must get changed because I am shadowing my mother tonight." Without another word, Contessa freed herself from Kalvin's grip and ran up the second flight of stairs to her room.

CHAPTER SEVENTEEN
In the still of the night

Frank pressed on the brake, coming to a stop right before they entered the Quarter on the other side of the river. "We need a game plan." Frank yawned, then spoke as he killed the engine to communicate with his comrades. "If this is going to work, we need to make all our moves in the daylight since our enemy plays in the dark," Frank spoke as he watched the lights in the old mill hotel go out. "What do we do?" said Lexi, re-adjusting herself in the backseat. "We find a place to rest, get up in the afternoon, and do recon on the situation. Don't speak about anything until you know there are no shadows around," said Frank. He then restarted the engine after getting everyone's sign of agreement.

Frank drove them across the river and stopped in front of a hotel. They all stepped out of the car. James stretched before he reached back into the car to grab his and Lexi's bags. James looked up and watched through the window. Frank and Celeste headed into the hotel. Celeste smiled at the hotel's night clerk. James pulled out the two bags and slammed the door behind him. "Oh, James, I could have gotten it," Lexi said. "It's fine. I need to work out more," James said as Lexi chuckled. "You need to work out? That is funny." This made James laugh as he hoisted it up onto his shoulder. "We will find her, won't we?" Lexi said with sorrow, letting it linger in the air.

"We will get Contessa back as well as her mother. You, Frank, Celeste, Contessa, and Grace are powerful. Knowing what we know now will win against this evil," James spoke as he hugged Lexi, the friend and confidante with whom he has become very close with. Sharing all the things he felt about her best friend and sister, he pulled back, smiling at Lexi, then ushered her towards the door, opened it, and let Lexi walk through it.

The two friends walked up to Frank and Celeste. "We have four rooms, all on the second floor," Frank spoke as he passed James and Lexi their keys and pointed them to the stairs. They all made their way up the stairs. James handed Lexi her bag, and they all headed into their rooms. The next afternoon James awoke with a knock at his door. "James, are you up?" Said Lexi from the hallway. "Yes, be there in a minute," James shouted from the bed, stretching out and rubbing his face. He popped out of bed and grabbed some clean clothes from his bag on the floor beside his bed.

The light beamed into the room through the burlap curtains covering the windows. James made his way out of his room across the hallway, knocking on the door across the hall. "Come in said Frank." James walked into Frank, laying out a game plan. First, the group would go to the main strip of the Quarter, where all the shops were asking around about the hotel and its people. Then, James would walk to the hotel and survey the situation. James zoned out of the conversation, letting his mind wander. Around the room were Frank's clothes piled in the corner. The desk lamp light was on.

Scraps of paper covered the desk, and the window let in a slight breeze. Lexi and Celeste were leaning up against the headboard. "James!" Celeste snapped her fingers at James. "Hello, child. Are you listening?" "Yes, we are running around today and trying to find out whatever we can about the hotel. "And the girls?" James casually said as he locked eyes with Celeste. "And what happens if you run into danger?" "Go for the juggler, then run he chuckled. "This is serious. You are not like us," said Lexi, trying to plead with him, mostly concerned with his safety. "I know, and I am. I was trying to make the moment not so gloomy," James sheepishly said. "Well, it is, and you are important to us because my baby girl loves you," said Celeste, nodding at James. "Well, let's get going."

The group got themselves together and headed out of the room. The street was crowded in the heart of the Quarter, with noise coming from every direction. The shop windows were lined with signs advertising ghost tours, spiritual walks, tarot readings, and more. The group stood together until Frank suggested they split up. When Celeste walked into a shop with Frank, Lexi pointed to another shop a few doors down the street. Grabbing James' arm to follow her, the two entered the shop with the doorbell still ringing in their ears. "Hello!" came the voice from the backroom through the curtains; the woman went through the curtain. "My name is Theresa. Welcome to my shop. Looking for a gift for the pretty lady?" said Theresa, looking at James with a warm smile. "No, mama, what we seek is some information."

James smiled back at the women as Lexi shuffled through the dress racks. She looked up as Theresa asked what kind of information. Theresa was weary of the two strangers. "All of a sudden, we are looking for my sister?" Said Lexi, smiling at Theresa. Lexi made her way from behind a manikin with a beautiful evening gown embroidered with crystals inlaid with lace. "She moved here quite some time ago and told us to come by anytime. She sounded so happy and told us she got a job at the old mill hotel, but she was not there when we asked for her at the front desk."

Lexi kept her eyes fixed on this woman, trying to do this intricate dance, saying a little so maybe she could get more out of her than she had given. "Yes, you must have talked to Madame Grace. She is a wonderful lady giving all those misfits a home," Theresa said as she grabbed her pearls. Theresa spoke with the warmest of smiles. "She must be running errands for her, James. Let the girls talk," Theresa continued. Looking around the shop as he passed by some dresses and looked out the window, his heart leaped when he saw his love walking with her arms full.

He reached the door but stopped when he saw Contessa absentmindedly walk into some man wearing a badge and gun. "Lexi, can you come here, please?" Said James nonchalantly. Lexi asked Theresa to excuse her, and Theresa smiled, walked over to the counter, and started rummaging through the paperwork. "What is it?" Lexi said to James as he pointed out the window at the scene unfolding before their eyes. Staring at their favorite person in the whole world were swooped up in the arms of the law and rushed inside the shop they were standing in. The sheriff ran past them and laid her down on a table lined with accessories.

Lexi tapped James and ushered him out the door. The two weaved in between the crowd, bumping into a few people sending back their apologies but never stopping until they reached Frank and Celeste. "What is it, child?" Celeste said as she watched them panting for breath, white as ghosts. "Contessa is over there in that shop," Lexi said between breaths. "Wait here." Frank moved past Celeste and gripped Lexi tight. "Tell me, girl! Were?" He kept shouting. James pointed at Contessa walking with the deputy around the corner and, moments later, drove off with him in his car. "Now, what do we do?" asked Celeste. "Now we head toward the hotel, and when it gets dark, we head back to the room so the shadows don't notice our presence."

The team agreed and took to finding the best way to the hotel and weaving between the Quarter's patrons until finally reaching the hotel. Celeste hid their presence behind a concealing spell when they reached the hotel. Hence, it was as if they were not there. She was getting as close as possible before they felt Contessa would see through it. Finally, they saw the end of what was going on. Contessa thanked him again, and then James' heart sank as he heard Contessa offer this policeman her hand for some ball tomorrow. Lexi looked at James and smiled at her friend, seeing the hurt in his eyes. Then Contessa waved away a young man while two other men lifted crates into their arms and followed behind Contessa into the hotel. "Listen, James, Contessa was just being nice, thanking that man," Lexi said, hoping to comfort him. "Also, she doesn't know if you are alive or dead. We know they're alive, but she doesn't know anything." Lexi kept trying to reassure her friend.

"You're right. When she sees me, we will be as right as rain." He smiled back. "Well, now we know our next move," said Frank. Celeste looked at him, confused. "And please do tell; what is that?" Celeste asked, looking bewildered at Frank. "We get into that ball," said Frank. "And how are we going to do that?" questioned Lexi. "With my Sweet's help," Frank said. "Frank, what about the shadows? What if she is under their spell?" Celeste said in a series of rapid-fire questions. "We must have faith and do what we can to get to Contessa. It is our best plan right now. Let's get off the streets before we raise suspicion." The three silently returned to the hotel and headed into their separate rooms to digest the day's events.

CHAPTER EIGHTEEN
Heaviest Is The Head That Wears The Crown

Madame Grace sat in her office, and out of the room's dark corners came the shadows fusing to form the same manly figure that appeared to her five years ago. "What do you think you are doing?" came a voice from the arm of the shadows. "We see all, and we hear all. Remember, you belong to us. Don't take our graciousness for granted." The harsher voice came from its neck. "Yes, I know that, but my soul is nearly mine, and I have to think bigger," Madame Grace said in a tone just as harsh as theirs. "Madame, you have been warned."

All the mouths smiled simultaneously, which made her a little uneasy. Before another word was spoken, the shadows ripped apart and returned to the darkness. They left Madame Grace alone with her thoughts. She picked up her cup of tea and threw it at the corner of the room where the last shadow retreated. It shattered on impact and stained the white wall brown. Madame Grace pushed herself out of her chair and fell right back into it, taking a deep breath. She patted her hands to her head and ensured every last strain of hair was still in place. She then collected her notebook with tonight's reservations, exited her chair, and left the office. As Madame Grace walked out of her office, she yelled, "ROLL CALL! CLIENTS HERE IN FIVE!" She then shut the door behind her.

In seconds, the eight street rats in a bawl this morning descended from the staircase. Now, they looked like the Gods of Mount Olympus, gracing the mere mortals with their presence. All the dolls stopped in front of Madame Grace and lined up straight. Contessa followed them, but instead of lining up, she came to the front and stood by her mother. Contessa just stood there next to her mother for the first time, usually not ever being downstairs for roll call when the hotel was open at night. This was because the supporting staff was not required to attend roll calls. She would occupy her time playing cards in the guest house the sisters lived in or practicing her magic by the forest's edge where no one would bother her.

However, tonight, she is front and center for her first training session as a Madame, her mother started. "Listen up. Contessa is no longer your maid. She is your boss. From this point on, call her Madame or Madame Contessa. Nothing outside of that. Do you hear me?" Her mother said in a sharp tone that told you if you disagreed, you would be dealt with swiftly without mercy. The Dolls, in unison, as if they were in class, said, "Yes, Madame Grace." Something was wrong. She could feel it in her bones. She stared at Bailey and did not see the fiery girl from this morning, but the girl before her looked like a hollow shell with no feeling. Like her movements were not her own. She was well-mannered, with no bite to her tone. She then looked at West; he looked more like a statue than a man of twenty-five.

"Now, the twins, you two will cater to our boys in blue. Kat, you will play with Mayor Bailey. You're assigned to Marcus Brash. He is here for the night from Chicago; Ceci, you have Mr. and Mrs. Brass' boys. You will host our bachelorette party. Four girls in all. Amelia, you have Kyle Cookson, a real estate tycoon who wants to improve the outer rim of the French Quarter, so take extra special care of him. He can be useful in my future endeavors," Madame Grace said and turned to look at Kalvin, coming out of the lounge. "Open the door," she told him before facing the entrance.

In his black pinstripe suit and fitted black hat, Kalvin walked over to the doors and opened one, then the other. He welcomed the first guest. "Mr. Mayor," he said as he tipped his hat hello. "Kalvin, you look dapper in that suit," said the mayor, fat and jolly in his favorite royal blue suit. Contessa watched as the mayor greeted my mother. They exchanged some friendly banter, like two old friends laughing on their thrones at all the little peasants they rule.

"Bailey, take the mayor in the lounge, have Monty make him a gin, and sit him at his favorite table. Hurry now, Brooke will be starting to perform soon," said Madame Grace with her usual impatient tone. Bailey then stepped forward like a lioness on the prowl. Every movement was intentional. The way she grabbed the mayor's arm allowed him to kiss her on her cheek and lead him toward the music. Reed was playing on the piano with light, fun, upbeat music. Contessa turned to watch one after another of the VIP guests making small talk with her mother.

Then, the dolls moved with one thing in mind. Making these select few feel there was no one else in the world. "Madame Contessa, let's go keep up," came her mother's voice as she walked behind West, who had two ladies, one on each arm. Madame Contessa went into the lounge. "Now, having to move past the locals who fill the rest of the lounge but could never afford a room or our services. They're here for cheap whiskey and to try their luck at a hand of cards." Finally catching up to her mother, Madame Contessa stayed on her heels to not upset her. Mother walked around the lounge to the bar. She stopped to chat with Monty. She told him something about watching the two shifty men in the corner.

Monty looked in the direction her mother was pointing and noticed the two rugged men watching the card game that was getting underway. The mayor was back facing toward the door, shuffling the cards in his hands. The twins wrapped their hands in the officer's hair. Bailey was on Marcus' lap, and Kat leaned over the mayor's shoulder, probably whispering some sweet nothings in his ears. Her mother walked towards the stage. Madame Contessa, West, and Miles were in the corner closest to the bar. West was sitting in the chair while a girl was on his lap. Milles was charming the girls with his boy next door charm with the tongue of a snake able to sell you back your shirt to prove that he could. Ceci was sitting between the Brass couple, passing an entire bottle of whiskey between them. Finally, Amelia traced Mr. Cookson's hand, laughing at something Madame Contessa could not hear over the piano.

Then her eyes went to the stage where Brooke stood in an emerald-green sleeveless dress with black heels, black lace gloves, and her hair up except a single curl beside her left eye. Then she started to sing. Her voice sounded as sweet as honey. Singing about lost love, staying with the melody that Reed provided her on the piano. She then focused on her mother, who was making her way over to the mayor. "Mr. Mayor, how is the game going?" "Just fine; I'm up by fifty and hot," he said. "Well, let me blow on them," said Kat as she leaned in further, slowly pursed her lips, and blew softly on his hands.

Madame Grace smiled and stepped around the table closer to him. "Well, well, well, what do we have here? Who is this pretty little thing? Madame, where on God's green earth have you been hiding her?" asked the mayor, eyeing Madame Contessa, licking his bottom lip. "Mr. Mayor, you surely remember my daughter Contessa. She was the maid and is now training to take over the hotel," said Madame Grace. The mayor still eyed her as if she were a prize to be won. He said, "Oh yes, I remember, vaguely in the market ten years ago, but very few other interactions since she never came to the lounge." "Well, we must make the rounds," said Madame Grace. "Come, Contessa dear." They both walked over to Mr. Cookson, most likely to talk business. As she walked away, Contessa saw the two fishermen ask if they could join the game. Then the mayor got up and let the two men sit. He told Kat to stay and entertain them and walked towards her and her mother, screaming over Brooke's singing, trying to get her mother's attention.

When he caught up, he said, "Madame Grace, please give me a moment of your time... Please." Her mother then turned around and smiled a somewhat civil smile. "Yes, Mr. Mayor, what can I do for you?" "Please, a moment in private. Please, in your office. You won't be sorry," he said. "Fine, Contessa, go into the kitchen and ask Deedee If she has everything she needs for Friday. I will come and retrieve you in a moment." Without waiting for a response, she moved past her and the mayor toward the lounge exit. The mayor followed both of them, leaving, and saw the door of her mother's office close before heading into the kitchen. "Mr. Mayor, you know very well that I do not conduct business during this hour of the night," she said with an aggravated tone. It was already a holier-than-thou tone.

She then walked behind her desk and sat in her chair. "Yes, I know that, and I'm sorry for that. However, what I want and am willing to offer will intrigue you, Madame," said the mayor, curling his lips at her as he stepped over to the purple chair and sat in it. "Go on," Madame Grace said. "I have a proposal. How would you like to join the **fleur-de-lys?** At this, she dropped the attitude and leaned in closer to let him know she was interested. "Well, as you know, fleur-de-lys run the French corner. The market you cater to. Nothing happens that they don't know about," the mayor said. "Yes, but what is so worth it to you that you would be so willing to let me sit at the head of the table of such a powerful club?" she said, reminding herself that nothing is for free, something she knows all too well. "I would like one night with your daughter in my bed. She is something of a flower untouched by another."

At this, Madame Grace looked at him with dagger eyes. She took her letter opener off her desk and into her hand in one swoop, shoved it into her desk, splitting the wood and letting it splinter around the blade's tip. In not her usual voice of arrogance but a viler one. A voice filled with venom. "Hell no! She is young and about to be named the new Madame of this hotel and has no business being in bed with any man!" said Madame Grace. "Please calm down. Think about what you will do when she takes over the day-to-day activities here at the hotel. What are you going to do? Knit a quilt in the corner? No! So, with you at the head of the table of the most prestigious organizations in New Orleans, you and I could control everything, which is better than running this hotel. Only doing things that will benefit you," he said as she pulled her letter opener out of the desk and twirled the tip in her fingers but had anger on her face.

"You listen here, you fat old washed-up bureaucrat! That is my child, and you can't have her now!" she shouted at him. Then he shouted louder back at her. "So how is this one thing, unlike the last five years when you have done some crazy shit? You're here because we allow it. A woman of color like yourself could never have what you have. Owning a hotel and running a full bar right in front of our faces. You will do what I asked or watch this place burn you WHORE!" After the mayor said this, he spat in Madame Grace's face. She was about to use the full force of her powers, but for some reason, she could no longer feel her powers. Now fear comes over her, and for the first time since she was a little girl, she felt herself unravel, and it showed on her face.

This made the mayor calm down and smile at her. "Now, take the deal and get something out of this. Because I will have her any which way I please, whenever I want," he said with a cocky tone. Then Madame Grace stood frozen, looking past him and watching the dark energy, following it past the office floor and towards the opposite wall, into the dark hole of the shadow's chest where a heart should reside. Then she moved her gaze to their face and saw it smiling. "Fine! You have a deal," said Madame Grace. "Good," said the mayor. He reached into his hand and handed her a **fleur-de-lys** pendant, telling her to have Contessa ready and in my usual room in twenty minutes.

Then, the mayor walked out, closing the door behind him. The shadows walked towards Madame Grace, and she felt her powers returning. The mouth in the face spoke deep and slow, with nothing to his tone. "Hope you know now that we are serious. If not, we have a few more surprises for you tonight. You are nothing without us, especially since we have your soul. We control all of you. But don't worry; we talked it over. We want you to join him at his little club, and maybe just maybe, there is enough dark energy to get your soul back and for us to sit on top of the throne that looks down on the French Quarter. Now go get Contessa ready." The shadows split apart again and disappeared. Madame Grace was alone. She collected herself, momentarily looked down at her hands, and made some purple sparks appear. To make sure she had her magic back. A calmness came over her, now having her security blanket back, and she put down the knife and walked out of her office.

CHAPTER NINETEEN
Sacrifices

Madame Grace walked through the lounge and passed the card game. Mr. Cookson stood up and was pulled toward the exit by Amelia. Then she entered the kitchen. Contessa and Alexandria played cards, and Deedee sipped wine while watching the girls. "Contessa, I need you to come upstairs with me now. Alexandria, please follow me as well," Madame Grace said. They followed her through the lounge, past the patrons listening to Brooke sing, then into the lounge. Alexandria pushed the number three button as they walked into the elevator. The elevator doors closed and rose to the top floor. When it reached the top floor and the doors parted, they walked out of the elevator door and went to Bailey's room.

Alexandria and Contessa were nervous because they do not usually enter a doll's room at night. They followed Madame Grace into the bedroom, and no item was out of place. Madame Grace pulled out Bailey's chair by the vanity and told Contessa to sit down. When Contessa did as she was told, Madame Grace started to speak. "Contessa, do you remember the night in the woods when we ran from the townsfolks five years ago? They had pitchforks, torches with blazing fire, and dogs at our heels." She said this with nothing but sorrow in her voice and none of her snooty tone that usually accompanied her words. Something no one had ever heard from her mother. Sounding like a mother about to tell her child something bad made Contessa nervous.

Then, there was a voice you would expect from a little girl. "Yes, mama, I do." "I was scared and did not know if we would make it out alive, but we did," her mother said. "Because we did it together, and now we are safe," she continued. Contessa looked at her mother for really the first time. She did not see the hotel's Madame or the first lady of the coven. She saw a woman with the lines of sleepless nights deeply carved into the sides of her lips and around her eyes. They were tired eyes, trying to stay open to watch the map of war in front of her and ensure the kingdom was protected from all around. "Yes, mama, we are. It is okay; we all are safe," said Contessa as she reached out and grabbed her mother.

She touched her hands, and they were cold. She rubbed them, trying to warm them up, and felt their smoothness. "Now I must ask something of you that I had wished never would have happened, but everyone must do their part. Because, as you know, one bad choice can ruin it all," said her mother. With these words, it made a glimpse of the memory of her and James in the back alley. Remembering his lips on hers and her body shocked the memory out of her head. Then entered the next memory of the aftermath of her choices in the ally. Seeing from the woods' edge. No longer the whimsical dance or coven members. Eating, drinking, and being merry to the battle that erupted. There was the sound of guns and dogs barking. Remembering the smell of gunpowder and smoke in the air further filled her eyes with tears. "What do you need me to do, mama? I will do anything for you," she said, tears filling her eyes. At this, Madame Grace stood tall and took back her hands.

Alexandria goes to the closet and finds something nice to wear. Something sexy and revealing. Alexandria did as she was told, as she promised so many years ago, walking past them and entering the closet. "But, mama, nothing of Bailey's will fit me. She has smaller breasts," said Contessa. "Contessa, I will make it fit, and tonight, something a little tight will help with what I need for you to do well," Madame Grace spoke. She grabbed a red lipstick from the vanity and put it to Contessa's lips, painting the red gunk on. She continued, "Whatever happens tonight, don't use your magic. Just breathe and follow the instructions that you are given. Don't resist." "Yes, mama," Contessa said, tears streaming down her face.

Realizing that she was now no longer a prize but a chess piece in her mother's game. But knowing that she would do whatever her mother asked because of that fatal night, she ruined her mother's happiness. Then Contessa looked past her mother and now sees Alexandria holding a revealing black number that would barely go past her butt. She looked up from the dress and at Alexandria's face as her eyes filled with tears. Knowing there was nothing she could do but help get her dressed. She smiled at Contessa and looked away from her and back at her mother. She had Contessa stand up as she walked behind her and undid her corset strings. She let the dress fall to the floor and grabbed her daughter's hand to help her step out of it. Then Alexandria walked over to them, asked Contessa to raise her arms, and tried to get the little black number on but could not until Madame Grace let her purple sparks fly.

The black number raised from Contessa's arm and hovered for a second above her head. The purple sparks undid the threads and sewed the dress back together, descending back over her hands and face. Touching her dragonfly necklace, hugging her breast and butt, and stopping passed her butt. Alexandria told Kat she was off tonight and would be bunking with you and your sisters in the servants' house. "Now, please Leave us," said Madame Grace. Alexandria then walked out of the room, but not before looking at Contessa, whispering, "Good luck," and closing the door. "Contessa, the Mayor, will be coming in at any moment, so hold your hands." Contessa did so without a word, and her mother held her hand over her daughter's, and just out of thin air appeared a vial of blue liquid. "Now, Contessa, drink. It will numb you and help with whatever pain this may cause you." Madame Grace knew this was the only solace she could give her daughter.

Thinking that she lost the battle, having her hands tied and standing at the end of a double-edged sword. Then she did something she had not done since Contessa was a little girl. She cupped her daughter's face and kissed her on the cheek, which startled Contessa. She then pushed the vial to Contessa's lips, and Contessa drank the blue liquid, which was sweet going down. When she finished the last drop, she placed the vial on the vanity, and her mother said she would need to get a secret from the mayor. Contessa just nodded then Madame Grace turned to leave the room. Contessa wanted nothing more than to run after her mother but froze in place. Then the door closed. Contessa stood alone in the room. After a second, she sat on the bed waiting, staring at the door as she waited.

The Madame, Contessa and the Dollhouse

Madame Grace headed down the stairs, watching West and Miles enter West's room. All she could hear was a woman laughing as West closed the door and headed to the elevator. When the doors opened, the mayor said the first meeting was tomorrow at eleven. Madame Grace just smiled, stepped past him, and entered the elevator, letting the doors close without a word, thinking his days were numbered. The mayor walked down the hall and knocked on the door he knew so well. Instead of staying home with his wife and three daughters, he would spend late nights in bed with Bailey. He left most nights after feeling satisfied and told his wife that he was working late. "Come in," said Contessa, and the mayor entered the room.

Instead of being frightened, Contessa felt alive and desired this man, noting that she had never had this feeling before. "Mr. Mayor, please sit next to me," said Contessa. The mayor let the door close behind him and walked towards Contessa, but instead of sitting down, he stood over her. She stared up at him, and he stared at her and she patted the bed next to her. Then, the mayor raised his hand and opened it. In one swoop, he slapped her with such force that he could feel the sting running through his fingers. "DON'T YOU EVER TELL DADDY WHAT TO DO!" the mayor shouted at Contessa. As she spoke, the words that came out of her mouth did not feel like hers. Feeling the sticky liquid entering, tasting the iron in her blood, all that came out was, "Sorry, daddy." Feeling weird as she said it, but grabbed his hand and kissed it, the blood staining his finger. "I am sorry, sweetheart. Daddy's sorry. Do you forgive me?" said the mayor. "Why?" said Contessa.

Without a word, she put her hands on his stomach and pushed him onto the bed, which made him fall back. She could feel herself not thinking about what she was doing. It was like her movements were not her own. She continued following the mayor's sensual moans, now grateful for a second for the blue liquid. She continued opening her mouth and licking the tip of his penis for a few moments. She then went down on him for a few minutes as he grabbed chunks of her hair and pushed her face up and down. When he let go for a second or two, clumps of her hair were left in his hand. He stood, told her to stand up, and then pushed her beside him. "Now, I will show you what makes your daddy happy." Contessa just smiled, and he rolled on top of her and slapped her one more time. Not like before, but playfully.

Then, with both hands, he ripped her dress in two, bent down to kiss her left breast, and took his hands down her body. He stopped to move her panties aside, shoving his cock into her hard and fast, which made Contessa scream. The mayor just laughed and kept going harder and faster, not caring how she felt, greatly enjoying her pain. Contessa could no longer look at him. Turning away, she thought she saw something in the corner, and the creature was smiling. She saw this blackness enter its chest like a flood, and then she moved her eyes away from the creature and followed the darkness back to the source. The mayor. She did not understand it but just watched the mayor finish panting next to her and sweating profusely. Then, after a moment, he got up and told her that she did very well. He got dressed and walked out.

Now, once again, Contessa was alone and hollow inside. Not feeling anything. No sadness or anger, and she no longer had tears in her eyes. She got up and examined the scene that played out as if she did not even realize she was the scene's star. Seeing the blood that stained the sheets and a smear of blood on the wall where she was thrown, she felt something hot hit her feet. Blood fell from her onto the floor. She touched herself and said a few words, and then the bleeding stopped. She walked to the door, naked and sore, and reached for the handle. She walked out into the hallway. It was empty and cold as she walked across the hall to her bedroom, opened the door, entered, fell onto the bed, and closed her eyes.

It only felt like a second when she heard the door open, and Alexandria entered with a glass and a bottle. "Go away," said Contessa. Alexandria did not comply. Instead, she put the glass down on Contessa's nightstand and poured the dark liquid into the glass. She handed it to Contessa, and Contessa grabbed it slowly, having never drunk it before. "Drink it, please. It will warm you up and help you forget what happened." So, Contessa thanked her, let the warm, hot liquid run down her throat in one swoop, and then handed the glass out for more. Alexandria poured more into her glass, put the bottle on the table, walked to the bathroom, grabbed a rag, and turned on the water. She then let the water run over the rag for a moment, turned the faucet off, rung out the rag, walked to the bed, and sat down next to Contessa. She placed the rag to her lip and smiled. "Looks like it hurt." Alexandria said, "I did not feel a thing." However, wincing now at the pain of the damp rag against her open cut.

"Hold that there. I will draw you a bath and lay some clothes out," said Alexandria. So, Contessa wrapped her hands around the rag and watched Alexandria re-enter the bathroom. Contessa saw nothing, but she heard the water running, hitting the ceramic of her claw foot tub. She just kept watching, still feeling like she was not here and her body was a million miles away. The water stopped, and Alexandria had her hands in her drawer and pulled out a night-gown, laying it on the bed. "Get some rest, Contessa. I will check on you in the morning," Alexandria said as she left the room. Instead of moving, she felt herself re-enter her body.

The rush of pain came at her all at once. She curled up into a ball on her bed and clutched her necklace. "Daddy, I am sorry. I miss you. I need you to forgive me, forgive me!" Contessa cried like that until she heard a noise from the balcony. She looked over at the door, and in the moonlight stood a tiny kitten. Its color was a swirl of browns and grays, and it felt like another present from her father. She called it over to her. "Meow, meow, come here, kitty," Contessa said through her sobs. The kitten came over to the bed, and Contessa rolled over and scooped it up with two hands, placing it on her chest. She cried, letting her tears soak the kitten's fur. She laid back in bed, petting the kitten until sleep overwhelmingly consumed her.

CHAPTER TWENTY
The Past is at Your Door

The doors opened to the elevator, and Madame Grace stepped out of the elevator composed and showing no feeling. She just put on the usual persona of the Madame of the house and heard a ruckus in the lounge. It was one of the shady gentlemen she asked Monty to watch. Monty was now trying to diffuse the situation as Madame Grace entered the room. She saw Kalvin enter the room from across the lounge because the noise traveled to the kitchen. That is when things turned from bad to worse. When the men saw Kalvin, one gentleman reached down, grabbed the table, threw it towards the bar, moved past the few local patrons, and lunged for Kalvin.

Seeing this man coming at him, Kalvin raised his hands, extended his claws, bared his teeth, and braced his impact. The other man entered the fight having his comrade's back but not before knocking two tables on their side and breaking a chair leg. Then reed intercepted him before he could get close to Kalvin. "Not today!" the five-foot Brit said, raising his hands into balled fists, ready to fight out of this. The man swung the chair leg at Reed and hit his elbow, but Reed went low and gave him a blow to the chest. Both men danced around the lounge and ended up by the stage. With his back to the door and the man's back to the stage, the man had given a heavy blow to Reed's side, knocking him to the ground. Then, the man raised to give one final blow to Reed before rejoining his buddy in his pursuit.

Suddenly, Brooke leaped off the stage and onto the man's back, sending them both to the floor. The man let go of the chair leg. Monty reached down to grab him and turn him around. The man faced Monty, looking up to be eye-to-eye with him, and then Monty struck him repeatedly until he saw the man start to grow fangs. He rolled to his back, slashing his claw deep into Monty's chest and painting his shirt red. Monty's blood dripped on the man who was ready to rip Monty's head clean off; until he could no longer move, no matter how hard he tried. Madame Grace walked past the frozen mess of Reed, Monty, Brooke, and the wolfman with Monty's blood suspended in mid-air and to the other scene of Kalvin, who was pinned against the wall.

She snapped her fingers, only allowing them to have movement of their heads. "SPEAK NOW, DOG!" Madame Grace shouted, not in the mood for the runaround. "Well, Kalvin here used to run with us, and upon his first full moon, he was in bed with my sister; even though he knew what he was and what that moon meant, he ignored every warning and ripped my sister to shreds. Then the next morning, my father found her in bed. If not for being in her bed, we would have needed dental records to identify the body." Then my father went outside to her window and followed the bloody paw prints into the woods to find Kalvin naked, covered in dirt and leaves, with dried blood smeared on his face. He picked him up, threw him over his shoulder, and brought him back to the elder's house, where my grandfather, the Alpha of our pack, stood before him as he woke and grabbed a rag to wipe the blood off his face.

All he could say was, "Welcome to the pack." No anger in his tone even though he had to help plan a funeral for my sister. Then he beckoned for some clothes and passed them to him like the prodigal son returning. "After what he did?" I said as my blood boiled, and I kicked him so hard that a few of the male pack members pushed me back. Kalvin snatched the clothes from the ground in front of him and bolted out the back, and I had been searching for him ever since. So, witch, you cannot deny me the revenge I want. Madame Grace looked at the man, fire burning in his eyes. She spoke with the same authority as she always had. "No one will be killing anyone! How much?"

The wolf shook his head. "NO! HOW DARE YOU! YOU BITCH! MY SISTER'S DEATH IS NO AMOUNT OF MONEY!" he snarled at her. "Fine! What if I could give you a potion so you can talk to your sister again and have the goodbye you never got?" said Madame Grace, never raising her tone and continuing as he seemed interested. "You nor any member of your pack can never step foot in New Orleans, and you drop your vendetta against young Mr. Kalvin here," she finished. "When can I get this potion, and can I get two extra for my parents?" This time, he spoke in a lower voice and said please. "Fine, and you can have three potions as soon as you leave this hotel. Do we have a deal?" said Madame Grace. The wolfman, just having an inquisitive face, finally agreed to the terms. She freed the group from her grip. The wolfman on the floor was about to strike Monty again when a loud voice broke through the commotion. "Get up, Cory. We're leaving!" "What?" he spat back. "Don't argue! I got something much better than his last breath."

Cory looked up at his friend, wiping the blood from his face. Now, it smeared onto his sleeve and allowed his friend to lead him out of the lounge, but before leaving, he turned to stare at Madame Grace. "You better keep your word, witch, or there will be more of us next time!" He left, walking out the door. Now, turning her attention to the mess before her, Monty stumbled back with blood dripping from his chest.

Kalvin rushed to help keep him on his feet, and Madame Grace moved closer to help heal his wounds. She got to him just as Reed was helping up Brooke, and they both stared at Madame Grace work her magic. She got close to Monty and let her sparks fly. The purple sparks now acted as a needle and thread, sewing Monty's flesh together. Monty screamed in pain until nothing was left but dried, smeared red blood on his chest. "Thank you, Madame, but you know that is not the first time I've had a near-death experience.

"Shut up, Monty!" said Madame Grace, and he did at once. "Now Kalvin, you caused this mess. Please clean it up, and it better look new when breakfast is served tomorrow. Do you hear me?" She continued with an announcement in her voice. "Reed, get Monty to bed. Kalvin will do your chores tonight, and Brooke will collect some extra linens from the closet and take them to your room. Kat will be staying with you and your sisters tonight. Go now! All of you!" Her icy tone sent a chill through the air. At this, they left, and Deedee pushed through the kitchen door into the lounge. "Madame, may I speak to you, please?" Deedee asked with tears, trying to push out the words through her blubbering.

"What is it, Deedee? It has been a long night, and I am tired," said Madame Grace. "My sister, the one who runs the restaurant, so I could come work here. Well, she said two policemen came in today, said they were from the town we had come from, and started talking about a cold case. They spoke of a fire and how they thought everyone had died for years until they got a tip that two of the maids who were said to have perished in the fire of said home were unaccounted for. Now you have to help us, please. I have been loyal to you and have kept the folks' bellies full. Please." Deedee pleaded, but before Madame Grace could answer, Lindsey interrupted, panting on her way in, not stopping to catch her breath.

"Madame Grace, the sheriff's niece, came in with some bags for the ball, and she said that I looked familiar. Then she said Some white man was stumbling through the streets asking if people had seen his three little daughters that he missed so dearly. She said he had not, but Theresa from the dress shop said we worked at the old mill hotel. I have been unable to tell my sisters, but I am scared, Madame. I am terrified. He can beat us dead for running, and nobody would ever bat an eye." Madame Grace just took a breath and babbled. "Deedee, grab Kalvin and pick up your sister, and let your daddy come here. I will deal with him here. Lindsey, tell your sisters not to leave the property, and if need be, for the time being, you three will bunk with the dolls. Lindsey, I swore an oath to you and will keep that promise until my last breath. Let's defend the hotel and protect each other. We're going to war. Get the others. Now go!" said Madame Grace. Both women ran out of the lounge and up the stairs. All Madame Grace could hear was Deedee calling for Kalvin.

"What is going on, Deedee?" Kalvin screamed, coming down the stairs shirtless. "We need to go now and get my sister. I need some muscles, and you're it," said Deedee. "No problem, I will get Reed. We will meet at the back door. Just give me two minutes, and we will go." Deedee watched Kalvin come down the stairs, and Lindsey ran down the stairs behind him. Kalvin ran to the door next to the stairwell and banged on the door. Then, Reed got up. "Now we have an errand to run. It is urgent," said Kalvin. "Fine, I am up," Reed said as he opened the door. "Let's go," he said as he passed Kalvin with an irritated smile and descended the stairs. Kalvin turned to follow Reed when he saw Lindsey and Alexandria at the bottom of the stairs. Alexandria was holding one of his shirts.

"Lindsey said you would need this," said Alexandria with a nervous smile. "Don't worry; everything will be fine," he said. "Yes, I know. Madame Grace is mighty, so I am not worried about that." She said to Kalvin, "What is it then? You can tell me anything. I will help you. Whatever it is." Kalvin reached out his hand to take his shirt as he spoke. "It's Contessa; she had a rough night, and I just am worried and would have rather kept an eye on her tonight." She said, "Well, I will check on her when I return. You go and get Brooke." She shook her head in compliance but still had a worried look in her eyes. Fearing that everything may just not be okay and thinking how stupid she could have been to think that he would not find them here, praying that Madame Grace would keep her word.

They both descended the stairs and walked across the lobby and into the kitchen, where much commotion was happening. Reed yelled at Deedee that she could not just surprise her sister with two men in the middle of the night. She would think you have gone mad, and you may even give her a heart attack. damn it, you toad-stool, waving her rolling pin in his face and Lindsey crying, afraid for her and her sisters. "Enough!" said Kalvin. "We're all family. Maybe not by blood but by fate, and I would die for each of you. "Now listen!" Madame Grace said. "We're going to get Deedee's sister. That is exactly what we are going to do. Then, when we get back, we will all take turns checking doors and windows to ensure nobody gets in. Then we will get the hotel ready for the ball tomor-row."

Now Kalvin was putting his shirt over his head and contin-ued to speak. "We will get the guests out and transform this hotel into the most spectacular ball the French Quarter has ever seen. Now move!" Kalvin shouted at the stunned faces before him, look-ing at him now more than before. A sense of hope washed over them. "Well, you heard the lad. You three lock up behind us. This is war, and I plan on being on the winning side of this one," Reed said as he laughed while walking toward the door. "You three lock up, and we will return in half an hour. Don't let anyone in; run into the office if someone gets past you. I don't think the Madame will be getting much sleep tonight." Deedee and Kalvin were right be-hind him. When the three of them were outside, Alexandria slammed the door shut and locked it, staring at it, half expecting them to walk back to the door.

She just stared until she heard the car leaving the ally and nothing. No sound or light was around her. "Aww!" Alexandria screamed. "Sorry," Brooke said. "But what do we do now?" Alexandria turned and looked at her sisters. "We do what Kalvin said! We prepare for battle. Lindsey, you take the top floor and check all the doors and windows. Then, Brook, you do the same to the second. I will check them down here, then we will reconvene here and wait for the others to return," Alexandria said as she smiled. Her sisters smiled back and then turned and walked out of the kitchen.

The car veered around the corner onto the street where Deedee's restaurant would be and stopped in front of it. Reed was getting out of the car, not even taking out the key from the ignition. All of them looked around, half-expecting for them to see a straggling patron coming home from the bar or a car parked on the side of the street. But nothing. Not a soul in sight.

Deedee clenched her jacket as a gust of wind rolled down the street. She looked at her comrades, walked towards the door of her establishment, and reached her fat, pudgy finger out to grip the door. She saw that it was tampered with, so she hesitated and retreated her hand. At seeing Deedee's reaction, Kalvin shoved passed her and quietly entered the restaurant. It was cold and dark, and Kalvin's senses were heightened when his incredible hearing picked up a woman crying in the corner next to the counter. Slowly he crept through, passing between tables and chairs. Reed watched him move, and Deedee was too scared to come inside. Then Kalvin saw the woman. "Deloris, do you remember me?" said Kalvin as he bent down to ensure she was not injured.

"Yes, I kind of do remember you." "We are here to take you to safety. Can you walk?" "Yes, I can," said Deloris. "Let me help you up," said Kalvin. "Is she okay?" Deedee said as she came from the entryway. "She is fine, but we have to hurry. Whoever was here may be back since they did not get what they wanted," said Kalvin. "They wanted to scare us and said it was not over." Deloris' voice was shaky, and her body shook from the traumatic moment that she just went through. "Two white men said they were from the town where we had been servants. They said they recognized me and told me the story and told me about how the plantation house went up in smoke. They thought everyone was dead, but then they just wandered in today and recognized me. They told me not to go anywhere, and then one broke the lock on the door and said, in case I need to visit you, I don't need a key. His laugh just sent shivers through me, and I had to take a deep breath. Unable to sleep, I stayed silent on the floor over in the corner," said Deloris as tears filled her face and soaked her cheek. "No one will ever hurt you again. I struck a deal with Madame Grace, and you will come to stay with us until this all blows over." CRASH came a sound from the kitchen. "Oh my gosh, they're here. They're going to kill us! Deedee, take your sister to the car," Kalvin whispered. "Reed, follow me. Let's handle this now." "Shall we?" Reed said with a smile. "Hold on to your knickers, lad? Let's sheer us some sheep," Reed said softly as they moved behind the counter and towards the kitchen, stopping at the door and just listening to the whispers of the two men.

"We'll grab her and wait for the sister to come home, then bring them home and string them up in the town square. Ha-ha," said the men, not even trying to be quiet as they stomped around. They were now on the other side of the door, and Kalvin stepped back, raised his foot, and hurled it into the door. "There will be no stringing today!" said Kalvin, sending the two men to the floor. One of the gentlemen just lay there cursing as he held his nose. His comrade rolled to his back, got to his feet, and grabbed the countertops, looking around for something to use as a weapon. After a second, Kalvin was at his side, easily making his way around the kitchen with great eyesight.

POW, then CRASH came the sound as Kalvin's hand connected with the man's face, and as he fell to the ground, a bunch of stuff went with him. Now, the man was disoriented but could wrap his fingers around the handle of a kitchen knife. Then when Kalvin went to reach for the neck and turn him over, the knife went into Kalvin's lower stomach. Pain shot through Kalvin all at once, and he staggered back and grabbed the counter for a second, which gave the man a chance to get to his feet. "Are you okay, lad?" Reed called out while standing over to a now unconscious man, but all Kalvin could do was laugh. He reached towards the wound and grabbed the hilt of the knife, let his blood soak his hand, and pulled it out, then licked his blood-soaked fingers and laughed, which concerned the man and made him step back and rethink his cocky attitude. "Listen, he said that woman and her sister killed my family, and all I want is revenge," he said pleadingly.

Kalvin laughed again. "No, you listen! Those women are my family, and no one is touching one hair on their head!" He threw the knife into the man's shoulder. "Let this be a warning to you," Kalvin said, walking away. The man grabbed the knife and pulled it out. "I am going to enjoy killing you!" "Reed, I'm going to need you to wait in the car for your safety," said Kalvin as he winked at Reed. "Are you sure?" "Yes, I would not want you to get blood on your coat," said Kalvin. At this, Reed just knotted and walked out of the kitchen in a sort of half run, half walk.

Then Kalvin turned to face the man. "May I ask you a question?" Kalvin said. "Sure you can. Everybody should get a last request before they die!" he snarled at Kalvin. "Has anyone welcomed you to the French Quarter or explained what happens within the shadows?" said Kalvin, now flashing the man a smile while watching him stand there with feet firmly planted on the ground. The man answered with a simple no. "But that does not matter to you since you will die before sunrise." "Well, let me be the first to welcome you," Kalvin said as his left heel cracked in half, startling the man again. Then crack went into his other foot. The man could not move, coming from a simple town with simple people not ever seeing or hearing the horror that unfolded before him. Kalvin was now on the floor, arms stretched out before him. His hair started coming over his back like a wave about to crash on the shore. His face started to grow into a long snout, and before this cocky, arrogant bastard stood Kalvin in his true form.

Without a second passing, he leaped forward, mouth open wide, and ripped a chunk of his throat out. Blood sprayed from the man, soaking the cabinets and Kalvin's fur coat. Now, the man gasped for air, but all he could manage was the gargling of him drowning in his blood. Then Kalvin heard a groan from behind him and turned a swift gesture. He saw the man getting up, so he lowered himself to the ground and watched him as he stumbled. When he got up, he stood to catch his bearing. "Steve! Steve! Where are you?" he called out, grabbing the countertop as he turned to see the bottom half of his friend lying on the floor. "Steve!" he called again, kicking his leg and walking around to see the horror on his friend's face. His eyes were wide open, and if it were not for the blood, he would think he was scared to death.

PLUNK came a sound from the corner. The man jumped back. "Who is there?" he said, but no response came. He could only see Kalvin's silvery eyes. The man backed up, fearing what the creature was that owned the eyes that stared at him. Then the man turned and ran, moving through the door. SMACK, down he went with the weight of Kalvin holding him down. The man tried to claw out of the restaurant, pleading for his life. Still, his cries fell on deaf ears as Kalvin took a chunk of flesh from the man's skin and bared his teeth into the back of his neck. That gave him the final death blow, silencing the man and making him motionless. When Kalvin knew his work was done, he walked around the counter and out the door, then jumped through the car window, scaring the occupants.

Kalvin just nudged his nose to the steering wheel, indicating for Reed to drive, which Reed did. "DAMN IT, DOG! You got blood on the leather seats." Kalvin snarled at Reed, and Deedee leaned forward and rubbed his head. "That is a good boy. You will get an extra special treat for what you have done." Kalvin just howled in excitement. "To the hotel!" Reed said. Deedee stared out the window as she sat back in her seat. Her sister leaned in and put her head on her big sister's chest as Deedee stroked her head, letting her fingers weave between her hair.

Some time had passed, and Alexandria could see bright lights lighting the ally and reached for the knife on the table. She just got up slowly so as not to wake her sleeping sister. SLAM went the car door as the headlights of the car went out. Then, just several voices and the turning of the lock. Alexandria could hear the thumping of her heart above all else, and when the door opened, she breathed a sigh of relief. It was Deedee, and the gang, except Kalvin, was naked and dripping with blood. "My dear, what happened?" Pushing Reed to the side and running to Kalvin. "I am fine; all is well," he said as he turned and bolted the door. "Have you been up this whole time? You must be exhausted," said Kalvin. "Yes, you said a half hour, and then I got worried and made the girls as comfortable as possible. Then they fell asleep. "You said we're at war. You don't sleep while in the middle of battle when you have men on the front lines," said Alexandria, trying not to speak too loudly. "We ran into a little problem, and then I solved it, and now Deedee and Deloris are safe, and now I will make you safe," said Kalvin.

Alexandria sighed and slumped back into a chair. "Yes, we're all safe, but Contessa is not." She spoke not really to anyone. "What do you mean?" said Kalvin. "Nothing; I should not have said anything," she said as she ran her fingers through her hair. Kalvin sat in the chair beside her and put his hands on her shoulder. "Please tell us," he said, pleading with concern since Contessa was like the little sister he never had. "Okay, fine, but nothing goes outside this kitchen tonight! Madame Grace gave Contessa to someone; I am not sure who, but my guess is the mayor," she said. "Sweety, what do you mean gave?" asked Deloris, not ever being at the hotel or asking her sister during one of their weekly talks.

"You know, making her have sex with someone," said Alexandria. "What do you mean? Isn't that her daughter?" Deloris asked in shock, making the sleeping girls turn over on the floor. "Yes, hush now and let the girl finish!" "I believe it was the Mayor, but I can't be sure as I saw him on the third floor but did not see what room he came out of as I stuck my head out of your bedroom," she said to Kalvin, with tears continued running down her cheek. "And there is nothing we can do about it." she continued. Kalvin then put his arm around her and just hugged her. "It will be okay. It will, and I, we will figure something out," said Kalvin. "What the hell would possess Madame Grace to do this to Contessa? Especially since she just announced her as her replacement for the hotel," said Deedee.

"I don't know, but we have to find out to help Madame Grace and Contessa. They have done so much for us. We could all be dead or worse. Let's get some sleep and reconvene tomorrow. We have a lot to do anyway for the ball, which is tomorrow. Kalvin, let's help Alexandria with her sisters and bunk them in your room," said Reed. Kalvin nodded, released Alexandria, got up, bent down next to Lindsey, and swooped her into his arms, which, with his werewolf strength, was no big deal for him. He carried her out of the kitchen with the others following him.

CHAPTER TWENTY-ONE
Fleur-de-lys

Madame Grace was up early and in the market when most people were still snuggled in their beds. "Kalvin, I have a lot to do, and we have a small errand that you cannot tell anyone about," Madame Grace said. "Yes, Madame," said Kalvin, walking in and stepping behind her like the loyal dog he has been for all these years. "Thank you for taking care of my past last night. I know I never told you why I was in the woods that night, but I apologize for allowing that to happen at the hotel. If I had any inclination that it would have happened, I would have stopped it," Kalvin said with a tinge of guilt to his tone.

"Kalvin dear, you do not have to explain to everyone who comes to me who has a past sob story. I don't care. I promised to protect you, and that is what I will do with my last breath, and that is what I intend to do. So, keep doing what you're doing, and I will continue doing as promised." "So, let's go, Madame Grace." As she entered the flower shop, ring went the bell attached to the door. "Hello, Madame Grace," said the shopkeeper. "What can I do you for?" The little old lady continued. "I was checking on my order, ensuring it was correct and will be delivered this morning." The shopkeeper screamed for her assistant, Savannah, in the back, who appeared within minutes. "Yes, Mrs. Barns." "Are the flowers for the Old Mill Hotel ready?" "Yes, eighteen centerpieces, five boutonnières, and ten corsages."

"Yes, exactly, and I will deliver them to the hotel this morning," said Savannah as she smiled at Madame Grace, and Madame Grace smiled back. "Very well," Madame Grace said as she turned to walk out. Kalvin grabbed the door and held it open for Madame Grace. "Oh wait; how is Contessa?" Savannah said. At this, Madame Grace turned around and gave Savannah an inquisitive simile. "What did you say about my daughter?" Madame Grace said. "Well, she bumped into my uncle, the deputy, fell, hit her head, and hurt her ankle. He took her home," Savannah said. "I was unaware of this. I will ask Contessa when I get home," Madame Grace spoke.

At this, she turned to look at Kalvin, trying to read him. If he knew anything about her run-in with the Deputy, it would have come from Kalvin. "We have a lot more to do." Madame Grace went to four more shops and made her way around town to several homes. She dropped off creams, knots, and candles and did a few run-of-the-mill love spells. She, unlike most witches, is not afraid to attempt such a touchy subject as love. Then she went to her last stop, the one Kalvin could not speak of to anyone, around four thirty in the afternoon. She stopped in front of a big two-story chateau. In front was an iron-clad gate with a brass fleur-de-ley In the center of it. Kalvin attempted to push the gate open but could not. He had tried several times using the full force of his brute strength, with nothing showing. Little beads of sweat formed on his forehead. "Oh, move, for heaven's sake!" Madame Grace pushed him aside and pulled a small gold pendant from her coat, now hanging from a gold chain. She placed it in the etched-out fleur de ley shape in the gate and stepped back.

The gate rattled momentarily, and the gold chain started to levitate. It popped from the gate and floated to Madame Grace's boney hand. She walked past the gates, Kalvin following right behind. Without a word, Madame Grace walked up the four steps to the porch, to the door, and knocked. They only waited for a few moments, and the door was answered by a mid-forties, tall, thin black man with no hair. "Hello, Madame Grace. The others have been waiting for you," said the man. "Good, please show them to me," Madame Grace said, and Madame Grace and Kalvin walked through. The man shut it. "Follow me to the billiard room."

They both did as they were told. More interested in finding out where they were, Kalvin examined the walls. All he could see was the oaked cherry frames with men and women in masquerade masks and small gold plaques that read: JOHN HALLTHE GRAND MARSHAL OF MARDI GRAS. Kalvin took this as they were the heads of whatever organization Madame Grace had gotten caught up in. Then the man opened two pocket doors and saw the police chief's cigar in his mouth, who leaned down to hit the ball. "Ha-ha!" said the police chief. "I guess the boys in blue will always be a step ahead of the boys in red," speaking to the fire chief who just took a swig of brandy. "We will see about that, Charles," the fire chief said to the police chief, placing his glass down and lining up his stick for his next shot. "Boys, please behave yourself," a woman in the corner by the fireplace said. But Kalvin knew nothing about her, never seeing her around town. He watched her as she talked to a very rugged man dressed in a lovely brown pants suit.

Another house servant handed her a crystal goblet, and Kalvin could smell iron in the room, concluding that the drink was not wine but blood. Kalvin let his eyes leave the corner and continued to watch the game, listening mostly to the friendly banter but letting his ears wander, collecting in the rest of the room's sounds. Then he heard the deep voice of the mayor, which made him tense up; scanning the room and trying to figure out where he could possibly be. Then, the police chief moved out of the way, and Kalvin saw him. The animal who had his way with Contessa. "Madame Grace, so lovely you could join us, especially with all you have to do before tonight," said the mayor. "Yes, Mr. Mayor, would not miss this for the world," she said. As she talked, the mayor got up from his chair and put his arm around her.

"Everyone, this is the new addition to our organization. As most of you know, she runs the Old Mill Hotel and will be a substantial addition here at the Fleur de lys." They clapped, and they all just said hi and returned to what they were doing. Except for the woman in the corner. She got up, and her movements were whimsical and slow. If you did not watch closely or have excellent eyesight like Kalvin, you would have never known she had moved. Hello, Madame Grace. I don't believe we have had the pleasure of meeting. "I am Tara, head of the Vampires in the French Quarter, and have held that title for the last one hundred years. I'm the only female member of Fleur-de-Lys, that is, until now. Tara smiled and continued. "Us girls have to stick together, or these men will get to have it their way." She winked. "I must get back to my friend Paul."

She pointed to the man who sat with her in the corner. "He is the head of the wolves in the bayou, and he is speaking to Aries this year's Grand Marshal." Kalvin sat and just listened to the mayor as he watched the mayor snugly on his high horse after doing what he did to Contessa. "Is there a problem, Kalvin?" said Madame Grace. "No, Madame," he smiled. "Young man, you have been my loyal servant for five years, and I know when you are lying. So what is it?" she said while smiling between her teeth. "Madame, this is not the time or place." He wanted to protect Alexandria from her wrath. "Well then, maybe you should wait outside; if you ruin this for me, those two men were just a preview of what will happen to you," she said, staring at him. Well, she fixed his collar.

"I will be in the other room. Summon me when we are leaving," and he stepped aside and walked out of the room. The mayor smiled at this, as he had despised Kalvin since they first met in the market five years ago. "Well, we shall go into the other room and start this meeting." They all stopped what they were doing and followed the mayor through the wooden pocket doors on the other side of the room. They all sat behind their chairs and said the oath that signified the start of the meeting, then pulled their chairs out and sat. In front of Madame Grace was a dainty purple mask. She looked up to see the others put theirs on, and she did the same. "Okay, everyone, who has something they want to discuss?" said the mayor. "I do," said Paul. "Okay, you have the floor," said the mayor. "As you all know, Mr. Cookson is trying to infringe on my land. The wolves own the bayou and need that land to hunt and do our ceremonies in peace. He needs to be stopped now!" Said Paul.

"Well, you can't fight progress, Paul," The police chief said. Paul growled at this and was insulted. "You would not say that if they shut down that damn doll house of hers where all of you go play and whore around with those soulless creatures you call humans!" Paul continued, showing a hint of his teeth and looking at Tara for support. "Well, I have lived here a long time, and I remember, unlike most of you, the dark ages where it was a constant war, and no outsider would dare come to the Quarter. Then the fleur de lys were formed, and our accords have made this place the place to be. Let's not ruin that now on behalf of an outsider." Tara smiled as she spoke softly.

"I know I am not a happy vampire without my food straight from the tap. The taste of it with a hint of liquor makes it much more delicious. So I stand by my fellow member and will help eliminate this, Mr. Cookson." "But he will bring more food for your kind," the fire chief butted in, and here came the Police chief. "Calm down! We all want the same thing: to keep us and ours on top and safe. So, let's come to a compromise. He can stay and build up to the bayou, but no further. Is that fair?" said the mayor. "Okay, I can live with that. But, if you try to double-cross me, I swear! Don't think for a second I am as weak as my father. Do you hear me?" said Paul. "Of course," said the mayor. "What is next on today's agenda?" "I have something to say," said the police chief. "A string of bodies has been coming up on shore or left in the cemetery. They all had Vampire bites on them," he said, staring directly at Tara. "I guess you can no longer control the night children. Maybe a change in leadership should be in order."

He gave her a half smile. "Don't you dare say I can't do my job! Hello, this is a sinner's town, and not every vampire that comes here is in my family," Tara said, keeping her calm with not even the slightest bite of annoyance. "But, you know what goes on in this Quarter regarding any nightwalker?" "Of course, and if not, I know someone who does." She smiled a smile that mimicked his. "Enough!" said the mayor. "Tara, can you make our problem go away?" "Yes, Mr. Mayor," said Tara. "So, Is that it? Then all problems are solved. Tomorrow night is the ball at Madame Grace's hotel, and we can all meet here and head to the ball together. Sound good?"

When the mayor asked the question, the members at the table agreed with a simple nod of okay. "So this meeting is adjourned and will reconvene tomorrow," finished the mayor as he rose from his chair and walked past them and out of the room. "We must be getting back to our stations," said the chief of police, and fire nodded their heads at the three other members and walked out. "THEY HAD NO RIGHT!" said Paul. "To speak to you like that. Be replaced? You're three hundred and fifty years old. You know more about this world than anybody at this table!" "Calm yourself, Paul, before you turn, which none of us need right now." "Don't worry; I will be on top soon enough." "Listen, Paul; I pay these humans no mind. They are just a blimp in the grand scheme of things. They will quickly perish as all the rest," said Tara. "May I intervene?" said Madame Grace.

Both Tara and Paul looked up at Madame Grace. They started to speak. "I will soon be handing the reins of the hotel over to my daughter and will need something to occupy my time, and because of that, I set my sites on something higher." "Oh, please tell me, what mountain are you trying to conquer?" said Tara. "The head chair of the fleur-de-lys, and that would mean the more powerful factions would run the Quarter." "Now, how do you propose they own the majority vote?" "Well, leave all of it to me; come to the ball and watch me work my magic. I'm willing to bite because it is dished out around these parts. The other reason is I want my piece of the pie, but if we are going to help, I want your promise on one thing," said Tara. "What is that?" Madame Grace asked. "I want to rework the territories for the factions." Madame Grace looked like she was looking at a chessboard to make her next move. "Fine. Leave it all to me. It will all come together at the ball." "So, do I get a say in this?" Paul said. Tara patted him and said, "You just did, sweetie, you just did." "Okay, I bid you a good day; see you at the ball." With a quick wave from Paul, she walked out of the room. "Come, dog; we have much to do," said Madame Grace. Then, they walked out of the chateau.

CHAPTER TWENTY-TWO
The Morning After

As the sun rose through the window panels and crawled up Contessa's bed, warming her body as it came over her eyes, it made her face sour. She squinted even tighter, praying morning would stop coming. Remembering that last night was not a dream. She felt small hints of pain around her body. Slowly, she turned to overhear a soft knock on the door. "Who is it?" She grumbled. "It is me." Alexandria opened the door. "Tessa, are you doing all right?" Alexandria asked as she opened the door.

Not waiting for a response, she went to bed, sat next to Contessa, and placed her hand on her back, making her cringe and cower into her mattress. "Oh, Tessa, I wish I knew why your mother did what she did, but I promise we are all here and will stand beside you," said Alexandria. I had to last night. My mother said we all have to make sacrifices. "Last night was mine, so let's get ready for tonight, and we will figure out the rest tomorrow," said Contessa as she slowly turned over. "Where is Kalvin?" she continued. Alexandria looked at her with sorrow in her eyes but just gave a slight smile. "He is with your mother on some final preparations." "Okay, I'm going to get dressed, get something in my stomach, and get this place in tip-top shape," Contessa finished speaking. She rose to her feet, walked over to her vanity, pinned up her hair, and threw her uniform on slowly over her bruised body.

She waved a hand at Alexandria to follow her out of the room, which she did reluctantly. In the hall were the rumblings of West and Bailey over the fact that she was out of the running tonight and West saying he is the shoe in to win. Contessa pushed in between them with Alexandria in tow, heading into the elevator, going down to the lobby, across the lobby, and into the kitchen. As they walked in, several pots were on the stove, sweet aromas filled the air, and chatter about gowns and table linens.

In walked Reed and Monty with crates full of tonight's liquor. Behind them was Kalvin, with a sour look, with her mother in tow. "Now, attention, everyone, I will not remind you how tonight will be one of the biggest nights in doll house history," Madame Grace said in her usual superior tone. "Contessa will take her place, and I will then take my place as the Queen of the Quarter, putting us and this house in a position where we never have to worry about losing our home again." Madame Grace spoke, as a matter of fact, sort of statement as if she looked into a crystal ball, seeing the future as she spoke it. "Now check the final detail, and Alexandria, are the dolls dressing?" "No, Madame," Alexandria said sheepishly. "Then why are you standing here and not telling your sisters to help wrangle them in and letting them know you need assistance?" Madame Grace continued. A knock came the sound on the back door. "Who is it?" shouted Deedee. Someone cleared their throat and said, "It is me, Savannah. I forgot to give you one more item left in my car for tonight's ball." "Who is this girl?" said Madame Grace, annoyed at this interruption. "It is the sheriff's daughter," Contessa said. "She helped me shop for the ball because I took a nasty fall yesterday."

Madame Grace looked less annoyed, all of a sudden forgetting she had even met her just yesterday. She smiled a different kind of smile from the one everyone was used to. All of you get back to work, and don't you dare disappoint me. Madame Grace walked to the door and saw Alexandria leaving the kitchen with Monty and Reed in tow. Kalvin walked over to Contessa with Deedee and Deloris cooking up a storm. As Madame Grace opened the door, she took a deep breath to compose herself. "Hello dear, come on in." Madame Grace stared at Savannah, holding a box of some sort. Grace stood aside and let her walk past her. "Wow, Ma'am, you look stunning!" said Savannah, looking at Madame Grace up and down in awe of her beauty. "Thank you, dear; now put that on the counter and tell me about this nasty fall everyone failed to mention," smiled Madame Grace.

Contessa and Kalvin looked at her, puzzled, trying to figure out why she would stop talking to this girl when there was so much to do. Savannah smiled and started talking about how her uncle, the sheriff, knocked Contessa off her feet, dropping boxes onto the sidewalk. "Oh, my word!" said Madame Grace, making Kalvin chuckle, which made Madame Grace scold him. Then Kalvin reached for his side, rubbing it in a circular motion. "Are you okay?" whispered Contessa, afraid to get scolded as Kalvin did. "I don't know. I felt like something kicked me." Grumbled Kalvin. Then he jumped again and started feeling around his jacket, which got him a good kick to the palm.

He reached into the inside pocket of his jacket, wrapping his hands around the last card of the deck that Madame Grace gave to him five years ago, pulling it out of his pocket, forgetting that there were others around. Kalvin laid eyes on the black card with a crimson red border, and a red Marinette doll was moving the strings to give the doll movement. It was moving faster as he pointed the card at Savannah. "What is that?" said Contessa, snapping Kalvin back into reality, pushing the card back down into his jacket pocket but not without catching the eye of Madame Grace, which led her to smile more. "Now, Contessa, could you come here?" said Madame Grace, who spoke gleefully, which made the people who still inhabited the room uneasy for the simple reason that this was not the Madame who had run this house for five years.

The one with her rules and her order kept the members of this house feeling obsolete most of the time. At this moment, she was like a friend having afternoon tea, laughing the day away without a care. "Dear, I like her and think you should have invited her to the ball." "I'm so sorry, Mrs. Savannah, for my daughter's rude manners. Honestly, Contessa, who raised you?" said Madame Grace. "Well, I can't recall?" said Contessa, making Madame Grace's eyes jolt and giving her a stern look. "Now, please accept my invitation to the ball tonight," said Madame Grace. "I would, but sadly, I don't own a dress that would be fitting for a ball," said Savannah sheepishly. "Nonsense; I will handle that. Come to my office and see if we can find something for you. I also believe I have a different mask from the ball's past. Kalvin, will you come to help me dig it out?"

Madame Grace smiled at him in what could only be seen as devilish as her tone, and he shook his head, standing and approaching Savannah to help her out of her chair. Madame Grace stood up. "Do you need my help, mother? I could help with alterations or a second opinion." Madame Grace took a quick pause, pondering this thought. She realized she had no choice when she looked at the corner of her room and saw the shadows gleefully looking at this as the opportunity they had been waiting for. Hence, she said, "Very well," and pointed them toward the kitchen door leading to the lobby. Following behind them, she stopped briefly to remind Deedee and Deloris that she was not to be disturbed until she emerged for the party.

She then exits the kitchen to see the back of Kalvin's head as he enters her office. Making her way around the front desk and into the office, she shut the door behind her, locking it. As she turned around, she imagined her next move. She would take Savannah into the basement, where the ceremony would happen. But, what paused her for the briefest of moments was Contessa. She has shielded her daughter for the last five years. Ever since she had to run from her home so long ago. She then walked toward the three of them. "You have to forgive me, Savannah. My desk is such a mess. So busy trying to keep this place running." Madame Grace was still trying to ponder her next move. What was so hard for Madame Grace was that Savannah was not like the other dolls. She was not running from anything. She was not hungry or poor. She was well-established; the biggest problem was that she was not an outsider.

She was breaking her rule, making her next words sound like a dance, not a conversation. "Now, Savannah, what is it that you want? You must want something in life, and as a thank you to you and your uncle, I would like to do something for you." Madame Grace spoke softly so as not to sound eager or mischievous but hopefully to put Savannah at ease. "It is okay, Madame. You're already doing so much by lending me the dress. My uncle is already going to flip. I'm even here since he says I should focus on useful things, like finding a husband and getting in with the ladies of the Quarter," Savannah said. "Oh, deary, I could teach you so much more than a room of stuffy old women who will do nothing but judge you. I could teach you about business so that no man could ever control you and no woman would ever cross you."

Madame Grace believed every word of what she was saying. Since, in a roundabout way, she would teach this naive girl the hard truths of this world, and when her contract is up, she could take care of herself. Even though no self-respecting man would ever take her for a wife. "Well, maybe you would consider working for me at the hotel. You could shadow Contessa tonight. She will become the hotel's owner. "Well, I'll take a back seat," Grace said as she smiled at Contessa. "Well, I would be happy to help Contessa. I don't have many friends and could use someone else to talk to besides my uncle and Theresa." "Excellent!" Madame Grace started shifting in her desk and stood in front of the bookcase, raising her bony fingers and moving them back and forth like before. Purple and green sparks shot from her fingers, and the bookcase moved, revealing the golden handle embedded into the floor.

Grace moved her fingers back and forth again, and the floor separated, revealing the staircase. "Follow me. I promise I will keep your uncle from being upset with you, and you will work with Contessa," Madame Grace said. Never seeing any of this, Contessa moved closer to Kalvin, and Grace spoke as they descended the staircase. "We will sign the contract here and get you the prettiest dress and mask you ever saw." The room at the end of the stairs was dimly lit, with the cauldron boiling with noises coming from the wall. "Don't mind the noises," Madame Grace said. "We had a small infestation of rats." She walked over to the armoire. "Sit, dear. On the table is a contract that all the employees must sign. Use the quill on the table," Madame Grace said as she whispered words over the armoire before opening it.

Contessa leaned into Kalvin as she was unsure of this whole thing. She knew about this place but did not know the staff had signed contracts. Behind Contessa came a slight wind that sent shivers up Contessa's spine. Kalvin grabbed Contessa's hand and told her she was safe, there was nothing to worry about, and that he had her. "Here we are." Grace pulled out a lavish floor-length ball gown with yellow canary crystals lining the dress with a low-cut neckline that was something straight out of a fairy tale. "Wow, Madame Grace! I cannot wear that. It is stunning," said Savannah. Kalvin and Contessa said nothing, just stunned at the beauty of this dress. "My dear, it is nothing. You will be the bell of the ball, but I see no signature on this contract. Are you having second thoughts?" smiled Madame Grace.

"No, ma'am, none whatsoever," said Savannah. Madame Grace reached for the quill and handed it to Savannah, but in a way where she pierced the side of her palm, which made Savannah push her hand back. "I'm so sorry, dear. Please forgive me," Madame Grace said as she watched the contract becoming stained in the crimson-red liquid like the other eight before her. "It is okay, deary, just sign it," said Madame Grace as she pushed the quill towards her again, which Savannah took with ease despite the pain from her palm. She leaned down over the paper, dipping the quill into ink at the upper edge of the desk, signing on the line next to the x. Her blood mixed with the ink and the quill's final swish as her hand moved along the line. Then Savannah dropped the quill, feeling the pain's intensity pulsating from her palm and dropping to her knees. Madame Grace knew she had the final piece of the puzzle to take her throne, ruling over the Quarter.

Kalvin released his hand from Contessa's and walked over to Savannah, grabbing her hand. He collected the blood from her open sore, then headed to the cauldron, throwing it in and watching the area above it filled with the crimson red smoke. Another doll appeared like so many times before. Kalvin picked it up, placed it in the center of the room, and walked back over to Savannah, dragging her to lie towards the lifeless, faceless doll. Next, walking over to the corner, was an outstretched arm to grab the vial. "What the hell did you do, Mom?" Contessa shouted, breaking the silent dance in the room. Madame Grace moved towards Kalvin, passing him to stand in front of the corner with the shadows to shield her daughter from what she could. "Let's get this done quickly," said Madame Grace.

Contessa ran over to Savannah, trying to save her, not knowing from what. Just knowing it had to be done. But only to hit an invisible wall that knocked Contessa off her feet. Leaning back onto her elbows, she watched as the once faceless doll was the spitting image of Savannah. Contessa had horror written all over her face. She watched the woman who did not raise her but was the vein of her existence step through the invisible wall and pick up the handles of the doll. She cut the strings and put it into another decorative cage. "Kalvin, you must take Savannah to her room and get Alexandria to get her ready. She needs to be perfect before the ball and interfere if Bailey or the others try anything to sabotage this night," Madame Grace said hastily.

Kalvin walked through the invisible wall and grabbed Savannah by the hand, helping her up as he was told. She walked past Contessa and up the stairs, leaving mother and daughter to speak privately. "Leave us!" Madame Grace spoke into the room but not at Contessa. "Who are you talking to, mama?" "It is not your concern," Madame Grace said to her daughter, watching her rise off of the ground. "What just happened"? Contessa said in the sternest voice she had ever used with her mother. "What needs to be done? What did you do to Savannah? Answer me now!" Venom spewed with every word that came from Contessa's mouth. "Little girl, you don't seem to realize that we have been allotted a certain lifestyle here in the Quarter, and what we do here is not what anyone would say is legal," Madame Grace said, matching Contessa's tone.

Madame Grace continued; she reminded Contessa of what they lost and that she needed Savannah to free herself of the chains she wrapped herself into. She will release her and her daughter, leaving this retched place behind, and leaving us in a better position than they currently have. "Now run upstairs and start acting like a Madame, not a child. Move!" screamed Madame Grace. Knowing it was a losing battle, Contessa turned on her heels and walked up the stairs.

CHAPTER TWENTY-THREE
Just Realized

Where are you going?" said Deedee as Contessa stormed out of the back kitchen door and into the ally. "Aww," Contessa screamed as she paced back and forth. "Is everything okay?" said a voice behind her, making Contessa stop. Peering over her shoulder, behind her stood a ghost. "Please don't scream." Contessa turned around to see the man she last saw as a boy. Standing before her was the son of a preacher who stood tall at 6'1 and was more muscular than she could remember. He still had impeccable cheekbones and beautiful wavy brown hair, and his silver eyes made her feel like she was staring at the moon.

"How? What?" was all Contessa could get out before his lips intertwined with hers, and she was lost in the abyss for a few moments. She did not think of what had just occurred in the secret basement of her mom's office. All anger left her body as she finally pushed him back. "Please tell me everything." "I will, my love. Please let me stare at you for a moment longer." James said as he breathed heavily with the biggest smile. He slowly caught his breath and explained how he escaped from his brothers grasp right before the fireworks lit up the sky as his brothers slept. He then ran the entire way to her house. "There, I saw a horror scene. From the edge of the property, I saw smoke filling the morning air. I ran up the front steps and saw the mayor die, then out into the back yard were the most horrifying scene was happening in front of me.

James continued, saying, "I raced in every direction, looking for you. I ended up in the backyard on the dance floor, where me and Celest watched your father hovering over a body." James paused as he saw his love-quivered eyes filling up with water. "What is it, my love?" "My dad is alive. Why did he not come for us?" she said with a shaking voice. "I will explain everything. Please bear with me. What I saw was Lenny lying there. Your father looked up at me and said, "The white devil has returned," which made Celest look at me, ready to defend me. Still, when I held my hands in protest, they waited, allowing me to apologize. Then we sat there wondering why no one had found you or your mom wandering in the woods. We thought the worst, and your father started to think outside forces construed this whole situation. Hence, we dug into it until Annie found out from your grandmother that these shadows were controlling the whole situation, watching your mom in her home country. With that information, it led us here," James said without taking a breath.

"Wait! My dad is here! We're here, James, we're here!" Contessa cried out, banging on his chest until James wrapped his hands around her wrist. "Contessa, please; no one can know we are here. I'm taking a risk showing up like this and may get a good beating from Celest for it," James, breathing heavily again, continued in as low of a whisper as possible. "You will see him tonight. We will free you and your mom from this place." "Wait," Contessa interrupted. "We're not prisoners. My mom runs the place, but we have taken prisoners or something of the sort," she spoke through the crackling in her voice.

The Madame, Contessa and the Dollhouse

"It is probably something to do with that creature controlling her. Something is not right, and I believe it will all come to a head tonight, so please do whatever you can to get us in," James hastily said. "I will but, but," Contessa stuttered over her words, looking around the ally and tracing the doll house wall, stopping at her open window. Snapping her head back at James, she said, "That is my balcony. My dad or Celest can get you all up there. I can sneak you down into the party that way," she said smiling.

James looked concerned at this notion and said there was no way we could get there. "Did you forget that you're in love with a witch with a father and family with magical powers? Getting up, there will be a Breeze," she chuckled, followed by a cough. "I'm sorry, I just forgot about all that, with seeing you tonight." "Well, I must go and tell the others," he said eagerly, kissing her for a moment, pulling away, and walking towards the street. "Wait," said Contessa. "What will you be wearing? You will all have masks on." "I will wear the face of a raven, Celeste will wear a black cat's face, your father a lion, and Lexi, a fox," he said. He then dashed into the crowded streets. Contessa then ran into the house and straight up to her room.

CHAPTER TWENTY-FOUR
The Missing Piece

As Contessa entered her room, she whirled around, flopping on her bed. She spun from what she saw and heard about her loved ones alive. She and her mother are prisoners. What to do? What to do? Then the lock on her door jiggled and turned, opening without a word from the other side. "What the?" is all Contessa could get out. "Please, shh, we are never alone," said Kalvin, sweat beating down his face. She tried to look at Contessa, only imagining the shame and disappointment she now felt about him. He moved about her room, making light illuminate every corner of her room and not saying another word until he was confident that no corner was dark for the shadows to listen in. Contessa spoke when he stood by her bed, looking down at the floor.

"It is okay." She smiled back. "I now know we are prisoners. Can't tell you how I know," Contessa said as she raised her hand, placing it on the surface of his sticky chin, pushing his face towards her so they could lock eyes. "But I don't know how we became prisoners in the first place," she continued. "Please tell me the missing pieces of the story." Kalvin, looking at her, took a deep breath, slumped down on the bed next to her, and began to tell the story of the first night he met Contessa and her mother. How he picked up their scent and knew he was meant to stay with them when they were asleep.

"Your mother woke. Next, I saw a desperate woman grasping at straws and this shadowy figure offering her the world. All she needed to do was do what you saw her do to Savannah tonight of her own free will. Give away her soul freely to the shadows. Then, in return, everything you have seen in the last five years happened." Kalvin talked with a few pauses, studying Contessa to find a glimpse of understanding in her eyes. "So, we were prisoners this whole time here. We have been a puppet in some demon's game. The dolls are dolls. I just thought they were different in the way, night after night, performing as they did and then being their true authentic selves during the day."

She could not rush the words out fast enough, going so fast that her thoughts and questions were jumbled. "Slow down, Contessa; there is not much time! The guest will be arriving soon." "I have to tell you; I know what happened last night. I didn't know last night until Alexandria told me when I got home. I have been pondering all night. Why? After everything your mother did to protect you, why would she allow the monster of a mayor to have his way with you? Then, today, she was at his secret club in some chateau, and after this meeting, she stayed behind to talk to another wolf and vampire. They devised a plan, so my thought was last night, your mother was forced to make you go with the mayor, which got the mayor in a good enough mood to invite her into the club. Now she wants to double-cross him to get more power." Now breathing heavily, Kalvin tried to get it all out as fast as possible, continuing to talk rapidly, stopping only briefly for a breath.

"But why did she have to be forced? What is the shadow's end game?" Contessa said, talking over Kalvin, which made him pause. "My best guess is the fact that the reason me and your mom call it the shadow or shadow man is because it can't come in the light. So, this demon has been collecting lustful energy every night to stay here on this plain for the last five years. It can't survive the sun. It does not notice, but I have watched it over the years. Testing its tolerance for the light, it now can last a long time since the dolls are good at what they do."

Kalvin chuckled at the notion as Contessa punched him in the arm for his insensitive gesture toward these defenseless people. "Sorry," said Kalvin, continuing. "I believe tonight, at this ball, it will have enough energy to live in our world full-time day or night, so the deal with your mom will be done. She will regain her soul, but your mom realizes what will happen to you when the shadow gets what it wants. She doesn't believe the shadows went through all this to run a brothel but has bigger plans. So, she wants to sit on the throne of the French Quarter." Kalvin said after a long breath before continuing. "So since you are older and need something to manage, she wanted to leave the dollhouse to you and all that goes along with it." "So, we must rescue my mom and intervene to stop the shadows from getting their way," Contessa said with a slight smile. So tonight, I might have a plan. All eyes will be on my mom, and when it is time for the dolls to go to work and have the yearly head doll announced, we could use that as a distraction to find a way to save everyone and their souls," she gleefully said with a small fire to her voice.

"But, that thing is strong. We are caged animals who are watched every second of every day." Kalvin spoke heavily, his words sounding like the battle was lost. "Well, as you pointed out and made abundantly clear with your actions of turning every light on in my room, making sure no corner was dark, we still have an upper hand tonight," Contessa said as she kissed him. "Go round up the staff. I'm calling an emergency staff meeting. Buck up and collect the troops. We are at war."

Smiling from ear to ear, Kalvin hugged Contessa tightly and repeated how brilliant she was. He stood up, saluted his new Madame, and ran out the door, leaving Contessa alone with her room, outfit, and thoughts. She got off her bed, walked to her wooden chair, and ran her fingers over the magenta fabric. Then, she slowly walked over to undress in front of the floor-length mirror. As her skin was exposed to the light, she saw the bruises left from the night before. In a few quick gestures, she watched as they faded into the background of her body. Then, she reached for her dress again and lifted her leg to step into it; she heard another knock. "Contessa, do you need any help?" came Alexandria's voice from the other side of the door. "Come in," Contessa responded. "Hey," Alexandra said with a half-hearted smile. "Let me help you with that." She spoke as she bent onto her knees to help Contessa step into her dress. "Thank you! I appreciate it. Is everything ready for the ball?" Contessa said, trying not to give away that she was worried about all the moving parts.

"Yes, the dolls are just waiting in their rooms for your mother to call them down," Alexandria said as she moved up the dress past Contessa's thigh, standing upright again, allowing Contessa to readjust her bust. "Kalvin said you were holding a private meeting without your mother. Is everything okay?" she sheepishly asked Contessa. "Yes, everything's fine; just a lot of moving parts. As your new boss, I want to start my rein on the right foot. Now that my eyes are truly open, I will do whatever it takes to keep you safe with no strings attached. Alexandria spun Contessa around and cried on her shoulders. "Thank you, Contessa. You are my only friend that I think of as more of a sister. I always feared that if your mother were not in charge, the bad juju in this house would come for my sisters and end up like the dolls."

She sobbed on Contessa's shoulder. Contessa lifted Alexandria's head off her shoulder. "Listen to me. I will save and protect everyone and take you all to a place where no one can hurt you or anyone else. As for my mother, she is redeemable, but it is time for me to go my separate way. But we will free her from her chains and find happiness far away from here." Contessa smiled at her friend, mustering enough that we got this attitude as one could muster in these rough times. "Okay, Madame," Alexandria giggled. "Now turn around, and let's make you a proper lady." Contessa turned as she was told, and Alexandria tied the corset that was fashioned after a dragonfly, the wings covering her bust and wrapping around her neck.

Then she stepped into her black shoes and walked past Alexandria to her desk, which had her dragonfly necklace and Venetia-laced dragonfly mask. She then took a deep breath and looked at herself one last time in the mirror, placing a hand on Alexandra's arm and squeezing it gently. "Let's give them the old razzle-dazzle." The two walked out of her room.

CHAPTER TWENTY-FIVE
Staff Meeting

Contessa and Alexandria entered the kitchen. There, she saw Deedee, Brooke, Lindsey, and Deloris standing by the sink, reviewing how to serve dinner tonight. Monty and Reed were playing cards at the table. Last, she saw Kalvin checking every corner of the room to see that the shadows could not hear what was happening. Finally, Kalvin stood up and gave Contessa a thumbs-up before sitting next to Reed at the kitchen table. Alexandria laid her hand on Contessa's shoulder before joining her sisters by the sink. Contessa cleared her throat before speaking, then started the staff meeting.

"Hey, you all; I need your attention, please." Contessa watched as not everyone was paying attention, locking eyes with the wall, praying she could do this. "Hey, shut up! Contessa has something to say!" said Alexandria from the back of the room, which made them jump back and perk up, giving their undivided attention to Contessa. "Okay then," Contessa said before clearing her throat once more. "Tonight is going to be very different from balls past. I'm pretty sure you all know more of what goes on here than I do, mostly because of my Mama, but the other part was of the night I lost my daddy, and so many others from my past. But no more. I'm your new Madame starting tonight; with me in control now and with my eyes wide open to the truths of this house, we are in a race against the clock in a game I did not know we were even playing."

Contessa continued, "The dolls and my mother will be free of this evil that has plagued us from the shadows." Contessa hastily got out before she paused, hoping to get a response. "What do you mean free us? We choose to be here," said Deedee with a curious look. "I know you believe you chose to be here, but I believe outside forces brought us together to further their position in this world." Contessa was surprised at Deedee's line of questioning. Kalvin then stood up and explained what had happened over the last five years and the doll ceremony. Deedee interrupted, explaining she did nothing of the sort, and neither did her sister. "They pledge loyalty to Madame Grace for protection against what brought them here to the Quarter. So, did anyone else become soulless in this room? speak up now and remove yourself before I do it for you!" Deedee said.

Contessa watched as they all denied ever giving up their souls. Kalvin jumped in and finished his grand explanation. "The demon that hurt you and your sister, the wolves that attacked us last night, was all because Madame Grace tried to take a stand and defied the evil because they wanted Contessa to end up with the mayor last night." "What in the hell!" shouted Monty. "Listen!" Kalvin went on and explained the whole story. None of them were surprised that the dolls were zombies going through the motions. But they thought it was just a potion Madame Grace made, not some demon controlling the situation. Now, time was of the essence. "So what do you want from us? How do we protect ourselves and get out of here alive?" said Dolores.

"Yeah, because if some scary demon thinks they can threaten my sister, I will send them back to hell where they can think twice about who they are messing with!" Deedee said, grabbing the butcher's knife from the counter. "Listen, tonight will have to go as planned, but the shadows are watching the festivities, thinking they are winning. We will have to play with smoke and mirrors in the dark of night; know we are not alone, and I have allies coming to our aid." Contessa rushed past her words, talking as fast as she could, holding up her hand to gesture in protest of people speaking at the moment.

"First, Lindsey, when you give your grand performance and the dolls are entertaining the guests, I will slip around to the bar, handing Reed an elixir that will change people's moods from lustful to something more innocent. The shadows will not be aware of this until the end of the evening. Then, Deedee, you, Deloris, and Brooke will serve those drinks at the start of my mother's speech after dinner, introducing me as the new Madame. So, every person in attendance must have one." The women nodded, understanding their part of the battle plan. "After dinner, Reed, Monty, and Kalvin, you get the girls out of the house and head out of town. We will meet back by the river at midnight." Contessa thought of it quickly, knowing that if this plan did not work, none of them could hide from the shadows. "What about you?" asked Monty. "I have to undo what my mother did and save her soul simultaneously. The allies I have coming will finish the night's events, hopefully with the nine dolls and my mother with us." She took a deep breath, looking around the room for reassurance.

There was nothing until she heard the smallest of the three sisters speaking up for the first time in a long time. "We will stand with you and save your mother's soul together." That comment gave Contessa and the room the confidence they needed to believe it would work. BAM! swung open the kitchen door, making the room jump. "What the hell are you all lounging around for?" Madame Grace stood in one of the standard purple dresses she wore night after night to work in as she checked in guests at the front desk or walked around the lounge with her hair pushed back with her emerald-green dragonflies. "We have guests arriving any minute, and you are all lying around like we don't have a ball to put on!"

Contessa, honestly, child, I'm going to put you in charge, and you can't control the staff in my absence. Brooke, Monty, Reed, lounge now!" Madame Grace screamed at them. "Lindsey, you take Contessa upstairs until after dinner, where I will announce her as the new Madame, and Savannah, the newest of dolls, will lead the others down, marking the start of the ball. Then cocktail hour will begin at seven sharp, followed by dinner at nine with the band playing in the background. Then, Brooke, you will come up and give the final performance, where you will finish up and announce me. I will make a grand entrance once more, remove my mask, and present Contessa as the new face of the doll house. Now move! Let the ball commence!"

Everyone without a word scattered like rats when the lights came on, trying to catch their breaths as they moved. "Oh, one more thing; remember my rules tonight! Don't fail me, or else!" Madame Grace said as everyone left the room. Madame Grace followed behind to return to the grand staircase and present the night's guests with magical dolls that cater to their every whim.

CHAPTER TWENTY-SIX
Chess

The evening began with Lindsey lighting the candle operas around the room and Kalvin opening the door for each guest and checking invitations as they walked in. Among the guests were shop owners of the Quarter. These top elite couples frequented the dollhouse daily, and then shortly after were the mayor and the fire and police chiefs. Behind them was the sheriff, all dressed in tailored black-tie suits. Then, at the end of the line were Tara and Paul. Tara is wearing a gold strapless number exposing her marble skin and hidden by a mask embroidered in charcoal black diamonds in the shape of a bat well.

On the other hand, Paul wore a tailored black suit with a silver bowtie hidden by a silver wolf mask lining the eyes with topaz blue gemstones. Everyone was elaborately dressed for the occasion as the invitations were specifically instructed. Clink! went the glass held by Deloris as everyone filled in the lobby. Then Kalvin gave her the signal for everything to begin. "Hello, ladies and gentlemen," Deloris said as she stood at the top of the stairs so everyone could see her standing in her chef's coat and a plain black mask that made her stand out. "I would like to welcome you to the dollhouse, where you will have a spectacular evening. But, without further ado, welcome the woman who has made all this possible. Madame Grace." Deloris finished as all the masked people raised their hands in applause for the evening hostess.

A cloud of maroon, purple, and green mist came down from the railing, and BAM! The crowd jumped back as the colors exploded together in a swirl of majestic delight, and her most beautiful gown to date stood when it cleared. Her hair, the most prim and proper it has ever been, pushed back with her. Not the emerald dragonflies she wore on most nights, but ruby red ones that complimented her red silk lace devil's mask, which sparkled in the room when the light touched its surfaces. Her gown was floor length with purple amethyst embellishing her breasts and white chiffon intertwined with her plum dress.

The crowd was in awe at the site of her. The applause got even louder for their host's beauty. "Thank you, Delores, for that marvelous introduction." "Now," began Madame Grace as the smoke cleared. "We are here to celebrate five years of success and prosperity, but tonight, we will have one major announcement after you have all filled your bellies." She chuckled as she spoke, being in a chipper mood and dazzling her guest as she continued, but not a second sooner. "But, let me present you with the most glamorous creatures you have ever seen. The dolls that make up the house." As the crowd clapped for this announcement, Madame Grace stood surveying the room and gathering all the praises the guests gave her. She then looked beyond them, noticing the movements in the shadows. She watched them as the room grew louder at the sight of the Greek statues that seemed to appear out of nowhere. She then watched as the shadows seemed to reach for the light, gaining more strength to possess a hold of a spot in this world.

She could only make out silvery silhouettes, telling her to speed it up, knowing that they were so close to getting their chance at the sun and the chance at these unsuspecting humans. Looking back at them, she saw Tessa notice the dark figures moving amongst them. "SAVANNAH! Is that you?" A voice from the crowd pushed Madame Grace back to the moment. "Yes," she smiled. "The newest member of the dolls is one of our local shop girls... Savannah." "No," Madame Grace spoke as she finally spotted her first disturbance of the night. The sheriff made his way through the crowd, throwing off his mask and staring at the unmovable, lifeless niece he raised.

Kalvin hugged the mayor, whispering in his ear so low no one could hear Madame Grace announcing that she would be tonight's winner of the top doll prize, which we hope you shower her with as many trinkets as possible to make her feel welcome. Madame Grace spoke, watching Kalvin push the sheriff into the elevator and watching the doors close behind them. She told the dolls to go play at the end of her grand speech. They did mingle at the party, moving in a grand formation, separating among the guest, and getting some control of their bodies to flirt and mingle with their guest. They dispersed amongst the crowd, with the twins locking arms with the fire and police chief. Then Savannah asked the mayor for some champagne. Miles smiled with his pearly whites at one of the many couples who frequented his room every night. Kat was crowded around a few gentleman callers, chuckling as she asked what they brought her. Ceci ran her hand through her hair as she reached for a hors-d'oeuvre.

Bailey made her way towards Kat but beelined it in the other direction as she felt her throat getting tight. A feeling she knew all too often as soon as she would start trouble. Lastly, Madame Grace saw West walk over to Tara and Paul. "May I get you a drink?" He flashed a devilish smile, making Paul step before her. "Now Paul, you know why we came, and our host brought me a gift to sample. Tara looked in Madame Grace's direction and snatched a crystal goblet from Lindsey's tray. "Paul, please step aside," Tara said playfully, and he did what Tara told him. "May I have your hand, please?" West raised it, smiling at her as she kissed his hand. "Aren't I supposed to meet your acquaintance? Sorry, I did not catch your name," West said. "It is Tara," she responded with a motion you could not see with the naked eye.

She turned his arm over to expose his wrist, sinking the tips of her fangs into his skin. Blood now surrounding her, she stood up and turned his wrist over the crystal goblet, letting it fill up half-way. "Paul, hand our new friend a napkin." Tara smiled, not taking her eyes off West. Paul did as he was told, and Tara released West's hand and pressed the goblet to her lips, allowing the crimson liquid to pass through her body, making Tara glow. When she finished, she handed the glass to West. "Will you boys lead me into the lounge for dinner?" West grabbed her left arm and Paul her right, escorting her through the crowd and out of sight of Madame Grace. Madame Grace headed down the staircase, making her way to the mayor. "Hello, Mr. Mayor. I hope our newest doll is to your liking," Madame Grace said with a smile. "Yes, of course, she is a delight. I never recognized her beauty when the sheriff brought her to work."

The mayor chuckled before taking a swig of his champagne. "Ha-ha!" Savannah laughed. "And I never noticed the charismatic charmer you were, Mr. Mayor," said Savannah. "Well, a match made in heaven if I say so myself. Well, maybe after dinner, you can show Savannah the ropes. "After dinner?" Madame Grace teasingly said as she slapped her hand on his chest. "Well, excuse me, I need to say hello to my other guests before announcing dinner."

Madame Grace readjusted the mayor's tie and walked amongst the guests, ensuring the dolls behaved and the guests were properly cared for as she entered the kitchen. "Lindsey!" Madame Grace barked her name. "Yes, Madame Grace." "Is everything ready for dinner?" She snarled at her. "Absolutely, Madame Grace. Just plating the last salads now." Lindsey tried to sound as if nothing out of the ordinary was happening. "Well, run out there and get Deloris and Deedee. I will head out behind you in a minute to announce dinner."

She finished looking at a petrified child. "MOVE!" She barked again, slamming her fist on the counter, causing her purple sparks to crackle like whips on the stone slab. Lindsey ran past her, bowing as she crossed her path. Grace opened and closed her fist, took a deep breath, and let out a muffled scream. Jolting around, she stood at the face of a golden lion that had a hold on her. "My love, please, I will move my hand away from yours. Don't scream," Frank said, releasing his hand from her mouth and removing his mask.

Frank was the only word that quivered out of her mouth. "I know you have many questions, but all you need to know is I'm here to free you, so please go on with the evening as planned," he said. He pressed his lips to hers. She inhaled him for the first time in five years. When she heard the gunshot echoing in the woods as she dragged her daughter out of harm's way into the devil's arms, she could finally breathe, shaking amongst the weight of his muscles. "I thought, I know what you must have thought, but can you do it? Can you wow them enough not to notice what is happening behind the scenes?" He said, breathing heavily and getting his words out in a commanding manner. "Yes," she said. "But you must go quickly. You won't be safe if it sees you," Madame Grace said, pushing her husband away and trying to push him out the door. He turned around to stare at his wife one last time.

Frank said, "What are you doing? The shadows know your thoughts." "I have to," he protested, and she went silent as he finished removing my face from her mind. "In this moment, she will forget I'm alive. To protect her from the evil, she needs to win the battle we are facing." Frank finished the words as Madame Grace stood staring at the back door, hearing a faint whisper. "You will never truly forget me, my love." Then, Madame Grace shivered when she felt the chill of the shadows fill the room with its presence. "What are you doing? We need you to continue the night's festivities. Your daughter has not made her grand entrance. Remember, you are still ours." The shadows spoke out at her from several unlit spots around the room.

Madame Grace turned on her heel. "How could I forget? I was looking over the first course before announcing dinner. Don't you think for a second I have forgotten what is at stake! By the rising sun, I should have my soul back if everything goes according to plan." Madame Grace snarled her venomous words at them; then the kitchen door swung open, leaving Grace in the corner looking crazy. "Is everything alright, Madame Grace?" Deedee said. "Of course it is! Now excuse me, I'm going to announce dinner!" Grace spat back. As she made her way to the door, Grace stormed past the crowd to the staircase, climbing a few steps and turning to face the crowd. As she rose, the crowd followed her until they fell silent to listen in. "Dinner is served."

CHAPTER TWENTY-SEVEN
The Allies from the Past

"What were you doing?" James asked as Frank returned from his escape into the kitchen. "I have not seen her in five years," he said in a loud whisper. James said that if tonight is the last night, you want to see her make more risky moves, matching his whisper. "Now you listen here. The two of you, don't you dare make me lose my chance to see baby girl again. Now you screwed up this afternoon. He screwed up. Now let's not screw up anymore!" Celeste said, scolding the two men. "Just for your information, I wiped her memory of the moment as soon as I knew I had to go. The shadows won't know I was there." He spoke through Frank. Actually, he spoke through his teeth.

"Oh Lord, I'm going to die again. I'm not going to see you tomorrow!" Lexi cried out. "Shut up, child! Tonight will be different. Baby girl and Mrs. Grace will be home with us tomorrow without question. We are going to win this fight," Celeste said as she slapped Lexi upside the head. "Ouch, woman! Why did you go and do a thing like that?" said Lexi. Celest spat back, "Why do you have to talk stupid?" She then turned to James. "Now, what did my Baby Girl say to you exactly? Word for word and leave nothing out." Celeste spoke quieter to James. She said her dad was a powerful witch and could get us to her room. She said, not sounding irritated that the complaint came out.

"Okay, big bad witch, get us up there," Celest said as she threw her hands up at Frank. "Fine! ascend," he whispered. Frank spoke as he reached out to grab the hands of his comrades, each grabbing onto the others as they made their way up to the third-floor balcony with the open window curtains blowing in the breeze. Contessa was sitting in her chair alone, working on a potion in her small cauldron mask lying beside her on the desktop. She heard a commotion rise to her, followed by the silhouette of someone hovering outside her room. Landing on her balcony one by one. Lexi, James, Celeste, then daddy. She raced over to the father that she lost for far too long. She wrapped her arms around him, burying her face into his chest. "Sweets, slow down! Let me get a good look at you, Contessa," Frank said.

As Contessa backed up, Frank shed a tear. "My sweets, never again will I leave your side. Let me look at my baby girl, Celeste, you, and Lexi. Lexi is alive and well, I see." Contessa laughed, choking back tears. Contessa ran over and hugged them both before the shouting in the hallway grew louder. James stood in front of them. "Who is that?" James asked. I hear Kalvin but don't recognize the other voice. She grabbed James. You have to hide. Please go into the bathroom now, she urgently whispered to them, pushing them into her bathroom. As she spoke to them, she closed her bathroom door. Her bedroom door swung open. First came in the sheriff, followed by Kalvin shouting at each other. Contessa ran past them, slamming her bedroom door and turning to face them. "What is going on?" Contessa demanded.

"He found out that Savannah joined the house," Kalvin explained. "And she would never wear something like that or do what those dolls do. I hear the mayor and the chief talking about their nights here." James screamed out at the two of them. "Sheriff, calm down!" Contessa said as she reached for the sheriff's hands. "A lot is going on that you don't know. I will get Savannah back home by sunrise. Please know that I will protect her," Contessa said, pushing the loose strand of hair out of his face. At that moment, the bathroom door opened. "And who is this young lady?" Said Frank. "Yeah, young lady!" echoed James. "Who am I?" said Lucas.

Contessa dropped her hands, and then Kalvin chimed in. "Contessa, what is going on here?" Kalvin said, looking at her and not understanding what he was looking at. "These are the allies I told you about earlier. My father Frank, the woman who raised me, Celeste, my best friend Lexi, and my love James," Contessa said, changing Lucas's facial expressions from confusion to sadness. "Now listen up because I must be downstairs really soon!" Contessa spoke with urgency. "Celeste, can you finish this potion? I need it done now, please. "Of course, baby girl; what is it for?" Celeste asked as she walked over to peer at the potion's ingredients. "It is to make people stop lusting. If I have planned it out right, it will affect everyone in the hotel later in the rooms, keeping the shadows from entering our world fully," Contessa said. Celeste sat at Contessa's desk and continued where she left off. Listening to the rest of the plan.

"Now, James and Daddy, you must open mom's office door. I have to get to the cellar but have no time to break momma's locking spell. I'm sure you, knowing her best, will breeze through it." She continued with just a simple nod from her father and James. "Lexi, head to the kitchen. We need someone to get us a vehicle that will hold as many people as possible. Last, Kalvin and Lucas, go downstairs and control yourselves. I have to know that if this goes wrong in any way, you two will save the dolls." When she finished, she held out her hand, and everyone in the room put theirs on top of hers. Contessa said, "Go, team!" All of them threw their hands into the air. "Done!" Celeste said, breaking the silence. "All done!" She handed a vial to Contessa, and Contessa took it and shoved it into her breast. "Now, we must get downstairs. Dinner will soon be ready," said Contessa. She walked past Celeste, grabbed her dragonfly Venetian mask, and led the troops downstairs to the battlefield.

CHAPTER TWENTY-EIGHT
The New Madame

The night was going well; Contessa could tell as she slipped back downstairs past the lobby, peering into the lounge. She watched all the guests eating. She pointed at the stairs and the office, which made Frank and James move. Then Kalvin and the sheriff brushed by Contessa. "Kalvin, your mask," Contessa whispered. "Kalvin," she whispered again, and then he turned at the last minute. He reached into his back pocket, wrapping his hands around the plain black mask the rest of the house staff wear. He then slipped back among the dinner guests.

The last to move were Celeste and Lexi. She pointed them in the direction of the kitchen. They moved from the stairs through the lobby and into the kitchen. Contessa followed them. In the kitchen were Deloris and Lindsey. Lindsey washed dishes, and Deloris set the last two dessert plates. "Who the hell are they? No, ma'am, no guests in the kitchen." Contessa peered from behind them a second later. "Deloris, it is all good. They're allies, Contessa said with hand gestures to calm down. Deloris laughed. "You were not kidding. We're going to die. Those demon things are everywhere." Lexi chuckled. "Ma'am, I said the same damn thing!" Lexi smiled at this charming woman. "I need to know if a vehicle in the Quarter can get all the dolls and staff out of here safely," Contessa said as she walked over to the counter. "Ummm, the firetruck would be the closest thing to get all of us out of here," said Deloris.

"Thank you, ma'am," said Celeste. Lexi was headed toward Deloris to shake her hand, and Celeste stopped her in her tracks. "We ain't got time for small talk, Lexi. Now let's go!" Lexi then pivoted and made her way to the back door and opened it. "Are you coming, your majesty?" She bowed as Celeste passed by her and stood up. All she did was turn and smile at Deloris. She shut the door, fading into the darkness. "Ohh my my, what a nice young lady," she said as she fanned herself with her hand. Deedee came in shortly after. "Now, Contessa, what are you standing around for? Brooke is almost done with her final number. Go on! Get!" She said, pushing Contessa back out into the lobby.

Contessa headed for the lounge, making her way into it. She saw Brooke hitting her final high note. No one noticed her slipping into the background of the festivities. She slipped over to the bar, not drawing any unnecessary attention to herself. Monty noticed Contessa just in the corner of his eye. He walked over to the bar's edge, watching Contessa pull out a veil of some simmering gold liquid. Then Contessa reached the bar and rolled it to Monty. He caught it, turned to the glasses laid out on the counter, opened the veil, and started to pour, watching each glass turn to gold them back to its original color. Moving past Contessa were Lindsey, Kalvin, Delores, and Deedee, all reaching for the trays of glasses. Brooke spoke about the generosity of their Madame and the amazing home she has provided for her and her sisters. "Madame Grace, could you please join me on the stage?" Brooke said with a tear streaming down her eye.

The crowd cheered their hostess, grabbing the microphone as she ascended the stage. "Thank you, my dear," Madame Grace said as she hugged Brook, which sent a shiver down her spine and put a shocked look on all the staff's faces. "Now I told you we have a big surprise. My time as the Madame of this house has come to an end. My sights are set higher, but you have nothing to worry about. I want to introduce you to my daughter, who will take my place. Madame Contessa." The crowd went into an uproar. They spent all night whistling and cheering. Before Contessa took the stage, Kalvin walked by with two champagne glasses.

Contessa reached out both hands, passing Brooke, making her way to her spot in the sun. A place she never thought would exist. She was always in her parent's shadows, never knowing what the sunlight felt like upon her face except for one brief moment five years ago when James kissed her behind the cantina. She reached out a hand to give her mother her glass of champagne and replaced it with her mother's microphone. "Thank you, Mother, for giving us a home." Contessa spoke, looking out over the crowd, watching them. Instinctively, she looked past them towards the room's dark corners, looking for signs of the shadows, making sure all their beings were watching her. Knowing if they were all there, the team could have a better chance of spotting them in the corner by the door rubbing their hands together. She raised the microphone, giving them all the charm and magic that, until tonight, she thought her mother lacked. "For my first act as acting Madame of the doll house, I ask you to raise your glasses to my mother and pray for her future success."

The crowd, in unison, raised their glasses, cheered Mama, and pointed their glasses to the crowd. Cheers and clinking were heard around the room from the masked guests who watched them. She said, "Our beautiful dolls are ready to take it from here. When you're ready, choose your doll at the highest prices and have fun." Madame Grace walked over to her daughter, hugged her, slipped the microphone out of her hand, and took her daughter wholeheartedly into her arms. Then she released her, turning to the crowd. Madame Grace raised the microphone to her lips. "Thank you, my daughter," Grace said some simple pleasantries as Contessa stepped down from the stage and returned to her comfort zone of the shadows, shaking the guest's hands as they watched her mother.

Contessa stopped as she felt a familiar sweaty hand pull on her arm. She stepped back and forced her hand out of the masked pig's tight grip that stared up at her little darling. "I'm sorry, but I must cancel with you tonight. I have bought time with this untouched angle tonight." Contessa recognized the voice as the sad, pathetic, slimy mayor who had stolen her innocence. As she watched him, she raised her hand to stop Kalvin and Lucas from interfering. Then, bending down to the mayor, she smiled and whispered in his ear, speaking so softly not even Tara could hear over her mother's speech. "I hope you get everything that you deserve tonight." She smiled and said, "If you ever address me other than Madame Contessa, I will put you out of the Quarter so fast you will forget the way back. Maybe I will put you out into the bayou. The wolves love a good hunt!"

Without another word, she walked to the back of the room, stopping briefly at the two masked men. "Both of you need to chill. watch the mayor find me when he takes your niece upstairs. She spoke early, like her mother. At this moment, she grabbed the sheriff's hand, looked him in the eyes, and continued. "You better practice your campaign speech. I believe the mayor's seat will be opening soon, as early as tonight." She said with a smile. She walked out of the lounge into the deserted lobby, quickly crossing it behind the front desk. She saw her father and James bent down on their knees. Her father uses counter spells to open the magically locked door. "Any luck?" She said behind them. "I think I almost got it. I used all the generic charms and have reached the most possible ones. I figured your mom was only in a house filled with one witch, not worrying about you entering her office."

Then, a click broke the silence. They all stood up, and Frank turned the handle to open the dark office. "I think it is empty," said Frank. The three stepped in. "You two must go to the kitchen, meet the others, and get ready to abstract the dolls. Use force on the guests if you have to," said Contessa seriously. "No sweets," said Frank. "I won't ever leave you again," James said. As he closed the door, he suddenly felt the resistance of pushback. As he closed it, Kalvin stood in the doorway. "Let me in. It is me," Kalvin said as he used more force than he should have. Contessa came over to the door, catching James before tumbling to the ground. "What the hell, man?" James spat at him. "Yeah, you're supposed to be watching Savannah and the mayor." "I don't have to worry about Lucas losing them. If he tries anything, then Lucas will be very close behind." Kalvin spoke quickly.

"Plus, I know this office, so please tell me what you are looking for," Kalvin finished, awaiting a response. Contessa spoke up. "I don't know. I'm looking for something to do for the bounding of the spirits from the dolls. Then, when I do that, the souls should return to where they came from. Then you and the others will get them out of there as I free my mom." Contessa stopped, and everyone stood there staring at each other. James turned on every light in the room. No dark spots were allowed. "Kalvin, where does my momma keep her contracts? The ones the dolls signed," Contessa urgently said. "They should be on her desk. They are signed down there but always brought up here for filling. "Okay, spread out and look for anything to help us leave here alive tonight," Contessa spoke to the men in the room.

Contessa then made her way to the desk and threw off her mask, letting it fall onto the stack of papers her Mama had cluttering her desk. "Daddy, can you open these locked doors?" she looked at her father, pleading with him. "I sure can, sweets!" He responded, "I can use the same incantation I used to unlock the door." He smiled at his daughter and moved towards the desk drawer. He reached out his hand and let his fingers do all the work. Red and green sparks leaped out of his fingertips and into the locks of the doors. Each clicked open one by one until there was nothing left to unlock. Contessa sat down in her mother's chair and opened the doors. She rummaged through the folders that occupied them. There were old receipts, work orders, and a journal stuffed in the back of the first draw.

Contessa removed it and spilled the secrets of the Quarter's most intimate secrets out loud. Like the mayor talking about what he does to his daughters behind closed doors. "Disgusting," said James. "That is horrendous!" He spat. Ignoring James, Contessa, with this puzzled look on her face, looked at Kalvin. "That is your mother's insurance policy. She had the dolls collect secrets for her and the energy for the shadows." So, she tucked that back in the drawer, closed it, opened the next, and pulled out the contracts. She passed out the pieces of parchment to the others in the room. "Study them quickly; we don't have long before they notice we are gone!" Contessa said before becoming silent, looking over the paper marked Ceci Bishop and the contract. She read the terms, reading that if Ceci's father ever finds her or touches her, the contract will be broken, and her soul will be returned immediately. "Urika, I have the way to win the war to get my Mama back. We need to get downstairs to get the dolls, which will be trickier but must be done.

CHAPTER TWENTY-NINE
My Soul to Keep

"Frank, you, and James must prepare for the next task. Head upstairs before the guests finish dinner and find Alexandria," Kalvin said. "I will not leave my daughter!" Frank returned with a cross between a shout and a whisper, spitting as he spoke. "I know the ends and out of that basement, and your wife is the only one with a doll not down in that basement. Your daughter did not share the thoughts tumbling inside her head." Kalvin sarcastically said. "Well then, what James said keeps them roused up and distracts the shadows. Your wife gives us time to save her and everybody else." Kalvin spoke as he walked over to the bookcase and opened the basement in the floor, exposing the staircase.

"Fine, I will make a spectacle of this evening, and James here will run upstairs and meet this Lindsey girl," Frank said as he walked over and hugged his daughter. "Be careful, sweets," said Frank as he hugged her tighter and pled, fighting back tears. He let her go, turning to James. "Come on, son. Let's move! We have your future mother-in-law to save." Frank placed his hand on James's back, turning him towards the door. James dug his heels in the ground and turned to Kalvin. "You better protect her with your life!" Kalvin looked him square in the eye, raising his hand for a handshake. "With my life?" Kalvin said as James locked hands with him.

When they released their hands, Kalvin and Contessa watched James and Frank walk out of the office door as they descended the staircase. "What is the plan?" asked Kalvin. "Can't say. As we continue down this path, there is always someone watching. Please! When I say jump, do it." Contessa spoke, following Kalvin into the room that would haunt her nightmares. The room was dark, giving off a chilling vibe. "Contessa, we need light," Kalvin said. "Your mother usually sends alight ahead to avoid too much darkness." Kalvin finished as he watched the room illuminate. "You're welcome," said Contessa.

The room was now lit, for the most part. Contessa saw dried blood on the desk, the contents of the vial that created the invisible wall on the floor, and the cauldron back in the corner. "What now, Kalvin? Where are the dolls?" said Contessa, eagerly speaking as she looked at Kalvin. "Calm down! It is behind this wall." She does some magic, and the wall goes away to expose the cages that house the dolls with the souls in them. He walked over to the wall, trying to reassure her. "Okay, stand back!" Contessa said, positioning herself as she prepared to break into the wall of souls. Sparks jolted from her fingers and cracked when they hit the wall, but nothing happened. Then she tried again. Another incantation after another. "Damn it! What am I missing?" She cried out. "Usually, there was a soul to keep when the wall opened up." Kalvin said. "We do the ceremony," Contessa said. Give it what it wants." "No, we can't!" shouted Kalvin.

"Kalvin, I need you to trust me. We don't have time to argue. Take my soul, free the dolls, then break the rules of the agreement at the last minute, and my soul will return to my body. It is the way to free them all." Contessa pleaded for him to understand. "Jump! I said jump!" Contessa chanted the words as Kalvin ran around the room and created everything that had been done in ceremonies past. "Contessa, light the cauldron and heat it." Kalvin spoke as he grabbed the ingredients from the cupboard. "You should change. You don't want to ruin your pretty dress." He spoke into the room, laser-focused on the task at hand.

Contessa made the sparks surround her in circular motions out of the sparks that left her hands. Her work clothes replaced the ball gown that Contessa wore. Then she flung her hands to the cauldron, making it smoke, bubble, and boil. "Now, the contract; Contessa, can you duplicate it?" Kalvin said, throwing things into the cauldron. "Yes, it should be a standard binding spell. Contessa conjured up a parchment that laid out the terms of the agreement, stating that if Kalvin hurt her, she would no longer be bound by the terms of the agreement; in exchange for her soul, read Contessa out loud to Kalvin. "Are you ready?" Contessa said. "Yes, I'll set the circle." Kalvin said. "The potion only needs your blood and a signed contract, and we are done. Hurt me, free them, in that order. It is the only way to have a chance tonight." Contessa said. "Okay, I understand," said Kalvin. Contessa walked over to the desk, picked up the quill, pricked her finger, dipped the quill into the exposed crimson color, and signed her soul away to Kalvin.

The pain was intense, and Contessa dropped to the floor. Kalvin dragged her to the center of the room, collected Contessa's blood from where the quill punctured Contessa's fingertip, and threw the vial into the Calderon, exposing another faceless Marinette doll. Kalvin walked over to Contessa, took her by the wrist, and dragged her into the middle of the circle with her screaming and cringing in on herself. Kalvin let Contessa's hand drop. When he reached the circle's center, he walked to the cauldron and picked up the marionette doll. He placed it beside Contessa's contorting body.

As Contessa's soul separated from her body, the wall separated behind him, revealing the tiny little dolls in grand design cages, all locked up tight. Grasping the bars, watching the next companion they will have staying with them. Kalvin left the circle, walked to the cages, and looked at the locks. He grasped the lock in his hand, turned around, and watched the faceless doll look like an identical match to Contessa. In a furious rage, he turned back to the first lock and crushed it with his bare hand, repeating the same motion to all nine locks. There was a crash as each hit the floor. Kalvin collected all nine marionette dolls in his hands, with each one squirming to get free. Kalvin felt a tug at his feet, and looking down was the tenth and final doll. Contessa's doll. Kalvin took a deep breath and kicked it. The doll flew back into the invisible barrier, crashing to the floor. Kalvin watched as Contessa's body was now lying on her back, and then Kalvin stepped forward and kicked Contessa in the face.

At that moment, the marionette doll started to look as if it had a seizure and imploded on itself. Contessa's soul floated in the invisible barrier, lowering itself as it saw its home. Contessa's body was lying on the floor, returning to its body. Contessa slowly started to get color back into her skin. She gasped for a breath. Kalvin dropped the dolls and kneeled beside her. "Are you okay?" Kalvin asked with tears rolling down his cheeks. "Kalvin, the dolls!" "What? They're fine." "No, you dropped them upstairs. Someone will know what is going on upstairs. The dolls are connected to their bodies." Contessa said urgently as she started to rise. "Oh shit! What now?" He spoke as he wiped his tears, scrambling to collect the dolls that were running up to them.

Both of them grabbed the dolls in their arms. "Contessa, this room must look like nothing's wrong, and your dress is not ballroom ready." Kalvin chuckled. "Now, give those to me and work your magic," he finished with a smile. Contessa raised her hands, making the room that she and Kalvin tore apart into a picturesque scene straight out of the Quarters society pages in the newspaper. Then, the final sparks swirled around her into a cloud of magenta purple into her masquerade ball gown. "Wow, that will never get old!" Kalvin said, trying to keep the nine dolls safe in his arms. "Contessa, your mask." Kalvin had a worried look on his face. "It is on my mother's desk Contessa responded. As they turned to walk up the stairs and the darkness closed in behind them, they felt the chill of what they feared most and made haste up the stairs, barely breathing until they reached Madame Grace's office.

Kalvin pulled down the book on the lever, closed the door to the staircase, and watched the bookcase return to its closed position. Contessa walked over to her mother's desk, grabbed her mask, and followed Kalvin out the door. "Aww!" screamed Kalvin as he bumped into Frank. "You got them?" Frank said. "Yes, daddy." "Take them and get them to the getaway vehicle. We will return their souls tonight at the docks." Contessa handed her father the dolls she was holding and slipped her mask back on. As the three of them walked into the lobby, spotting her mother trying to escape the many guests talking to her.

No doubt, she tried to run downstairs to check on what was happening in her hotel. Her mother's back was turned away. Frank and Kalvin walked behind her into the kitchen, and Contessa up the stairs. As Contessa reached the top of the stairs, she turned and watched her mother talking to guests. Then, she saw Lucas and Lindsey wave to her from the second-floor hallway. Contessa turned and made her way to the two allies. "What is it, Contessa?" She said. The dolls have been upstairs for about five minutes, and Savannah and the mayor are at the end of the hall. Then Lucas spoke urgently. "Calm down. I know how to free Savannah and ensure the mayor never hurts anyone again. Wait here. Savannah will be joining you soon.

CHAPTER THIRTY
The Charade At The Masquerade

Frank headed to the lounge. He was in the tux he wore the night of the solstice, but this time, he wore the golden lion mask concealing his identity. Watching just out of reach of the shadows, his wife was talking to a couple in a way he knew all too well. She was indeed in her element, loving every minute. Being in control like this was divine. James was by the bar, mostly watching the room's dark corners where light could not reach. Frank spotted a shimmering hand reach for the light and recoil, unable to bear it. This made Frank smile. Even if it were a small one, since with the potions circulating in the guest's veins, the shadows would get suspicious when it reached for the light later in the evening.

"I don't believe I know you." Said a voice that made Frank's smile go from a half smile to a full one. "Well, how could you?" "I just came into town last night, invited by one of your patrons I do business with." Frank smiled. "Oh well, who might that be?" Madame Grace smiled back, having a small smile, as she allowed the glass of champagne to touch her lips. "That pig over there!" Frank pointed in the direction of the mayor and Savannah. Frank spoke. "The young lady on the pig-faced man's lap." This made Madame Grace chuckle. "Well, he has no real power here." Madame Grace chuckled. "Tell me what business you are in." Madame Grace said inquisitively. "I'm an in-politics kind of a town council mayor, but I don't want to talk business tonight, Madame."

Frank smiled at her playing coy with his wife. Frank grabbed the goblet from Madame Grace's hand, put it on the tray Deedee was carrying, and then reached out his hand. "May I have this dance?" He bowed and looked up at the woman he fell in love with. Madame Grace took his hand, and Frank escorted Madame Grace to the dance floor. The piano was soft, and the music swirled in the room with so much soul and sorrow following the tempo. Frank took his wife. They spun and swayed, having light banter, forgetting so much was happening around them. James asked for another champagne and watched with one eye the beautiful scene of the happy couple dancing. Then, in the other, the shadowy demons repeated the same motion over and over again until they stopped feeling the atmosphere change.

The shadowy demon froze and looked confused, and mist evaporated out of the room. "Think! Think!" Said James in a panic to himself. "Something is not right." So, James threw a punch at the guy next to him, and even with human eyes, he saw a little bit of darkness come out into the room where he saw them. The shadows from across the room. The first glimpse of the darkness that was needed since the dolls would not be going to do their best work. The shimmering smile on their face for several minutes as the man punched James in the gut was all he needed to start a brawl. Madame Grace unlocked her inner-laced fingers from the lion-faced man. "Excuse me, please." Madame Grace said to her mysteriously charming dance partner. Frank nodded his head, and she walked over to the fight, but Monty and Reed had already had the two men by the scruffs of their necks. "Madame, this man over here with the cow mask hit this other bloke in the stomach."

Monty lied to Madame Grace for the first time. Not knowing if she bought the lie, Reed stepped in. "Don't worry, Madame Grace. We will escort this troublemaker out!" Madame Grace became pleased as she turned and smiled at the guest. "My valued guest, please don't let two drunk men ruin your evening. My lovely dolls, take our guests to your rooms and make sure they leave happily in the morning." Madame Grace said as the room went into a celebratory cheer. Madame Grace turned to the four gentlemen and spoke. "Now listen, Monty, please take this one out back and dispose of his body. He tried ruining my grand ball with his childish behavior. And this one, Reed, get him some time with Bailey or something to make up for the trouble."

The two men nodded and escorted James and the masked man out of the lounge. Monty escorted the masked man out of sight through the kitchen door. "Sorry, sir, Bailey is headed up the stairs with that man, so if you wait, I will make sure you have a turn." Said Reed. "That is not necessary," said James. Both men kept up appearances to not alarm the guests to the rouse. As the lobby became empty, Reed smacked James on the arm and said, "That was a close one, right?" Reed smirked at James. "Yes, it was," James said, rubbing his shoulder. "Let's grab Monty and head out. The rest of them will catch up." James finished, and Reed hugged James. "Good luck," Reed said as the door to the kitchen swung closed behind him.

CHAPTER THIRTY-ONE
Death of a King

"Come on, baby girl, tell Daddy how much you like it!" The mayor grunted under his golden Venetian pig mask. "Tell me how much you need it!" came from his whiskey-stained breath as he squeezed Savannah's inner thigh and hit her ass repeatedly. Savannah responded in a low growl, "Yes, Daddy!" is all she could say as the mayor pushed her up against the wall, guiding her hand behind her back. All Savannah felt was the leather coiling, one strap around another, wrapping tightly around her wrist.

Then the mayor turned her swiftly around, holding one end of the leather-bound rope with his free hand. He reached his hand up around her neck, leaning into her and licking her cheek with the tip of his slimy tongue. Then he threw her on the bed. Taking the strap in his hand, he wrapped it around the bedpost to fully control this delicate flower. The mayor reached his hand over his mask, pushing it off his face and allowing it to fall on the floor. Taking a few steps forward, he lifted his leg onto the bed; then his other one went over Savannah's body to straddle her, pressing his body weight down on her. His sweat was dripping onto her collarbone. Savannah was lying there, tugging at the strap that bounded her wrist. The mayor kissed her cheek. The mayor pulled his arm down, and she screamed in a passionate, painful scream.

BAM! The door slammed open, and the mayor flung back into the wall and was held against it by Contessa's magic. With sheer rage, she watched Savannah jump up in disarray, not in control of her full body and reacting robotically. "Sheriff, get in here now!" Contessa screamed from the room, not removing her eyes. "Oh shit!" the sheriff said as he ran into the room, then landed back on the door, stabilizing him from the fall. "I need you to be mad at Savannah!" Contessa barked at the sheriff. "Get mad at her now!' she shouted louder, watching the mayor squirm. "You stupid bitch; you are mine when I get down from here!" the mayor spat. "You will never make it past the bed!" she scowled at him. "Now, sheriff, get mad at Savannah," Contessa repeated. "I'm not mad at her; I'm just worried, damn it."

"Man, just do what I say!" she said with the utmost annoyance. "Alright, fine!" "Savannah, what the hell were you thinking? I have told you about this place and what they do here, and you are just out of nowhere in this room with that piece of slime!" The sheriff screamed at Savannah until the cold brush of air passed him, and in front of them was Savannah's soul hovering above her for a moment. Then, inside of her, the life returned to her face. "What just happened?" the sheriff said in bewilderment. "Uncle!" is all Savannah could say. "Has the sheriff hopped on the bed and just held her?" "My mother made a contractual promise that she would make you okay with the fact that she is in this house working for my mother in the capacity that she is doing it," Contessa spoke, shifting her eyes from the scene that lay on the bed and the mayor struggling on the wall.

"So, when I told you to get mad at her, she broke the contract's terms, making it null and void," Contessa finished. The sheriff got to his feet, reaching out a hand to help stabilize his niece, but as she got off the bed, she sprung back. Being tugged by the leather strap bounding her wrist to the bedpost, she tugged at it, tears welling up in her eyes. "Get it off! Please get it off!" Savannah screamed in a panic. Her uncle rushed to aid her, and then Contessa spoke gleaming as she did. "Allow me." Contessa twisted her wrist, and the purple sparks reached Savannah's constraints. They unraveled around her wrist and moved towards the mayor, coiling around his body, tightening every time the mayor squirmed or moved even a muscle.

"Tell me you like it, Daddy!" She laughed. "Tell me you want more!" she shrilled. "Fuck you, you stupid bitch!" he said as the leather strap covered his face, squeezing his bodily fluids through the seams of the ropes. Contessa released the mayor's body, and Savannah brushed past Contessa. The sheriff stopped in front of Contessa and smiled. "Thank you. It is over now. Let's get out of here." the sheriff said, sliding past Contessa. Contessa turned and followed them out as Lindsey ran into Contessa's arms. "I'm fine," Contessa reassured her, and Mayor Lindsey asked, "Let's just say the mayor's kids can sleep soundly tonight." From the staircase, she heard footsteps. "Quick, get behind me!" Contessa ordered the others. On the top of the stairs, she saw her mother madder than she had ever seen. "What do you think you are doing? You are ruining everything!" she said, walking towards her daughter. "Mom, you're not yourself." "You will be okay soon. I will save you."

Contessa pleaded with her mother, "Save me? I chose this life. I was in control. I never have to lose anyone or anything again. It's not your place to save me." Madame Grace chuckled at her daughter. "We can talk about this later, but let them go, and we can figure out our next move. They're free to leave. They don't matter to me. The contract no longer binds the child; they are just a spoke on the social ladder. Thanks to you, that pathetic excuse for a housekeeper is no longer needed. So, go, goodbye." Madame Grace stepped aside, snapping her fingers quickly. I won't ask twice." She spoke, and the sheriff pushed the girls forward. "Lucas, catch up with Kalvin and the others. They will take you to safety," Contessa said as she raised her hands, waiting for the double-cross, but nothing happened.

All she saw was the three of them running down the stairs, leaving Contessa and her mother alone, or so she thought. A figure swaying back and forth in every corner of the room, grasping at the light, scared she ruined their chances to walk in the sun. "As you see, child, you have pissed off the powers that be. You will not ruin this for us!" Madame Grace scolded her daughter. "Ruin your what? Your fancy prison? Your soul-sucking best friend? please share with the room what I'm ruining!" Contessa shouted, then turned her anger to the audience in the room. "You can't have her! You can't have any of them! You will never see the light of day as long as I live. You will die in your shadowy prison, you bastards!" she screamed out into the room.

Then, from the stairs, she saw her father. He was raised into the air, the darkness surrounding him. "I just want my family," Frank gasped in an attempt to plead with the shadows. "You took something from us; now we will take something from you!" came voices from every corner of the room. "You are forgetting something, demons." Contessa now screamed even more harshly. "My name is Contessa Grace Montgomery. My parents are Frank and Grace Montgomery." Contessa walked closer to her father. Contessa continued, "Of the Montgomery coven. one of the most powerful covens in the south, and I will show you what I can do. I'm no longer in the shadows of my parents, and neither are you!"

In all her rage, Contessa let her magic fly, letting the purple sparks light up the hallway. They engulfed the room in flames, and the shadows dropped Frank and moved swiftly to Madame Grace. They swarmed around her and evaporated into thin air, leaving only Frank and Contessa in the hallway. Contessa ran to catch her father, who was teetering on the edge of the top stair of the staircase. They turned and ran down the stairs, moving as quickly as possible to beat the wildfire that was engulfing the world around them. They went through the lobby, past the lounge, and into the kitchen. The ceiling above was scorched with racing flames when they reached the kitchen. Frank reached for the back door, opened it, and they entered the ally.

CHAPTER THIRTY-TWO
At Long Last

Frank stepped out, first in the alley, to shield Contessa from any danger that lay ahead slowly. He reached out to grip Contessa's hand and slowly walked toward the street, not knowing if the shadows and his wife had gone through the smoke. Frank saw figures running toward them, so he raised his hands, ready for another fight, until he heard a familiar voice. "Mr. Frank! Mr. Frank!" Yelled to Lexi from ahead of them, reaching out a hand to help move them along toward the main street. They started running as the flames engulfed the doll house and exploded out the kitchen windows.

When they reached the road, there was a fire truck with everyone already on board, holding on to the sides or in the cockpit. Contessa was hoisted up onto the back. Frank wrapped his body around her to shield her from the flames, and then Lexi jumped into the passenger seat next to Celeste. Let's go, Monty!" Lexi shouted over another window, blowing glass out into the street. Monty revved the engine as the streetlights illuminated, and they sped off towards the bayou. The people crowded the road, looking towards the towering flames. They then whipped their heads around when they realized the fire truck was heading away. Some people even jumped and waved at the fire truck. Still, Monty just kept moving forward, stopping for nothing and no one until they reached the dock for the Redfin Ray's riverboat cruises.

The riverboat that brought Contessa to New Orleans so many years ago. When Lexi came to a complete stop, he shouted to every one of the passengers, "End of the line!" Monty and Reed opened the doors and walked to the back of the truck. Frank was already on solid ground helping Contessa down, and Kalvin jumped off the top of the truck, helping to head towards the ladder to help Savannah and the dolls down. "Well, what do we do now?" said Deedee. "Well, ma'am, if you and your sister want, you can live in Blackwood. We have a plantation there and plenty of room for all of you, and I can give you all work or find work for you. If not, I wish you all the best." said Frank, smiling at Deedee. "Thank you. Mr. Frank is a good man I have known my whole life. He is honest and fair," said Lexi, patting Frank on the back.

Then Lindsey spoke up behind Kalvin. "You mean all of us? Me and my sisters?" "Yes, young lady. What you all did over the years, especially tonight, for my girls, you all will always have a home." Frank opened his arms at Lindsey, who was crying as she ran into his arms and cried. "Thank you so much, sir, thank you," Lindsey said through the tears streaming down her face. "Now, we just wait here for the riverboat." "What about the dolls?" said Alexandria. "Well, we will get them back to Montgomery plantation where we will reunite them with their souls and either get them to a safe place, or they can find a home with us in Blackwood. We will all figure that out when we get home." Frank reassured everyone that he had a plan. Monty stepped towards Frank and said, "Reed here could run errands for you like we did your wife, sir. There could be some work like that. Plus, you're good with cars. You can help keep mine up and running."

Frank reached out a hand to the two gentlemen, and they shook on it. "What about you son?" Frank asked Kalvin. "I don't know, sir, where I would fit in. I did a lot of bad stuff here. I hurt a lot of people." Kalvin spoke, talking down at the ground. "Kalvin, I have been married to my wife for a long time, and that woman has made me do many stupid things that sometimes I'm not proud of, but I would do it again because it gave me Contessa and the plantation." Frank said, walking between Monty and Reed and stopping in front of Kalvin. "But all I need to know is my sweets and wife are both alive because you have protected them for all these years. So, you will always have a place under my roof."

Frank grabbed Kalvin and hugged him, squeezing him tightly for a moment, and then Kalvin cleared his throat. "Sir, I would like to ask Alexandria something." He stepped aside to look at Alexandria, who was holding her sister's hand. "Me? What?" Alexandria said. "I wanted to ask you if you would take me, a broken man, and turn him into the happiest man alive and become my wife." Kalvin smiled as he dropped down to one knee. "Ooh, child, I will make the cake. Celeste, Deloris, you can make the food. Deedee said gleefully. "Hush up!" said Deloris. "Well, child," said Celeste. "Yes, I would love to be your wife," said Alexandria. With that response, Kalvin jumped up and ran to Alexandria, wrapping her up in his arms. He swung her around, and after they stopped spinning, he stared into her eyes, cupped her chin, and slowly kissed her. "Congrats!" said the sheriff.

"I hate to leave this love fest, but Savannah and I are going to take this truck back to the hotel and clean up the mess the mayor left in the Quarter." "Yeah, maybe take Contessa's advice, run for mayor, and clean up the Quarter," Savannah said, smiling at her uncle, as he smiled back. "Now, that doesn't sound like a bad idea." He hugged his niece, tears rolling down his cheek. "I'm glad you are safe," the sheriff said as he kissed Savannah on her forehead. Then, with his arm wrapped around his niece, he hugged everyone goodbye. They hopped into the fire truck and sped off towards the rising smoke. Kalvin walked over to Contessa. As everyone disbursed into their little groups, Alexandria, Lindsey and Brooke huddled, chatting about what to expect in their new life.

Deedee and Deloris were laughing, with Celeste and Deloris calling Monty handsome. Monty and Reed shared a smoke over on some benches. Frank walked to the end of the dock to check the riverboat schedule. "Is your mom really gone?" he quietly asked her. "I don't know. My best guess is the shadows knew I knew how to break the binding contract, and with my mom, her contract was that she and I would always be safe. Since I controlled the fire, that left my mother vulnerable. To work on a new plan, they must need my mother still. But, that is just a theory, but all I know is we have not seen the last of them because I will save my mother one day." she said with radiating confidence, smiling at Kalvin. "I will do whatever it takes to keep you safe. Therefore, if you are planning for another battle, so am I." He smiled at Contessa. A cough interrupted them.

"Congrats, man," said James. "Thanks, man, I appreciate it. May I steal Contessa for a moment?" "Yes, of course." Kalvin said as he walked over to Monty and Reed. "I don't want to piggyback off of anyone, but I would also like to ask you something." James dropped to one knee and reached out for Contessa's hand. "I have loved you and have never stopped, even knowing I may never see you again. You are the reason my heart beats. I want to be your husband until the end of days. Will you, Contessa Grace Montgomery, be my wife?" As he spoke, he heard the onlookers gasp and shout things, making Contessa do a half giggle and half cry. "Yes, I will be your wife." He hopped up and passionately kissed her. She embraced them. The world was spinning around them until they separated. The two of them walked towards the dock where the riverboat was easier to see in the rising sun's light. After Frank bought everyone a ticket and exchanged pleasantries with the captain, they boarded. The gang crowded around the back of the boat, locking arms, listening to the horn blow, and setting sail after about a half-hour wait for a few other passengers to board. She looked at her father and said, "Down came the doll house, the Madame and all."

The end

www.ingramcontent.com/pod-product-compliance
Lightning Source LLC
Chambersburg PA
CBHW070837280626
47161CB00015B/1030